THE FIVE STONE STEPS

by John Orton

Typeset in Dante MT Std and Gotham

Design and publishing by UK Book Publishing

UK Book Publishing is a trading name of Consilience Media

www.ukbookpublishing.com

ISBN: 978-1-910223-17-8

Foreword

Thomas 'Jock' Gordon joined the South Shields Police after the First
War, became Station Sergeant, and remained in the Force until after
the Second World War. In his old age he went to live with his son,
Tommy. Tommy had kept his father's 'stave' or truncheon which his
Dad called 'Fagan', and when I asked Tommy if he knew anything
of Policing in the early days, he produced a dog eared manuscript
of his father's Memories. The hand written pages gave a wonderful
insight, not only into the details of Police procedure, but also into
life in Shields in the twenties and thirties.

The Five Stone Steps is my fictionalised version of the memoirs.
I have intertwined Jock's reminiscences with some of the tales told
by my Grandmother, Gertrude, who was a real Geordie Hinny. She
was the daughter of John Pells, a mariner from Norfolk who later
became a North Sea Pilot. The family had lived in Maxwell Street,
and Gertie worked as a cook in the North of England Café.

My aim has been to bring Jock Gordon's Memoirs to life – in
doing so some of the story lines have been exaggerated, or invented
for dramatic effect. The characters have also been given fictitious
names apart from one or two who are mentioned in passing but do
not have any part to play in the tales. I have researched the stories as
best I could, but if there are any errors or anachronisms, I apologise.

I would like to thank Marilyn Gordon, Tommy's widow, who
gave me permission to make use of all the material in the memoirs,
and who has encouraged me throughout.

Thanks are also due to South Tyneside Libraries for allowing me
to reproduce the images of South Shields in the 1920s which appear
in the book and which can all be found on the South Tyneside
Historic Images web site.

This book is dedicated to and written for the people of South
Shields.

John Orton

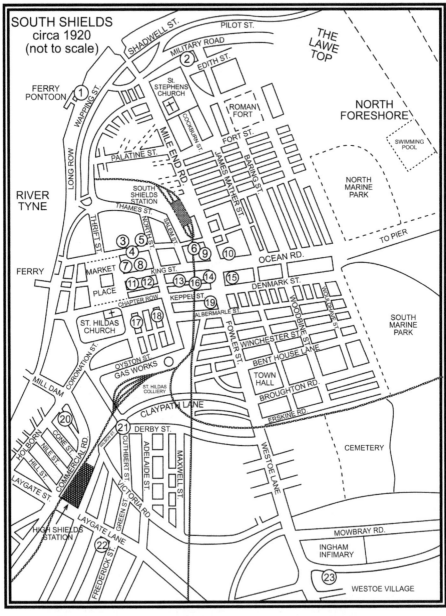

SOUTH SHIELDS
circa 1920
(not to scale)

THE LAWE TOP

FERRY PONTOON

NORTH FORESHORE

SWIMMING POOL

SHADWELL ST.
PILOT ST.
MILITARY ROAD
EDITH ST.
St. STEPHENS CHURCH
ROMAN FORT
WAPPING ST.
MILE END RD.
COCKBURN ST.
FORT ST.
BARING ST.
JAMES MATHER ST.
LONG ROW
PALATINE ST.
SOUTH SHIELDS STATION
THAMES ST.
THRIFT ST.
SALEM ST.
NORTH ST.
RIVER TYNE
NORTH MARINE PARK
TO PIER
OCEAN RD.
FERRY
MARKET PLACE
King ST.
KEPPEL ST.
DENMARK ST.
ALBERMARLE ST.
WOODBINE ST.
MOUNT DALE ST.
SOUTH MARINE PARK
CHAPTER ROW
ST. HILDAS CHURCH
CORONATION ST.
OYSTON ST.
GAS WORKS
FOWLER ST.
WINCHESTER ST.
BENT HOUSE LANE
ST. HILDAS COLLIERY
CLAYPATH LANE
TOWN HALL
BROUGHTON RD.
ERSKINE RD.
MILL DAM
DERBY ST.
CUTHBERT ST.
ADELAIDE ST.
MAXWELL ST.
WESTOE LANE
CEMETERY
HOLBORN
COMMERCIAL RD.
CONE ST.
NILE ST.
HILL ST.
LAYGATE ST.
VICTORIA RD.
GREEN ST.
LAYGATE LANE
HIGH SHIELDS STATION
FREDERICK ST.
MOWBRAY RD.
INGHAM INFIMARY
WESTOE VILLAGE

1. The Burton House
2. The Turk's Head
3. The City Of Durham
4. Union Alley
5. The Black & Grey
6. The Bridge
7. Crofton's Corner
8. The Golden Lion
9. The Scotia
10. The Roma
11. The Tram
12. The Mechanics
13. Smithy Street
14. The Wheatsheaf
15. Oliver's
16. The General Havelock
17. The Douglas
18. Barrington Street
19. Police H. Q.
20. Nelson's Bank
21. The Queen's Head
22. The Adam and Eve
23. The Westoe

Contents

List of illustrations

CHAPTER ELEVEN
Long Bank – STH0001407

The images are available to purchase through South Tyneside
libraries using the reference codes above.

www.southtynesideimages.org.uk

Lower Thames Street

A piece of pie

After three years in the trenches and fresh out of the Army, I had hoped for better in civvy street, but four months of door knocking with a suitcase of household goods in my hand had been enough. When the chance of going back into uniform cropped up, I jumped at it.

My first day in the South Shields Police was hardly memorable. I was given a second hand uniform, second hand boots and was told to be prepared to go on duty the next day in the Market Place where I would double up with one of the old hands for a fortnight. After that I would be on my own.

My accommodation was in Tyne Dock – a single room with a range to cook on and not much else. There was a cold tap in the yard but no toilet. I had a bucket which I would empty on the common midden out the back.

It did not take long to unpack my suitcase – my worldly goods comprised a change of underwear and socks, a tooth brush, a razor, shaving brush and mug – together with a half bottle of whisky and a dog eared edition of Burns' poems.

My father had been a Scottish drover who passed through Carlisle each year. A young farm lass had caught his eye one year and he had married her on his way back to Scotland. My inheritance from him had consisted of two books: Burns and a Bible. He had carried them on his droves – they were the only company he needed.

My first days as a Shields Bobby were spent with Sam Beecroft – a big bluff fellow who liked his beer. We were standing at Crofton's corner in the Market Place one Saturday afternoon when I made acquaintance with the newly appointed Inspector Mullins. He came striding up to us and without any word of introduction just asked, "Any trouble today?" Sam replied that things were quiet. I didn't know Mullins then and tried to impress.

"There was an old drunk who'd fallen over outside the *City of Durham*. He lives in North Street so I took him home. His wife was pleased to see him." She'd shouted so loud at the poor old bugger that half the doors in the street had opened.

"You did what?" Mullins took out his notebook. "Drunkenness in a public place is a criminal offence. The man should have been charged."

Sam tried to say something but I realised now which way the wind was blowing. "Officer Beecroft did say that I should arrest the man but I took pity on him."

"Pity's not a word we use in the Shields Force. As you've just started out I'll make nowt of it, Constable Duncan, but watch yourself in future." Mullins said no more and stalked off on his way down to the Mill Dam.

"You made a mistake there, Tom. Mullins is best ignored, but I'd watch out for him in future." Sam was right. Mullins was a Methodist who had taken the pledge. It soon became apparent that he wanted to make everyone's life as miserable as his own. Burns knew his kind:

> "Oh ye wha are sae guid yoursel,
> Sae pious and sae holy,
> Ye've nowt to do but mark and tell
> Your Neebour's fauts and folly."

Sam waited until he had disappeared, looked around, rubbed his chin and said, "Let's have a scout down Union Alley, I've not been in the *Black and Grey* for a while."

Sam knew all the pubs round the Market and there were dozens of them. It meant that he could have a pint or two every day without becoming a burden on any landlord in particular. He'd look in, normally in the Snug or the Jug and Bottle. "Everything all right, Landlord?" A foaming pint would be placed on the counter and Sam wouldn't take long over it. He took a shine to me in those early days as I am not a beer drinker. I'd normally take a couple of sips from my pint while Sam was emptying his, and then pour the rest into Sam's glass. I never had a taste for it. Whisky was my tipple, but you didn't get that buckshee in Shields' pubs.

As we came out of the *Black and Grey* five minutes later I collided with a one legged man with a crutch – no harm done. I put my hand on his arm to steady him.

"Keep your bloody hands to yoursel' and watch where you're gannin'."

It was my introduction to Hughie Ross. He was a character all right, with a shock of white hair that used to be red and a temper to go with it. He made a few pence washing up in cafés and hotels, and when they'd had enough of him he'd be a lookout for bookies' runners. Whatever he earned he spent in the boozers.

Sam told him to bugger off. As Hughie went on his way over the cobbles muttering to himself Sam remarked, "If you ever have to arrest him when he's drunk, watch out for his crutch. If he catches you with it he'll knock you into the middle of next week."

Saturday was a big day in Shields. The Market started early and finished around midnight. After two o'clock in the afternoon we always doubled up on duty. It was mostly drunks and fights but you had the odd bit of sneak thievery and pickpocketing.

There was every type of stall on the Market: clothes, curtains, materials, haberdashery, boots and shoes – old and new – butchers, greengrocers, tripe stalls, fish stalls. There was the man who made toffee on the spot; quacks selling potions that would cure everything; and the famous gypsy with his hedgehog ointment. The fish was fresh from the North Shields Fish Quay. If you were up early enough you'd see Annie Mountain with her barrow coming back on the Ferry to set up her stall. There were no fridges in those days and it all had to be sold. Those who did not have much waited until late to do their shopping. Many a poor family owed their Sunday joint to a Shields butcher clearing his stall for what it would fetch before midnight.

At about four o'clock Sam was starting to feel a little peckish. We sauntered over to the Pie stall. There were pork pies, steak pies, rabbit pies, cow heel pies, but the pie that was the cheapest, and many said the best, was the plate pie. Nothing but pastry and minced beef and onions cooked on a tin plate. It was a penny ha'penny a slice or ninepence for a whole pie if you brought your own plate. Sam knew Mrs. Hankey who served on the stall, and as soon as he caught her eye she finished serving her customer, cut two slices, put them on a piece of newspaper and brought them over.

We stepped into the small alley between the stalls to eat our pie. It was delicious – I licked my lips as a trickle of gravy ran down my chin. I looked round and saw that I was being watched. A young bairn who couldn't have been more than four or five was staring at the pie in my hand. I could almost feel the hunger in his belly as his little eyes savoured the flaky pastry and the thick meat filling. He was standing by a pram which his mother was gently pushing back and forward. She was pale and thin with ash blonde hair and blue eyes – she would have been a beauty but for the suffering and worry etched on her face. They were not poorly dressed but it was plain to see that they were in want. As her eyes took in the look on the boy's face the woman looked round, and when she saw two well covered Bobbies eating pie, she became even paler, put out her hand to move the boy on and then fainted clean away.

I wolfed down what was left of the pie and ran over. The little lad was crying. A woman had his mother's head cradled in her lap, and was gently slapping her face to bring her round. A man in a bowler hat came forward with some smelling salts. The woman slowly recovered consciousness.

"Do you want a doctor, hinny?" the woman asked.

"Oh no, I think I'm all right. I've been feeling run down."

She was not a Shields woman, but spoke with a London accent. I bent over. "Let me help you up." She was still unsteady on her feet.

"She wants a good feed if you ask me," muttered the woman who had helped her. "Where do you live, hinny?"

4

"Just down Lower Thames Street. I'll be all right if we take it slowly."

"That's on my beat. I'll walk with you to see you home." I took her by the arm, and with the other hand held the bairn's hand. The mother pushed the pram and we made our way out of the Market.

"I'll not be long," I told Sam. He said nowt – he didn't need to, the look on his face said it all.

The woman's name was Annie Burnett. She'd met her husband during the War, when he'd been on leave in London. She didn't say so but I suspected that the young lad holding my hand had been the fruit of their meeting; a gallant soldier in uniform going back to the trenches with a pretty girl reluctant to say no. He was a riveter at the Middle Docks.

Lower Thames Street runs parallel to the river and like all the streets in old Shields had seen better days. It was a narrow cobbled street with soot-grimed houses. The family had one room on the first floor of a narrow three storey house – his wages should have brought better than this. A stout woman in a black dress and a white pinny was standing on the step as we went in.

"Eeeh, what's the matter, hinny?" she asked. Annie said nothing.

"She had a fainting fit in the Market."

"Oh the poor soul. Here I'll come up with you."

The room was clean but that was all. There was one bed, a table, two chairs and some wooden boxes for cupboards.

Mrs. Black, the neighbour, was a typical Shields woman, kind hearted but mouthy. "All she needs is a good feed. It's that man of hers. It's the same each pay day – he stops in every pub on the way yem. Last Saturday he didn't come home till past closing time. She feeds the bairns but starves hersel'."

"He said he'd come straight home tonight." Annie tried to defend her man but I could see by her eyes that she feared another late night with half or more of the wage packet gone.

"Well, she won't gan roond the pubs to find him. That's the only way with some men." She looked at me and whispered, "She's a bit

5

hoity-toity. She'll have to learn."

"She's in no state to go looking for him tonight. Could you make her a cup of tea?"

Annie had run out so Mrs. Black went to get some tea. "I'll lend you half a cup."

I went over to one of the boxes and picked up a plate. I took the young lad by the hand and said I was away out for a while. Little Jackie, named after his dad, was only too glad to go for a walk with a Policeman. Half the street was out on their doorsteps by now but we took no notice. As we entered the Market and headed towards the pie stall Little Jackie began to hope.

"Are you getting us pie, Mister? I like pie."

Mrs. Hankey didn't make us wait in the queue.

"Can I have half a pie, please?" I had not forgotten the little lad's eyes when he'd watched me eating and I reckoned that Annie had not eaten herself for a couple of days. What could I do? I'd thought of buying a whole pie, but ninepence was a lot of money for me, and I didn't want any left over for John Burnett, whether he came home drunk or sober. Mrs. Hankey cut a pie down the middle and deftly lifted the half onto my plate. She looked at Little Jackie.

"Is it for the poor woman who fainted?"

"Aye." She took my fourpence ha'penny and then scooped up a large dollop of pease pudding onto the plate. "That's from me. There's nowt like pease pudding to fill you up."

Little Jackie was so excited we nearly had to run back. I didn't stay; I just put the plate on the table and told Annie that she had to have some as well as the children. She blushed but hunger will always overcome pride. "There might even be enough for a slice for Mrs. Black," I said. Annie would need all the friends she could get.

As I came back to the Market Place I saw Inspector Mullins with Sam, standing by the Pie Stall. I was in for it but as I approached them it was Sam who spoke first.

"Did you catch the little beggar?"

I said nowt. Mrs. Hankey looked over. "I was just telling the

Inspector how that little devil had pinched a piece of pie right from under me nose." She was in on it with Sam.

"Aye, I was just about to collar him, but he dashed down one of the alleys off Thrift Street. I lost him, and myself, for five minutes."

"It's a warren down there," Sam added.

Mullins scowled. "You should know the terrain, Duncan – you're ex-army, aren't you?" He looked at me. "Would you recognise him again?"

"Well I only saw him from behind." I thought I'd better use my imagination. "But he had no boots on."

Mullins looked at me. "You mean you couldn't catch a barefoot runner over cobbles." He turned away in mock disgust. "Now you haven't been feeding these lads too much pie, Mrs. Hankey."

We all laughed. Mullins was in a good humour for once. I was lucky; on another day I might have been in his book.

It was night duty for me for the next two weeks but I was never one for sleeping long in the day, and in the afternoons I would often go for a good walk. There was always something to see along the riverside, and I would stroll around the narrow lanes and alleys of Old Shields ending up in the Market Place. It all helped with my local knowledge. I'd quite often go down Lower Thames Street, and not long after the day I'd first met Annie Burnett I saw Little Jackie playing on the step outside his house. As I stopped to say hello, his mother came out with the pram. She had a black eye or what was left of one. I asked if she was feeling better. "Yes," she replied, "thank you very much," and taking Jackie by the hand walked briskly away down towards Long Row. I'd seen the curtains on the first floor window move and Mrs. Black came down the stairs.

"He came back drunk as usual last Saturday. Mind he wasn't as bad as he normally is, and he'd bought some fish and chips. I think the bairn must have said something about the pie. Well, he was furious. I could hear every word. He'd given her what was left of his wages, but he took some back and said he was going up to the Market to tell you that his family didn't take charity. He was going to throw the money back in your face. He got as far as the *Silent Woman* in Thrift Street. When he finally came back he thumped her. She'd be better off without him.

"She's off down the Long Row to see Mr. Cleghorn. He keeps the lodging house at number 33. He was telling me last week that his wife's pregnant again and he was thinking of taking on some help. I told her to go and see him. He's a canny fellow. She won't earn much but it'll be her money and won't go down her man's throat. I said that I'd look after the bairns for her."

I was in two minds. I told myself that I should keep out of it, but I couldn't stop thinking about those pale blue eyes. We used to keep an eye on the lodging houses, and I made a mental note to check out Mr. Cleghorn's next time I was on duty in that part of town.

I was stirred out of my reverie by a commotion across the street. Hughie Ross was walking along the pavement and a gang of young lads were walking in front of him, pretending to have crutches, limping and talking to themselves. Hughie was going mad. He was shouting something terrible. If I'd been on duty I could have arrested him for swearing in a public place. I crossed over the street and told the lads to bugger off and leave old Hughie alone. They ran off laughing. I didn't receive any thanks.

"Why dain't ye mind your own bloody business? I'd have caught the little buggers and given them a taste of this." He swung his crutch from the ground in an upwards strike that nearly took my head off, and left Hughie sitting on his bum on the cobbles as he overbalanced. I helped him up, and he went on his way muttering under his breath.

The next time I saw Hughie Ross was a couple of weeks later. I was back on the afternoon shift in the Market. It was a Saturday and I was doubled up with Sam Beecroft. We'd been busy – three drunks and a fight in the *City of Durham*. Sam had taken the last drunk down to Keppel Street, and Inspector Mullins had come back with him to lend a hand.

Things seemed to have quietened down for a while, and Sam

went off to patrol down Thrift Street, while Mullins and myself stayed put at the Market. He must have smelled trouble coming up. The doors of the *Tram* swung wide open and Geordie Hardcastle, the barman, put Hughie Ross and a small red faced man out onto the pavement. "And divvent come back until you're sober!"

Hughie and his fellow drunk had fallen out over something and continued a vituperative altercation that brought quite a crowd of onlookers. Hughie was always good value, particularly if he had had a few. I was minded to let them be for a while – not so Inspector Mullins. "Drunk and disorderly – they'll spend the afternoon in the cells."

As we walked over, the little red faced fellow saw us, and made off quickly across the cobbles, into the Market, and away. Hughie stayed where he was, shouting and bawling at no one in particular.

"You make the arrest, Duncan. I'll back you up." As if I needed back up to take Hughie down to Keppel Street. I made my way round the back of the crowd as I intended to come on to Hughie from behind to avoid the crutch. Mullins thought I was shirking. "For heaven's sake, man, we haven't got all day." He pushed forward and as he confronted the little man, Hughie's crutch shot up in Mullins' direction. I reached out, just managing to grab Hughie's shoulder in time. Instead of having his head knocked off, Mullins just lost his helmet.

"I'm arresting you for being drunk and disorderly," I said to Hughie who couldn't have cared less and continued shouting and bawling as I walked him off down Chapter Row. Mullins, who had recovered his helmet, had no option but to stay on duty at the Market Place at least until Sam returned.

The Station Sergeant's face dropped when he saw Hughie. "Couldn't ye have just sent him packing down to Long Row. He's nowt but a bloody nuisance."

"I'm sorry, Sergeant. Inspector Mullins said I was to arrest him."

He took the charge of drunk and disorderly. In those days it was the Station Sergeant who was responsible for the charge book, and it was his job to accept or reject the charge, no matter what the rank of the arresting officer. The rejected charge book was an unpopular little volume. The arresting officer could appeal to senior officers to have the Sergeant overruled, but this rarely happened while Bob Jamieson was Sergeant.

We'd just locked Hughie up for a while to sober him up a bit before bailing him, when Mullins came down the five stone steps. The powers that be had selected Mullins as Inspector over the head of Bob Jamieson, who had been favourite for the job. What made matters worse was that Mullins came from the Durham Constabulary, and there was little love lost between the two Forces. Being a Bobby in South Shields might have its rewards, but it was not always easy to keep law and order in a big town with a lot of hard men from the mines and the ships who liked their beer on a Saturday night. Durham was mainly a rural area and they didn't put themselves out.

"I hope you've thrown the book at him, the vicious little bugger," Mullins snarled.

Sergeant Jamieson looked up. "I don't know why you even bothered with him. He's no harm if you just ignore him. It's more trouble than it's worth to bring him in. He'll be bailed when he's sober and fined a tanner on Monday."

"He'll be sent to Durham for three months. Assaulting a Police Inspector's a serious offence."

I'd told Sergeant Jamieson about Mullins' helmet. We'd both had a laugh. I did not know Bob Jamieson well at that time. He may have been a bit too blunt in his way of talking to certain people but he was a good copper.

"The charge is drunk and disorderly," Jamieson replied to Mullins showing him the Charge Book.

"Well it will have to be changed. Ross assaulted me with his crutch. He nearly had me head off me shoulders."

"The arresting officer felt that the drunk and disorderly charge sufficed. We all know about Hughie's crutch."

Mullins of course did not. "He knocked my helmet off and that's an assault. I'll make the charge myself if Constable Duncan won't," he said, giving me a distinctly old fashioned look.

Sergeant Jamieson did it by the book. He asked the Inspector to go over the facts and then asked me if I had anything to add. I said nowt.

"Charge rejected," was Jamieson's reply, and he wrote the particulars in the Rejected Charge book. I went back to the Market on my own. Mullins was furious and marched off upstairs to see the Senior Officer on Duty.

Mullins was lucky: the Superintendent was in. Henry Burnside was a big man who liked his beer. He'd worked his way up through the ranks because he understood Police work the old fashioned way. 'Hit 'em hard before they hit you.' The Chief could not have asked for a more loyal deputy, and Burnside would always back his men, sometimes too readily. His major weakness was the drink. He came in on Saturdays, even if he was not on duty, just to get out of the house; he would have several drinks before he arrived at the Station, and a few more on the way home. He never did much while he was there but technically he was in charge. He was easy meat for Mullins, who did not let his Methodist principles stop him from taking advantage of a man slightly the worse for wear. 'A savage assault on an Inspector with a blunt instrument,' was how he described the attack. Henry Burnside signed the note to Sergeant Jamieson instructing him to accept a charge of assault. He insisted afterwards that Mullins had not mentioned that the assailant was Hughie Ross or that the blunt instrument was a crutch, but in all other details Mullins' account was strictly accurate. Henry had thought he ought to support the newly appointed Inspector – by the time he spoke to Bob on his way out the damage had been done. The charge had been taken and as it involved an assault Hughie was not bailed but stayed in the cells until Monday.

I was in Court when the case came up. Hughie pleaded not guilty. He was bailed until the following week when a special date had been set down for the hearing. The bail was conditional on his remaining at a fixed address.

"Well, I was staying at Cleghorn's lodging hoose, but I've missed two neets and he may have given me bed to someone else." Hughie cut a pathetic figure in the dock. The Chief Constable, who in those days dealt with all the prosecutions personally, paused and looked back to me. I stepped forward from the back of the Court, whispered a few words and the Chief then addressed the Court.

"Your Worships, the arresting officer in the case is happy to accompany the accused to Mr. Cleghorn's Lodging House to confirm that he has a bed there. If not, he will make sure he finds a lodging nearby, and report back to your Clerk, who can amend the bail notice accordingly."

On the way back to the Long Row Hughie kept muttering away about Mullins.

"Just stick to the facts, Hughie," I told him. "Admit you were making a nuisance of yourself and were the worse for drink. You didn't mean to hit Inspector Mullins, did you?"

"Wye of course not. But if folk get in the way of me crutch it's their own look out. I didn't start the trouble anyway – it was that bastard little Jimmy Olliphant."

I was waiting for Hughie to explain.

"I'm saying nowt more, I'm not a nark."

I thought no more of it but made a mental note of the red faced man's name.

We arrived at 33 Long Row. The door was open and we went in. Mr. Cleghorn was sitting at the kitchen table sipping tea from a saucer with the papers open in front of him at the racing pages.

"I hear ye've been knocking Policemen's helmets off, ye auld bugger."

Hughie said nowt.

"Is there a bed for him?" I asked. "It's a condition of his bail."

"Well, I've got a bed but this is a respectable lodging hoose. I'm not sure we should be taking in gangsters and the like." Cleghorn was having a little joke but Hughie didn't see the funny side of it.

"Listen to him. You should see some of the sods he lets in here."

"You'll have to put up with him for the week."

"Aye, well, so long as he behaves himself and pays his way."

Hughie was definitely relieved. "You wouldn't want any washing up deein', Mr. Cleghorn? I could do with a few pence for a pint."

"I'm sorry, Hughie, I've taken on a young lass. Wor Agnes is pregnant again."

Cleghorn had one of those deep, nasal Shields accents and it must have carried into the kitchen. Annie Burnett came out wiping her hands on her pinny. She looked a lot better than last time I'd seen her, although she was still pale.

"If you want me to fetch those messages this morning, Mr. Cleghorn, the washing up will have to wait."

"Gan on then, Hughie. I'll give you thre'pence."

"You look tired, Mr. Ross, I'll make you a nice cup of tea. Would you want one, Officer?" Annie asked in a friendlier voice than last time she had spoken to me. I accepted.

"Aye, well gan in to the kitchen. If you stop here folk'll think you're after me." He laughed and returned to the racing pages. Hughie would most likely put the bet on for him and earn a few more pennies.

Hughie started on the pile of dishes left from breakfast. I asked Annie how she was keeping. "I'm just about managing. It's hard work but Mr. Cleghorn lets me have a meal and if there's any left over I can take some home for the children. The main thing is that Mr. Cleghorn gives the wages to me every few days, and I can spend it on what we need."

"Is your husband still drinking then?"

"He has to work hard and there's so many pubs on the way home. He tries his best though." She was still being defensive.

"I don't know how long this job will last. I'm pregnant again." She spoke without any great feeling but I could detect a note of resignation in her voice. She could hardly manage with two children. How would she cope with her wastrel husband, another mouth to feed, and all without the money she was now earning? She was up at five and had to make her man's bait before starting at the lodging house at six prompt. She'd light the fires and make a start on the breakfast. It was porridge for most but some of the working men with a bit of money might have a kipper or some bacon. Some cooked for themselves but Annie had to do the washing up and she'd then tidy the rooms, make the beds, change the sheets if need be, clear up any mess and slop out the night pails. Customers of lodging houses down the Long Row were not of the highest quality, but she was at least lucky that it was a men-only establishment – the women who were reduced to seeking nightly lodgings were pitiful characters. She finished at noon, then came back again at four o'clock and would stay until the evening washing up was done. Cleghorn paid her fourteen and six a week.

I left the Long Row with mixed feelings. I didn't know what more I could do to help and there were many in Shields worse off than Annie Burnett. I promised myself that I would look in occasionally at No. 33 to check that Hughie Ross was still living there. If I saw Annie, then all well and good.

From what I'd heard about him Hughie Ross had been a cantankerous piece of work for years. He had no real friends as he would soon fall out with anyone because of his mouth. But on the odd days when I looked in at Mr. Cleghorn's lodging house, I noticed that Hughie was normally hanging around Annie and being half pleasant. He'd still grumble but without any real nastiness. It must have been her fair hair and blue eyes, or perhaps it was because she treated him like a human being; and all the while Cleghorn sat at the table drinking his tea and reading the racing pages.

It was the following Monday when things turned for the worse. I was on nightshift. I'd just collected the old bull's eye lamp from the Warder and was on my way out of the Station, when Sam Beecroft came up the steps.

"Tom, there's been trouble down at Long Row. Annie Burnett's been hurt bad." He knew I'd been keeping my eye on her. "She was leaving about half past seven. Cleghorn had given her half her wages – apparently he paid her on Mondays and Thursdays to help her out. Her husband was waiting for her and he wanted her money – we all know what for. She wouldn't let him have any so he hit her, banged her against the wall hard. Hughie Ross set upon him with his crutch but Burnett flattened him then took his crutch, hit him with it and then smashed it in two. By the time I got there Burnett had gone. He'd taken the money from Annie's purse while she lay groaning on the cobbles. The doctor was called out. She's lost the bairn she was carrying and she's in a sorry state, but the doctor says she'll be all right so long as she rests for a few days. She's in a bed at Cleghorn's in one of the back rooms. She won't press charges against her husband, and auld Hughie's saying nowt except that he's not a copper's nark."

I knew straight away what I was going to do, and Sam could see it in my eyes.

"I'll come with you."

"No, I'll do it on my own, Sam."

"Aye, you will, but I'll watch your back."

I wasn't in the mood to stand and argue. We headed off down Chapter Row. "I've heard he drinks in the *Silent Woman* down Thrift Street," was all that Sam said on the way across the Market Place.

John Burnett was there. The barman pointed him out, sitting in the corner with a few mates. Sam had stayed outside and held my lamp for me. I went across.

"Burnett, outside." He started to gobshite me and I slapped him hard with my gloves. The others moved away quickly. I grabbed him by the arm and took him outside down the side alley.

"You hit your wife again and you'll get worse than this." I gave him a hiding he would not forget for a month of Sundays. Sam called me off after a few minutes when Burnett's squeals were attracting attention. I let go of him and he fell on to the cobbles.

"That'll teach the bastard."

That was the way things were done. It was rough justice but it was sometimes necessary, and it worked.

The next morning I was walking past the CID Office towards the five stone steps. The door was ajar and I heard the Big Fella, Detective Inspector Norman Lamont, talking to Bob Jamieson. I probably would have heard if the door had been closed and I'd been half way up Fowler Street. The Big Fella had a loud voice and he wasn't one to whisper.

"I'm sure the Olliphants are at the bottom of it. We sent Tommy down last year but Freddie's still about." I had stopped when I heard the name Olliphant, and the Big Fella must have sensed my presence.

"You got nothing better to do than skulk in corridors and listen at doors, Constable?"

I mumbled an apology for eavesdropping but asked if Tommy and Freddie were related to Jimmy Olliphant, Hughie Ross's sparring partner of last week.

"He's a cousin," Bob Jamieson chipped in. "Not in the same league as Tommy and Freddie but all the Olliphants are scoundrels of some sort. You think he's up to something?"

"Hughie Ross had a right barny with him just before he nearly decapitated Inspector Mullins. He told me it was all Jimmy's fault, but when I pressed him he said he wasn't a nark."

The Big Fella looked interested. "There's been a spate of burglaries – evenings, when the owners are out. The crooks mainly take jewellery and sometimes a small ornament, nothing too bulky. It's the Olliphants' trademark but if Freddie's on his own he'll need a fence. Tommy used to look after that end of things.

"Sergeant Jamieson, can you spare Constable Duncan for a couple of hours? I want someone to check round the pawnshops to see if anything has turned up. If he draws a blank he can have another chat with Hughie Ross. I heard he got a pasting yesterday."

News travelled fast. I said he was more worried about his Court appearance next week.

"He should be – with two black eyes he'll look a right villain. If he gives you a lead on the Olliphants I'll have a word with the Chief."

There were pawnshops galore in Shields in those days. I started off at Smallman's in Smithy Street and ended up at Lush's at Laygate. None of the stolen goods on my list had been pawned. I took a tram back to the Market and headed down Thrift Street to the Pawnshop Dock where something there had caught my eye on my earlier visit – a crutch. It had seen some wear and tear and the leather on the arm rest was all worn away, but it was solid.

The Pawnbroker was none too pleased – having Polis in the shop twice in one day was bad for business. I took the crutch and said I'd be back with the money for it. "Divvent bother. Ye can keep it but I dain't want to see ye for a twelvemonth."

When I reached 33 Long Row, Cuddie Cleghorn was in his usual place at the table reading the racing pages, Hughie Ross was sitting on an old settle up against the wall, and right beside him was Jimmy Olliphant, the little red faced man I'd last seen running across the cobbles in the Market. There was an enamel jug on the floor between them with a cloth over the top and they each had a glass of beer.

I caught Cuddie Cleghorn's slightly anxious glance. No alcohol was allowed in lodging houses. "It's medicinal," he grunted.

Hughie looked up. "Can't you leave us in peace for a minute? I'm sick of the sight of ye." I was ready for more but Hughie paused a while as he took in the crutch I was carrying.

"What ye got there?"

"Nowt that can't wait."

I handed the crutch to Cuddie Cleghorn who stood up and tried the crutch himself. "Wye, it's solid man. The rest will need recovering but that'll be nae bother." Cleghorn pulled Hughie up and put the crutch under his arm. It was a bit high.

"I'll just saw a couple of inches off in the yard and ye'll be well away. How much?"

"That depends on what these two tell me."

Cleghorn got the message and went out to the yard.

"Right you two, I want to know what you were arguing about just before Hughie was nicked."

"It's nowt to do with you, you interfering sod."

"Something's going on and you better tell me what it is, or the crutch'll go back, and you'll be spending three months in Durham."

"Ye blackmailing swine, I'm saying nowt."

I looked at Jimmy.

"Is it anything to do with your Freddie? If you're mixed up with burglary you could go down with your mate Hughie, and I wouldn't fancy your chances in Durham."

Jimmy poured himself another glass and topped up Hughie's at the same time. His hand was shaking so much that he slopped some beer on to the floor.

"Ye hopeless bugger. It's all because of ye. If ye'd given me what ye'd promised nowt of this would have happened. Well, I'm telling ye noo I'm not gan' doon for the likes of that bastard Freddie."

"It's not my fault, man. I keep trying to tell him, Officer. Freddie would pay me five bob for information on people who went out regularly of an evening. I let Hughie in on it – if he gave me a name and Freddie did the job I'd go halvers with him. Hughie told me about the Coulthards but Freddie already knew that the Coulthards went out to play whist every Friday. He said half o' Shields knew that and I could whistle for me money."

The Coulthards who lived in one of the big houses on the Lawe Top had been one of the burglar's victims.

"Where does he fence the stuff?"

Hughie took Jimmy by the arm. "Tell him nowt more. Your Freddie's a nasty piece of work with a lot of friends as bad as he is. If he thinks we shopped him we'll be right in the shite."

"I'll keep your names out of it and if we nab Freddie I'll have a word to see if we can do something about your attack on Inspector Mullins." That clinched it. They told me all I needed to know.

Cuddie Cleghorn came back in. "I've made a good job of that even if I do say so myself. Ye ganna try it out, Hughie?"

When I told Bob Jamieson how the booty was fenced he laughed and so did the Big Fella when we went to see him.

The next morning I was standing outside the *Bridge Inn* in plain clothes, alongside Alec Dorothy. Alec was also a new recruit who, like me, had joined the Force after the War. We both had our eyes on an undistinguished looking shop in Queen Street. There was nothing in the window to tell you what was sold and we hadn't seen a rush of customers.

"There's no way I'm going into there to ask for a French letter," Alec said to me as we both puffed away at our tabs. I was beginning to have similar qualms when help came from an unexpected source. 'Dapper' Digby Johnson, the bookies' runner who worked for Jack Conway, came out of the Bridge Public Bar and nearly walked into us. He looked worried when he recognised Alec. Digby was a nice looking fellow, very smartly dressed in a three piece suit and sporting a good quality cloth cap at a jaunty angle.

"Morning Digby," was Alec's greeting.

"I cannot stop, Constable Dorothy, I'm off to see someone." He didn't get far.

"We're not after betting slips, Digby, we're not even on duty," Alec reassured him. "You got a girl friend, Digby?"

"Well I might have one. Why you asking?"

Alec nodded towards the shop. "Me marra here's going courting tonight, and he wants to take precautions, if he gets lucky, like." Alec sounded embarrassed at the thought of it.

"Is that all?" Digby relaxed, took out a packet of Senior Service, and lit one up. "I've known the owner, Gerry O'Dowd, a while now. He's a customer of mine an' all, ye kna'." He winked. "There's nowt to be worried about. Ye just gan up to the counter and say you want something for a lady."

Alec looked interested. "You mean you use them yourself?"

"Wye aye. The thing is I meet a lot of women on me rounds. Most of them are married and their husbands don't know they bet. If they get too deep in debt to Jack, and if they're not too old, I offer to sort things out for them, for a little something in return. They always put up the same argument – they don't want a bairn – so I show them a French letter and that's that." He had a self satisfied smirk on his face. Much as I took a dislike to him I thought he might be useful. I spoke for the first time.

"Could you do me a favour, Digby? If I gave you the money could you buy one for me?"

"Wye aye. If you're a first timer I'd go for the new rubber ones. They're trickier to get on but they're more comfortable than the old skin ones. Mind, you can only use them once."

"How much?"

"The rubbers are thre'pence each but I can get you a pack of five for a bob."

"One will do fine. While you're in there could you spin him a yarn as well?"

"Wharraboot?"

"Tell him you're not sure your girlfriend will go all the way so you're thinking of buying her something."

"Like what?"

"Well, like some jewellery, but you don't want to pay too much."

"Ye must be soft, ye. If they're not paying off a debt, the most I'd ever give for it would be a tip – mind my tips never fail. Ye must be desperate."

"It's not that. She's a romantic sort of girl, always at the flicks. I just thought that if I gave her a nice brooch or a pair of earrings she'd think I was serious."

"Funny enough, I was in there the other day and Gerry was selling something like that to another customer. What do I do if he has something?"

"If you think it will do the trick then buy it. Mind, don't offer what he asks for it, knock him down."

"I'm not daft, ye kna'. Ye'll have to trust me though, I doubt if he'll give me a receipt."

"That's all right." The Big Fella had given me ten shillings but I just gave Digby five bob. "If you can get something for less I'll see you all right."

Digby might have been blessed with good looks but I doubt if he had much in the brain box. He never twigged for a minute what we were up to.

Ten minutes later he came out smiling all over his face. "Here you are," he said as he handed me over a brown paper bag which I very quickly put into my pocket. "And look at this."

We moved back into the doorway of the *Bridge* as Digby took out a pearl necklace. "I had to pay the full five bob for it. You've still got a bargain. He said he'd taken it in payment for a debt."

I took the list the DI had given me from my pocket. I looked at Alec. "We're on."

Alec took Digby by the arm. "Come with me and just look stupid. It won't be hard."

We hustled Digby into the shop to confront a startled Gerry O'Dowd. "We're plain clothes Polis, Mr. O'Dowd. We've just arrested Digby Johnson on suspicion of carrying betting slips, but when we searched him we found this."

Alec held out the necklace. "It was stolen from the Coulthards' house a couple of weeks ago."

Gerry didn't make any trouble and said straight away that he was fencing jewels for Freddie Olliphant. He owed him money for a gambling debt so it was either selling the stolen goods or a broken leg. Alec stayed with O'Dowd to sort out the rest of the stolen property, and I marched a worried looking Digby outside. "You're not going to arrest me?" he asked as we walked past the *Bridge*.

"No, you did us a good turn; we'll keep your name out of it. We'll need to ask Mr. O'Dowd to give us back the five bob though."

Digby looked even more worried. He put his hand in his pocket and gave me ninepence. "I only paid Four and Three so I thought I'd keep the change as a tip like."

I pocketed the money and said nowt. I had thought as much. "Bugger off then."

He seemed reluctant to go. "You're really a Polis?" I nodded. "So you don't want the French letter after all?"

"Certainly not." I nearly asked him what sort of person he thought I was, but I think he'd already worked that one out and that there wasn't a queue of lasses waiting for me.

"Well, I could always put it to good use." Digby was back to his normal self. I handed him the paper bag.

"You're welcome."

I went back into the shop. There was a pile of jewellery on the counter and Alec was ticking the pieces off one by one from the list.

The DI was a happy man when we took O'Dowd down the five stone steps and along to the Charge Room with the haul of stolen goods. Freddie Olliphant was arrested. The Big Fella had promised me that if we made an arrest he'd intervene with the Chief to see if he could do anything for Hughie. He was good to his word. The Chief didn't take long over it and the charges were dropped. As a special Court had been arranged the Chief still had to go before the Magistrates for the quaint custom of the presentation of the white gloves. Whenever there were no cases to bring before the Court the Chief Constable presented the Chairman of the Bench with a pair of white gloves. I'd never seen or heard of it before in my native Scotland but then we Scots are not as profligate as our English cousins. It was not a completely wasted morning as the Chief then invited the Magistrates and their Clerk back to his office for a glass of whisky.

Inspector Mullins was not pleased. He thought I'd gone behind his back and he had it in for me from then on.

The next time I saw Hughie Ross we were both on the platform at Shields Station seeing Annie Burnett off to London. I had been round to see her at Cleghorn's the morning after the attack to tell her that she would not have any more trouble from her husband.

She said she'd had enough, she was going to swallow her pride and go home to her parents in London who would look after her and the children. She had asked me a favour. She'd once before written to ask for money for the train journey to return home, but Burnett had taken the money and her parents had said they would not send any more. She asked if I could write to them and suggest that they send the money to me. "They'll trust a Policeman."

Her parents sent rail tickets but not money, and asked me to make sure she used them.

Thoughts of Annie Burnett were never far from my mind after that. I had her address in London from the letter her parents had sent. I was thinking that if we kept in touch then at some time in the future I could transfer to the Metropolitan Police, and I would be able to keep an eye out for her. Then I received a letter from her which came care of Keppel Street. As soon as I opened it and realised who it was from I put it back in the envelope, and did not read it until I arrived home.

She had settled in well with her parents, and had found a job working in a tea shop. Her mother looked after the children who were doing so much better now that they were getting proper meals. She had been thinking though, that she might have been a little too hard on John, her husband. She wondered whether she should give him another chance. She would not want to return to the North but he would almost certainly be able to find work in the capital. Did I know where he lived now? Her letters to Lower Thames Street had been returned 'not known at this address'.

I crumpled up the letter and threw it in the fire.

Union Alley – The Black and Grey is the building on the far left having its windows cleaned!

A nip of whisky

I could have done with a nip of whisky as I made my way back
to Keppel Street nick for a break. It was one of those bitterly cold
Shields nights when a Nor' Easter is blowing in off the German Sea.
Even with my greatcoat and cape the icy blast was enough to chill
the bones.

I'd not been in the Police Force for long and my beat was further
away from HQ than most. By the time I got to the Parade room the
air was thick with smoke. I can still taste the atmosphere. A dozen
or so old hands sat at the top end of a long table in the middle of
the low ceilinged room. Some had already been in for more than an
hour, the dominoes were out and a game of 'fives and threes' was
in full flow. A box of onions was on the table and the men ate them
raw with their tea and sandwiches. The new recruits were down the
other end away from the fire. Alec Dorothy, who like me had joined
the Force in 1919 as soon as he was demobbed, gestured to me
to sit beside him. Although I hailed from Scotland and Alec was a
Shieldsman, we got on well. Alec was normally a cheerful lad but he
had a side to him that I did not share; he was by nature envious of
others and always wanted more than he had. If he condemned the
property owners it was not out of working class politics but because
he wanted their wealth for himself.

"You look as though you could do with something hot, Tom,"
he greeted me in a loud voice – I could sense trouble coming. He
poured me out some tea from the pot. When I held the mug in both
hands I could hardly feel any warmth – the tea was lukewarm and
stewed.

"Hey, can you smell whisky?" he asked. He looked round. "It
comes from ower there. You'll have had a few tonight, Bill?"

Bill Spyles ignored him and continued peeling an onion. Bill
was an old hand and they didn't come much harder. He was not
tall but he was solid, and even though he measured more round the
waist than the shoulders he could still hold his own. He was not

the brightest of men, but if you were going to get into a scrap then you'd want Bill beside you.

The old hands shared out the best beats, closest to Keppel Street with the most licensed premises. In the heart of Shields, particularly around the Market Place, the Publicans were thick with the Police. It was the practice of many to leave a small pot of whisky just outside the back door of the Pub so that the Constable on night shift would have a little warmer. The younger Bobbies like Alec and me rarely got a sniff. We were given the beats furthest away from the centre of Old Shields where there were not as many pubs, and where Landlords were not so generous with their spirits. I was prepared to bide my time; others like Alec were not so happy.

"Aye, I could really have done with a drop tonight. Couldn't you, Tom? And auld Bill there would have had a skinful. Now if it was me, I'd let me young marras have a share."

A raw onion sailed past Alec's left ear and splattered against the wall. If it had caught him it would have knocked his head off. He turned white. Bill Spyles looked straight at him with his little piggy eyes.

"When you've been in the Force as long as me you'll get your whisky. In the meantime just shut it, and next time I'll not bloody miss."

I was not going to get involved in this. I stood up. "This tea's like dish water. I'll make another pot. Anybody else want any?"

John Burgess came over. He was an old hand, like Bill, but of a friendlier disposition. "Sit yersel' down, 'Jock', and finish your bait. You've just come in. I'll make the cha."

Peace was restored. Bill picked another onion out of the box and the 'fives and threes' continued. I knew of course that Alec would not let things drop, but he said nowt about it though for several weeks. His thoughts were elsewhere. We were having a break in the Parade Room one morning on the early shift. Alec was full of himself.

"Ye kna' that new shop girl I was telling you about that works in Oliver's. She's called Katie." Alec bought his cigarettes at the tobacconists in Fowler Street. A new assistant had started a few weeks ago, and she was, as they say in Shields, 'a bonny lass' – a redhead, like me, but a lot prettier.

"I've asked her oot. She says she'll think about it and let me know tomorrow when I get me Woodbines."

He didn't stop talking about her, and when she agreed to go to the pictures with him he was over the moon. He was less happy the day after the big date. He'd walked her home to Cockburn Street on the Lawe Top but she'd not let him kiss her goodnight. She was already going out with someone else.

"She said she did like me though, and we could go out again if I wanted to, but I wasn't to get serious."

"I'd be very careful, Alec. Did she say who the other lad is?"

"Aye, ye might kna' him – Nipper Nesbitt."

I knew him and I could see why Alec was worried. Nipper was a nice looking fellow who probably earned a lot more than Alec ever did. He was a bookies' runner and was one of Jack Conway's top men. He'd never been caught and boy, could he run. If they had ever put him in the Powderhall Sprint he would have left them standing. He only had to hear a Policeman's whistle and he was off like a whippet. Nipper had his own style of running, back straight, head held high and arms pumping up and down. Jack Conway had a gammy leg so he usually had Nipper around when he was holding a lot of cash, just in case. It wasn't only the Polis he was afraid of. Bookmakers were often the target of robberies and had to look to their own protection. Nipper would never fight; he just took off with the money and that was that. For all that, he was a likeable lad who would always pass the time of day with you.

Alec didn't say much over the next few weeks. You'd always know when he was taking Katie out – the day before he'd be smiling and joking but the day after he'd be down; he wasn't keen at all on her seeing Nipper in between times. Then one break time he came in to the Parade Room smiling all over his face. It was the old Alec again who came and sat down beside me.

"Ye'll nivver guess who I had a drink with last neet."

"Alec, there's a lot of folk in Shields and most of them frequent public houses so I don't think I ever will."

He laughed. "Nipper Nesbitt."

"Well at least you're drinking and not fighting."

"Aye, he's a canny lad when you get to kna' him. He bumped into me and Katie the other neet when we were coming out of the *Golden Lion*. I thought he was going to turn nasty but he didn't. He said Katie would have to make her mind up sometime, but there was no point in us falling out over it. He also said he knew how to make a woman happy." Alec paused. "When he said that, ye kna', wor Katie blushed. Ye don't think he's been..."

"Well how would I know? He probably meant kissing, or buying her presents, or he might be giving her tips on the horses."

"Aw man, hadaway, she wouldn't bet. I don't like the sound of that kissing though. Anyway he suggested we have a drink together, so we met last night in the *Black and Grey*. He likes his whisky."

"The man's got taste then!" was all I could think to reply.

And so it went on. Alec and Nipper became quite friendly, but I knew the way Alec's mind worked and I was sure that he would be plotting or scheming something to put one over on Nipper. Nipper, on the other hand, was not worried. He was not daft and could have got a good job, but standing on street corners and at bar counters taking bets and dodging the Police was what he enjoyed – and it was good money. He'd never been nicked but if he ever was he'd be fined a couple of quid which Jack Conway would pay and he'd be straight back on the street. Nipper was a good judge of character – you have to be in his line of work – and I suspect that he had more experience of women than Alec. He knew that whatever Alec might do, Katie would eventually choose him. He was not too worried then, when the Police started to clamp down on street betting and on Jack Conway and Nipper Nesbitt in particular. Why the powers that be should have chosen that particular time was a mystery to many. I had my suspicions but I'll say nowt; others did. I wasn't the only one that knew about Alec's love triangle – he'd talk to anyone about his Katie, particularly when he'd had a few drinks.

When orders came down from above that the beat officers were to be on the lookout for bookies' runners and in particular a certain Percival 'Nipper' Nesbitt – the Percival was a surprise to us all – several of my colleagues put two and two together. Alec had recently joined the local Lodge and had cosied up to one or two of the Councillors on the Police Committee. The odd word here or there could be very effective if you were saying what people wanted to hear, and not everybody thought like our Chief that the prime job of the Constable was to keep order – street betting was illegal but it rarely caused a breach of the peace, and Police resources were better spent on crimes that ended up with people being hurt, robbed or cheated. Amen to that. Some of our Councillor masters were known for their desire to make everybody's life as miserable as their own, so Alec's little whispering campaign had its effect.

As I'm sitting at my desk by the fire sipping my whisky and writing these memoirs I can see the humorous side but at the time it was not so pleasant. Jack Conway could smell a copper half a mile away and was never caught with anything like a betting slip on him. As for Nipper, as soon as he saw one of us getting close, he was off, back straight, head high, arms pumping. Even Ernest Armstrong who played on the wing for Westoe Rugby Club, and was reckoned to be fast, was left standing. He had tried to come on to Nipper from the doorway of the *Tram* as he was taking a bet on the corner opposite Crofton's. Nipper saw him at the last minute and took off straight across the Market Place and down one of the side streets. All of Shields laughed. Nipper became so popular that people were queuing to put on bets with him in the hope of seeing a race. It was said that Jimmy Crimbone, the bookie from Taylor Street, was offering odds of 20 to 1 against any Constable catching Nipper from a standing start, but could find no takers. The Chief put a stop to it. He came to the Parade Room one day and spoke to us in his usual no nonsense way. He said the Force had been made to look a laughing stock. He looked to us, 'the Bobbies on the Beat', to carry on our normal duties as keepers of the peace.

"Don't fret about Nipper Nesbitt," he said. "Shields is not a big place. One day, one of you will walk round a corner and bump into Nipper Nesbitt taking a bet, and if you do you'd better hold onto him until you get him to Keppel Street. You can let go when you reach the top of the five stone steps!" It went down well.

One night, not long after, I'd managed to do my round in good time and was in the Parade Room early. The dominoes were taken of course but at least the tea was piping hot. I'd just settled in when Bill Spyles came in. He slammed his truncheon down on the bench, glowered round the room and spoke.

"Some bastard's had me whisky." We all looked up. "I was all right at the *Scotia* and the *Bridge* but when I got to the *Black and Grey* the pot was empty – same at the *Golden Lion* and the *City of Durham*. The bugger had cut the tie and left the pot on the ground." He looked towards me and Alec and one or two other of the new recruits. "If I catch the sod that did it I'll ram me stave right up his arse." Bill didn't make threats lightly and the truncheons in those days were solid wood.

"What makes you sure it's one of us?" I asked quietly. 'Poaching' on someone else's beat was just about the worst offence a Policeman could commit. "It might have been someone who'd seen you take a drop and thought they'd try it for themselves."

"The folk of Shields have long memories. Someone did try it before your time, Geordie Daws. It was on Joe Hand's beat. Joe lay in wait for him one night and Geordie ended up in hospital for a week – he still walks with a limp. No! You mark my words. It'll be someone in this Parade Room."

I said nothing but as I bit into my lump of cheese I detected a faint but unmistakable smell of whisky mingled with peppermint coming from right beside me where Alec Dorothy was sitting and, for once, not saying a word.

The next night was the same. Bill had had his tots at the *Scotia* and the *Bridge*. The pot which should have been tied to the lock on the back door of the *Black and Grey* was on the ground. The pots had lug handles and the Landlords would tie them to the bolt on the door with a bit of twine. The Constable would usually untie the knot, have his drink and tie the pot back on. In freezing weather you just cut the tie. Bill's sneak thief was taking no risks by lingering to untie the twine – he just cut, drank, and scarpered.

Bill was calmer that night. As he lit up his pipe he looked at the bottom end of the table.

"I warned you last night. I'm saying no more. Gentleman Jim'll do my talking from now on." The old hands had a pet name for their truncheons, which some of them still called staves, and Bill's was Gentleman Jim.

I made a point of leaving the station with Alec. As we walked down the steps I put my hand on his arm.

"I know what you're up to, Alec. I smelt it on your breath the other night. You've had your fun, now lay off it."

Alec smiled. "Divvent fash yersel', Tom. I'll be fine. The fun's just beginning."

As I did my rounds I became more and more worried. In later years I would let people look after themselves. I've learned the hard way that you are never thanked for interfering, but in those days I was young and keen. My concerns for Alec kept niggling away at me all the next day so I decided that I would start my shift a little early, and then make my way back to the town centre after midnight to have a scout around the pubs near to the *Black and Grey*. It did not need a Sherlock Holmes to deduce that if the whisky thief struck again it would be at the *Black and Grey*. Even Bill Spyles, limited as he was in the skills of logic and reasoning, would have worked that one out. It was one of those cold, damp, foggy nights, and it was not too difficult to pass by unnoticed. I made my way up Bridge Street, and at its corner with North Street found a perfect spot to observe Union Alley and the back door of the Black and Grey without being seen myself. The fog was starting to thicken but I could just about see all that I needed.

I heard the footsteps before I saw the figure coming down North Street. He slowed down and stopped just by the corner of Union Alley. You could not see much in the fog but I could hear his breathing as he looked around. One thing was certain: he was not Alec Dorothy – no helmet, no great overcoat. Whoever it was, he walked quickly over to the back door of the *Black and Grey*, pulled a knife out of his pocket, and started cutting the twine. He seemed to be having trouble.

Bill appeared out of the shadows so fast I almost didn't see him. He didn't say a word but his truncheon was in his hand as he came on to the villain, and he struck down with an over-arm blow that would have killed an ox. I shouted out 'Police' at the top of my voice – just in time – the shadowy figure at the gate moved quickly. Gentleman Jim hit his shoulder and then thudded against the door with a resounding crash. I couldn't see much of what happened next as I ran across the street but as I came close I saw Bill stagger backwards clutching at his chest.

"He's stabbed me, the bugger," he shouted out as he slumped to his knees.

The other man did not wait around for me to arrive; he turned and ran. I didn't see his face, I didn't need to – there was only one lad in Shields who could run as fast as that – back straight, head high, arms pumping.

As I got to Bill, he was slowly sinking to the pavement, the whisky thief's knife sticking out of his chest. He recognised me.

"It's you, Tom. He's done for me, the bastard. Stabbed in the heart. I'm a goner."

His eyes flickered and he fell at my feet. As I looked down at Bill's prone body I heard someone else come on the scene – you wouldn't believe it: Alec Dorothy. The back entrance of the *Black and Grey* was proving to be a popular place.

"He's been knifed," I said as I carefully unbuttoned Bill's overcoat and tunic. Alec put his hand on Bill's neck and felt the pulse. "Well his heart's beating all right."

I moved my hand under the tunic – there was no blood, but then I felt the knife. It had just pierced the flesh; there was a trace of moisture but not much. I could feel something hard and flat holding the knife blade. I put my other hand between the greatcoat and the tunic and found Bill's pocket book – it had saved him.

"He's all right, Alec. His pocket book's stopped the knife. He's just fainted; it'll be the shock."

"Jesus, he's a lucky bastard. I'll go after the other one." Before I could say anything he was gone. I pulled the knife out. It was an old army knife and it would have been fatal if it had gone straight in. I knelt forward and put my mouth next to Bill's ear. "Bill, Bill…" I whispered quietly and his eyelids began to flicker. "It's the Angel Gabriel. You've reached the promised land."

His eyes slowly opened and he looked round with the happiest smile I've ever seen on his ugly mug – that is until he saw my own equally plain features. I got out of the way quick as his right fist came over.

"Ye bugger. Where am I?" He then remembered what had happened and clutched his chest. I showed him the knife.

"Take your pocket book out."

He sat up and undid his tunic pocket. He pulled the book out and inspected the cut that went right through it. "I never thought I'd see the day when I had a good word to say about this bloody thing."

Like most of the old hands who were recruited for brawn rather than brain, Bill detested having to write up his calls in the blue-bound note book. "I could have been a goner. Hey Tom, pass me that whisky pot. I've had a nasty shock."

I had a job untying the pot – it was held on with wire.

"I asked Jock Dunn, the landlord, to put wire on. I saw him this evening before coming on duty. I wanted to make sure whoever tried to take it would stay put till I could get at him."

I finally freed the pot and handed it to Bill who took a deep swig.

"Pass it here, Bill. I've had a bit of a shock too. Seeing you fall to the ground like that when you were hardly scratched." He handed me the pot.

"Well, what was I supposed to think with the knife sticking out of me like that, right where my heart is. The mind can play tricks on you." He stood up and started doing up the buttons on his greatcoat. "I think it might be best if we kept this to ourselves, Tom. No harm's been done. I doubt if the bastard will take any more of my whisky. I gave him a good belt on the shoulder which he'll feel for a few days."

Of course I knew exactly why Bill wanted to keep things quiet. He would be the butt of all sorts of jokes, fainting like he did when he was not hurt, and it would be the old hands who would be the worst. They could be a cruel bunch.

"I'm not sure I can do that, Bill. Attempted murder is a serious offence in my book."

Bill had taken back the whisky pot and after a last drink was tying it back to the door.

"I don't think the lad meant any harm. He was taken by surprise. He probably didn't even see that it was the Polis that was on to him. He just hit out with the hand that was holding the knife."

"I didn't mean that," I said looking straight into Bill's piggy little eyes. "It was the vicious attack from behind with a truncheon, and the man was just after a drop of whisky. You'd have nigh killed him had I not shouted out."

Bill started to say something then stopped. I could see that he was trying to work me out.

"That was a good drop," was all I said.

"Aye, come along Tom. Keep me company for a while. There'll be a pot at the *City of Durham*."

We went halvers at all Bill's stops until break time. It says something about Bill and his mates on the 'whisky beats' that even

on half rations I knew I'd had a drink by time we returned to Keppel
Street. I'd agreed to keep stumm and hadn't mentioned that Alec
Dorothy had turned up. He lodged close to me and I would see
him in the morning. I was sure that he would want to keep things
quiet as much as Bill did. As for me, I overcame my scruples. Bill
promised to have a word with the other old timers to see if I could
be squeezed onto a 'whisky beat' from time to time.

Nipper Nesbitt vanished. Jack Conway, who had spent his entire
life avoiding the Polis, actually approached the Constable on duty
in the Market Place to ask if we'd arrested Nipper. Charlie Nesbitt,
Nipper's brother, a pitman and a nasty piece of work, came into the
Station to ask if we knew where he was. We didn't. It was a relief
to many in the Force that he was no longer running rings round us,
and no one in authority lifted a finger to find the missing lad.

Alec had never been happier. He'd seen Katie every day since
Nipper had gone AWOL. One morning he came in the Parade
Room smirking to himself more than usual.

"I think Katie and me are going to be married. I've not asked her
yet, but I'll be surprised if she says no after what she gave me last
night."

I said nowt. Sure enough, not long afterwards, Alec announced
to the Parade Room that he was to be wed. It was then that Alec's
problems started. When Katie took him round to meet the folks,
he said it felt like a funeral. Her father, Teddy Ollerenshaw, was a
blacksmith at St. Hilda's Colliery who just sat in his chair by the
fire smoking his pipe. Katie's mother was the trouble – she was a
big woman with fleshy features and an ample bosom. She liked her
snuff and her horses. That's how Katie had met Nipper who would
do home visits for regular customers – straight in the backdoor
without knocking and up the stairs – 'Teddy's cousin' if anyone
asked.

You'd have normally expected that a respectable family like the
Ollerenshaws would not have welcomed the attentions of a bookies'
runner to their daughter. Not so. Nipper was like one of the family

already and Mrs. Ollerenshaw knew the advantages of a bookie who would give you a bit of credit when times were hard. From the first day she met Alec she took against him.

"I hope you're not one of the Dorothys from Maxwell Street," was her greeting, and when Alec confessed that he was – "Well I'm not very happy about that. We hoped that our Katie would be going up in the world."

In the end she had no choice. Katie was pregnant and would have been put out on the streets if she had not been engaged to Alec. Nipper Nesbitt was still missing so Mrs. Ollerenshaw gave in. The wedding took place at St. Stephen's. Although the Force was well represented at the Church, I was the only one to be invited back after the wedding. It was close relatives only but their upstairs flat was full to bursting – the Ollerenshaws and the Dorothys were big families. I'd only taken a light lunch as I had fond memories of the tables bending under the weight of victuals at weddings in Scotland and Carlisle. I was disappointed. The few tongue sandwiches went before I could get to the table and cold cow-heel pie and pease pudding is not my idea of a wedding feast, but there were plenty of pickles and bread and butter so I did not starve. Katie's mother had not put herself out for the food but there was no shortage of drinks. Katie's brother, Little Teddy, worked at Turnbull's brewery. There were two barrels on trestles in the hallway at the top of the stairs and a long table with bottles of stout and spirits. I had my share.

Little Teddy, who towered over his father, took after his mother – he was a right gobshiter, as we would have said in the Army. The Ollerenshaw men had all met in the *Beehive* before the wedding and some had managed a quick one on the way back to the house. I'm not saying that Little Teddy was the worse for drink but he was even more talkative than usual. Most of us were trying to ignore him until he started telling Alec about how he had been drinking with Charlie Nesbitt in the *Douglas.*

"Charlie says that there's only one explanation of why Nipper's gone missing. He reckons that someone must have murdered him.

Nipper would never have gone away without telling his mother. She's worried sick, the poor auld hinny. He also reckons that Nipper was going to ask wor Katie to marry him. Then Nipper disappears and you marry Katie..."

He hadn't time to finish as Alec had him by the throat. "You repeat that again..." Two of the Ollerenshaw clan were quick to come to Teddy's aid. Fists were clenched and ready to be thrown as I quickly pushed my way to Alec's side. There was a resounding crash as Big Teddy brought his hand down onto the table.

"There'll be no fighting in my hoose on the day of me daughter's wedding. If anyone starts anything they'll finish it with me."

'Big' Teddy was just over five feet tall but he was broad round the shoulders and as strong as an ox. There were no takers.

I didn't stay long after that. Katie of course had overheard; Alec's wedding night was going to be interesting, but his troubles did not stop there. Charlie Nesbitt had convinced himself that Nipper was dead and that Alec had done away with him. He was going round Shields telling anyone who would listen, and he had started taunting Alec when he was on duty in the Market Place. Charlie was usually half cut, of course. He wasn't married and lodged with another pitman's family in Cornwallis Street. If he wasn't down the Pit he'd be in the boozers until his money ran out.

It has often struck me how two brothers can be so different. While Nipper was happy go lucky, Charlie was dour. Nipper would always run away from trouble; Charlie went looking for it. It may have been that their character was influenced by their looks. Nipper was a nice looking lad; Charlie had a squint in one eye and sticky out ears. Mind, no one ever made fun of him.

On Saturdays there were always two on duty in the Market and they stuck together. Alec was on duty with Henry Milburn, but Henry had had to take a drunk back to Keppel Street so Alec was on his own for a while. Charlie Nesbitt came out of the *Grapes* and saw Alec. He started on him straight away. Alec just ignored him but then Charlie pushed him on the shoulder – that's one thing you didn't do to a Shields Bobby. Alec went to arrest Charlie, Charlie nutted him, Alec went down, and Charlie put the boot in hard. In those days people didn't just stand by and watch when an officer was in difficulty. A couple of fellows managed to pull Charlie away. A young lad who'd seen it all ran round the corner to the *Mechanics* where the old timers used to drink when off duty. Bill Spyles and John Burgess were playing 'fives and threes'. They were out fast. Charlie had started on the two fellows who'd helped Alec but Bill and John went in hard and put him down. Reinforcements arrived from Keppel Street and Alec was taken to the hospital. Charlie arrived there under arrest not long after as a result of an unfortunate accident in Police Headquarters. As he was being taken into the Station he fell down the five stone steps – black eyes, broken nose, three cracked ribs and a broken wrist. It was a common occurrence and the Magistrates did not ask any questions. Alec was badly bruised in a very sensitive part of the body, and Charlie was sent to Durham for six months.

After that things calmed down. Katie gave birth to a boy, and she and Alec moved into married quarters at Keppel Street. Everything was going well for Alec – that is until Nipper Nesbitt turned up in Shields eighteen months later.

I only learned some considerable time afterwards what had happened to Nipper on that fateful night. He had a room over a shop in Cuthbert Street and he'd gone straight there after his fight with Bill. He was getting his money from under the floorboards when Alec arrived. Alec had put Nipper up to taking the whisky in the almost certain knowledge that Bill would be in wait. He had hoped that Nipper would get a hiding, and be put out of commission for a while so that he would have Katie all to himself. Things turned out even better than that when Alec told Nipper that Bill was dead, and that he'd go to the gallows for sure if he was caught. He agreed to help the unsuspecting and very worried

bookies' runner. As soon as Nipper had his money the two left
to make their way down to Holborn. Alec had spent his first year
on the beat there and like all the Polis had come to know the
Arab Boarding House Keepers. They were leaders of the Arab
Community who looked after the seamen who lodged in their
houses. They knew the Ship's Masters and would sign the men on,
keep their money for them and generally look after them. Alec took
Nipper to Abdul Said. He had done him a favour once and knew he
would help him. The next day Nipper was on the *Oberon* bound for
Fremantle. He went aboard with half a dozen other Arab firemen.
Abdul Said had persuaded one of his men to let Nipper have his
papers. It had not been difficult; the young Arab had just been
married and could spend a few weeks with his wife before coming
to the Station to report that his papers had been stolen – he'd be
well paid. Abdul Said had had a quiet word with the Skipper and no
doubt a few pounds had passed between them. With his dark hair,
swarthy complexion and dressed in Arab clothes, Nipper passed
casual inspection. He had never done any hard work in his life and
the first couple of weeks nearly killed him. The Arab firemen, who
had been told to look after him by Abdul Said, carried him until he
got used to the graft. He was paid off in Australia and decided to
settle there. He soon found work as the Aussies liked their betting.
He'd always look out for the Shields lads on any ships that arrived.
No one seemed to have heard anything about the murder of a
Policeman. Then one day a young Shields seaman told Nipper how
he'd been arrested and given a hammering.

"I'll nivver forget the bastard, he was called Spyles, Bill Spyles,
and I was only having a bit of fun."

This had taken place a good three months after Nipper had left
Shields, so he had found a ship to South America and then back to
Liverpool. From there he'd checked out that he was not wanted by
the Shields Police and had come home.

I saw him once walking up Mile End Road but as soon as he saw
me he was round the corner and off. The next time I saw Nipper

41

he was in the Ingham Infirmary. He'd been found in a back lane off Woodbine Street badly beaten. The Police Surgeon had had a look at his injuries and reckoned that he'd been struck with something hard, a club or a cosh. It took him a day or two to come round properly so I was sent up to see if he could remember anything. He could hardly talk as his front teeth had been knocked out – but he was saying nowt, he had seen nowt, heard nowt.

It was fairly plain that Bill Spyles had had his revenge. It surprised me as I thought that Bill had forgotten the whole thing. I started having a battle with my conscience. We all stood by each other, but it was not right for someone to be beaten half to death. I decided to talk to Bill first before going any further. I went round to the *Mechanics* one evening when we were both off duty. He was playing 'fives and threes'.

"I need a word, Bill."

"Well you'll have to wait. I'm busy."

I leant over. "It's about Nipper Nesbitt and it won't wait."

He'd just finished a round. "John," he called over to John Burgess who was standing at the bar, "come and keep me hand warm while I have a chat with Tom." He got up out of his chair and we moved to a seat at the back of the bar.

"I went to see Nipper Nesbitt the other day. He's in a state. So far as I know there's only one man in Shields who bears him a grudge and that's you. It was only a nip of whisky, Bill."

Bill sipped his beer. "Your memory's not that good, Tom. You never told me who had been at my whisky that night at the *Black and Grey*. I'm not saying I didn't have my suspicions when Nipper went missing, but even if I'd known it was him I'd not have gone looking for him. If I'd bumped into him I might have given him a slap with me gloves and warned him not to pull any more stunts, but I wouldn't have used Gentleman Jim on him. Not for something that's long forgotten." He looked at me. "When was he attacked?"

"It was last Friday night about ten o'clock."

"John," he called over to the 'fives and threes' table. "Tom here wants to know if he could have a game this Friday night."

"Nae chance," came the gruff reply. "There's already half a dozen waiting to get in."

"You were lucky last Friday."

"Luck doesn't come into it – pure skill."

Bill turned back to me. "I was here until closing time, and a bit. You can ask any of the lads."

I sat quiet for a while and finished my whisky.

"I'm sorry for troubling you, Bill, but if it wasn't you, then who else?"

"Try a jealous husband," was all Bill said.

As I hammered on the door to Alec Dorothy's house at Keppel Street later that same day, his words came back to me. One of the wives had come down to complain to the Station Sergeant about the noise – she said it sounded as though murder was being done. As I knew Alec I was sent up. It seemed to be just my luck to be around when something unpleasant was going on. I could hear the voices as I ran down the long stone corridor. After a few moments the door was opened by Katie holding the bairn in her arms with Alec trying to pull her back inside. She had her coat on and a small suitcase was by the door. She'd been crying but that was not why her face was red and puffed – she'd been given a hiding. I pushed myself into the room and came between Alec and his wife. He glared at me threateningly.

"If you don't get out of my house now, I'll throw you out. This is between me and Katie. She's my wife and she'll do as I say."

I looked him straight in the eyes. "If you want to be arrested for assault on your wife and threatening a Police Officer then go ahead. You'll be downstairs before your feet touch the ground."

It was known in the Force that I did not make idle threats. Alec backed off. "Well she's not leaving me. She married me and she stays here."

Katie had other ideas. "I am, Alec Dorothy. Do you think I can stay knowing what you've done to Nipper? You trick him into leaving Shields so that you'll have me all to yourself, and then when he comes back you beat him half to death."

"Aye, well he only got what he deserved. I know you've seen him. He was after you as soon as he was back in Shields. You chose me and you can stay with me."

"Alec, you can't force Katie to stay if she doesn't want to. Give her a chance to think things over."

He wasn't budging.

"Mind, Alec. I'm saying nowt to anyone about what I've heard here, but if Nipper changes his mind and agrees to testify you'll be away in Durham for a few years and Katie can do what she wants."

Alec was never stupid and he knew that he had no choice. "Aye, well so long as it's only for a few days. Here, let me kiss the bairn goodbye."

He seemed to have calmed down and he took young Eddy from Katie. "Right, you can bugger off, but little Eddy stays with me and you can't do anything about that, Tom Duncan. If she wants him she'll have to go to court. If she loves the bairn, she'll stay here."

Katie picked up the suitcase. "I'm going. I'll be at me mother's. Eddy's not yours, Alec. He's Nipper's."

Alec said nowt. He just stood there.

"Why do you think I was so keen to get married after Nipper was gone? I didn't know what to do but you were only too happy. I thought you might realise when the baby was early but you just didn't think. You'll look a right fool looking after another man's bairn and I'll make sure folk know."

"But he looks like me. Everyone says."

"Of course they do; they'd say it whatever he looked like. But you've said yourself how quick he is, and how he's nearly running now before he can walk."

That clinched it. Alec gave the bairn back to Katie. "Good riddance," was all he said.

I could not feel any great sorrow for him as he had brought it on himself. I left with Katie and carried the suitcase for her. I walked her to her mother's but neither of us said much.

Katie and Nipper left Shields as soon as he left the hospital. They moved to Sunderland. Nipper started taking bets on his own account and soon had a good business going. Alec divorced Katie some time after she'd left, and Nipper and Katie were wed.

It was years later before I saw Katie and Nipper again. I'd retired from the Force and the letter inviting me to their twenty fifth wedding anniversary had been forwarded on from Keppel Street. It was a big do and I was greeted like an old friend. Katie said it was a belated thank you for my help on the day she'd finally left Alec. She pointed out to me a tall, good looking fellow. "That's Eddy, our eldest."

I could not believe my eyes. He was the spitting image of Alec Dorothy when he was that age. I said nowt; I didn't need to. My face must have said it all. Katie laughed. "I wasn't going to leave Eddy behind and I wasn't going to stay with Alec. It was all I could think of. Alec didn't deserve any better after what he had done to Nipper."

"Does Alec know?"

"After I left he never wanted to see me or the bairn. We offered him every chance. He didn't want to pay any maintenance.

"I'll be quite honest, I wasn't sure myself when he was born. I thought he was Nipper's and that's why I gave in to Alec after Nipper disappeared. The other one, Percy, is Nipper's all right." She pointed to a young man standing on his own. "He was faster than Nipper ever was. Everybody said he would have run for England in the Olympics after the War. As it was, he lost both legs in the Normandy landings." The young lad moved over to where a pretty girl was standing. He walked slowly and jerkily on his false legs.

Mill Dam and the Cumberland Arms

A bonny lass

It was just after closing time on a Saturday night, and I was walking up East Holborn with Walter Heron who'd joined the Force a few months after me. I'd found my feet but Walter still had a long way to go. On Saturday nights we usually doubled up for the first couple of hours until the streets were clear.

Holborn ran along the Riverside. It was a warren of alleyways, narrow streets, clinker houses and steep banks. On East and West Holborn, the main streets, there were pubs, lodging houses for sailors and all types of shops. Cockroaches and rats were plentiful. It must have been a public health nightmare for the authorities. By the twenties the Arab seafarers had made Holborn their home. There were many lodging houses for Arab sailors and coffee shops were as common as pubs.

It was a pleasant, balmy evening that Saturday, and we hadn't had any trouble until a drunken seaman came staggering out of one of the alleys. He looked as though he'd been in a fight and was roaring drunk. He grabbed hold of Walter and when we tried to push him away he started throwing his fists around. We decided to take him in for his own safety. He was Norwegian and kept trying to tell us something – it could have been double Dutch for all the sense we could make of it. We got him back to the Station and he was locked up for the night. The Officer in Charge of Laygate nick was Charlie Nicholls – nearly time expired.

"Drunk and disorderly?"

"Aye, that should cover it."

As I started writing up my note book I said to Charlie, "He was worked up about something. It might be worth asking Jan Christiansen to have a word with him."

Jan Christiansen ran a lodging house for sailors and most of the Norwegian lads stayed there. He was always willing to come in and translate for us, and would stand bail if necessary. They'd stay in his lodging house and he'd sort them out and tidy them up all ready for

Court.

"You can do me a favour then, Tom. If there're lights on in the *Banks O'Tyne* when you go back up Holborn, have a look in. Jan should be in the back room with Chrissie Andersen. Ask him to pop round in the morning. We'll need to sort out bail in any case."

Charlie knew Holborn like the back of his hand and he knew where to find people. Walter came in carrying a mug of tea.

"Write your notes up, Walter," I asked. I'd taken Walter under my wing – he needed looking after.

"I'll do it later; let's have me tea first. Anyway I can't see the point – your book will have it all in, and there'll be less spelling mistakes for Inspector Mullins to complain aboot."

Walter Heron should never have been a Police Officer. He was a big lad but he was not very clever. He became one of my closest friends so I am well qualified to comment. Walter's main trouble was his good nature and his gullibility; he was easily taken in. The first time I met him he was standing outside the store room looking lost. It was his first day. He was nearly six feet tall, very thin, with a mop of straight blond hair and ruddy cheeks. His new uniform, second hand like everything else we were given, had last been worn by a shorter, stouter man and it showed.

I walked past him and then stopped. "Are ye waiting for something?"

"Aye, Sergeant Jamieson sent me down to the stores for a long stand. The storeman said to wait in the corridor."

I remembered from my Army days seeing many a new recruit wandering round barracks for hours with a tin in his hand, looking for the last post which needed a lick of paint.

"Well, if I were you, I'd go back to Sergeant Jamieson and tell him you've stood long enough."

He looked at me for several seconds. I could almost sense his brain slowly getting into gear. "The bastards," he finally said, his cheeks blushing red with embarrassment. They'd seen him coming a mile off.

I put out my hand. "I'm Tom Duncan."

"Walter Heron. I'll buy ye a drink the neet." I never said no when someone else was buying.

Walter's uncle was on the Police Committee and as the new recruit's ineptitudes became clear, word spread that he'd only got the job because of nepotism. Anyone who knew anything about the Chief would have dismissed any such suggestion out of hand.

Walter was the son of a butcher who had a little shop on the corner of Denmark Street. Business had been bad during the war and his father had just started getting back to normal when he'd had a heart attack and died. Walter had taken over the family concern. Now I've no reason to doubt that Walter could cut up a carcass as well as the next man but he was not a businessman – he was too trusting and would give tick to anyone. Word soon spread and he did a roaring trade for a while but very little money was coming in. When he started going round to the addresses people had given, he found that they had never lived there. He'd been had. He had to bail out and sell the business before he was bankrupted. His uncle had helped him out and decided that Walter should join the Force.

Two vacancies had been advertised around that time and Walter applied. His uncle went in to see the Chief, explained Walter's circumstances and asked that the Chief should give him favourable consideration. The Chief very politely but firmly told Alderman Heron that he only made appointments on merit, and that he'd consider Walter's application like any other. Walter did not get the job.

At the next meeting of the Police Committee when the Chief reported the appointments, Walter's uncle started to stir things up. He wanted to know why the Chief had taken on two men from outside the town, one from Glasgow and the other from Cumberland, when there had been a perfectly acceptable candidate from Shields whose mother and sisters depended upon him. Walter's uncle had a lot of friends on the Committee who, like him, saw nothing wrong with the appointment of Committee Members' relatives to jobs as Constables. The Chief made a tactical error. He did not want to antagonise Walter's uncle any more than he already had, and he therefore commented favourably on Walter's application, saying that in normal circumstances he would have stood a very good chance, but the two men he had appointed had been outstanding applicants – one had been a Regimental Sergeant Major and the other had won the Military Medal. Walter had spent the war years in the catering corps at Aldershot.

"So," enquired Walter's uncle, "had these two worthy candidates not applied then Walter would most likely have been appointed?"

"In all probability, yes," replied the Chief.

Everybody seemed satisfied and the Committee moved to the next item on the Chief's report. He was expecting a battle with the Committee as he was asking for an increase in the number of Constables. To his surprise his report was accepted and he was authorized to appoint two more Constables, one in the current year and one in the next. He had not twigged what was coming and when he did it was too late.

One of Alderman Heron's cronies suggested that it seemed to be a waste of time and money for the Chief to advertise the vacancy when Walter Heron, who he had mentioned earlier in the meeting as being suitable material, could be appointed straight away. The Chief had no option, but Walter would not have it easy, and although he somehow managed to keep his job, it was not for want of trying to lose it.

Inspector Mullins, who had recently been appointed, had been given a brief by the Chief to improve the standard of note-taking by officers. It was the sort of task the Mullins of this world revelled in, but it was not an easy one. Most of the old timers who made up a good half of the Force had been recruited at a time when brawn rather than brain was the main requirement. New recruits had compulsory night classes but some would never improve. Walter was one of these.

Every so often Mullins would come into the Parade Room before a shift to inspect the note books. He'd look at two or three and if he found anything of interest he'd share it with everyone. He soon realised that Walter was easy meat. He was looking at Walter's notes this particular morning when an item caught his eye which he read out for all to hear.

"'3pm. Called to Salem Street. Man had broken leg. Helped man home.

"'3.30pm. Left man at home in Smithy Street.'

"You've omitted any reference, Constable Heron, to any medical assistance. It must have been miraculous if the man could go home half an hour later."

I thought that I'd better help Walter out. He'd told me what had happened. "Can I help, Sir?"

"No you cannot, Constable Duncan. Officer Heron will explain."

Well, I'd tried my best. I just let Mullins get on with it.

"He didn't need a doctor. I just gave him a hand yem."

"And I suppose you left him lying on the doorstep with his broken leg?"

"Wye of course not. He just hopped along the hall."

I've never seen so many Policemen trying to keep a straight face. Most of them like me knew what had happened. Mullins didn't – he was furious.

"He just hopped along the hall?"

"Aye, and then I carried his broken leg in for him."

It was no good. Sam Beecroft nearly choked. Bill Spyles was weeping and John Burgess looked as though he'd got a kipper bone stuck in his throat.

"I dain't kna' why you're laughing. It was auld Jack Chew. He cleans the Conveniences. He caught his wooden leg in the gutter and it snapped."

Mullins said nowt; he didn't need to. He thought that Walter had set him up. He handed back his book. "Parade dismissed." He marched out of the room, the muscles on the back of his neck twitching.

We'd both been relieved to be moved to Laygate as it meant we'd be out of Mullins' way, so while Walter sipped his tea I finished my notes and headed off to the *Banks O'Tyne*. When I reached the Pub it was well past midnight. There were no lights showing so I was about to walk on when I heard the door opening. A man and a woman were leaving. The fellow was a tall, well built chap with a peaked cap, probably a sea captain. He was holding the young lady very tight. I stepped forward showing my lantern and asked if the Landlord was about. The young lass shouted out 'Chrissie,' and the couple went on their way just as a bald headed man in shirtsleeves appeared from behind the door. There were no lights on in the bar but I could see a shimmer of light coming from behind a curtain that led to a back room. Laughter and a clink of glasses gave the game away.

"Ja, Officer, is there any trouble?"

I put his mind at rest.

"Constable Nicholls sent me." Charlie's name was all it needed.

"Well come in. I'm just having a drink with a few friends. Come and join us."

"I will if Jan Christiansen's with you."

"Wye of course he is. Where else would he be on a Saturday night?"

Where indeed? I was to learn that the back room of the *Banks O'Tyne* was a favourite meeting place after closing hours – a haunt for seafarers, mostly Scandinavian. Charlie Nicholls himself was a regular. There was a lively crowd there that Saturday. I went to sit beside Jan Christiansen who was a large robust looking man with blonde hair now beginning to thin and turn grey.

"So Charlie Nicholls sent you to keep an eye on me, did he? He's a canny fellow."

Jan spoke in a broad Geordie accent with just a trace of his Nordic origins. He'd lived in Shields since he was a young man when he had decided that looking after sailors was far more profitable than sailing beside them. Chrissie Andersen brought me my whisky and I told Jan that he was wanted at the station next morning.

"I'll be there, me bonny lad, bright and early."

I had a couple of drinks and enjoyed the company before going back on my rounds. I had a bit of time to make up so I didn't arrive back at the nick for my tea break until well after two. The place was in an uproar. The Matron was lying flat on her back on the floor in a faint. Charlie Nicholls was giving her smelling salts. Walter was looking on with a face like a pickled herring, and the other lads were having a good laugh to themselves. I soon found out why.

Walter had patrolled up to the top of Victoria Road where he'd stood a while waiting for Alec Dorothy who he knew would be coming down Westoe Lane. They had a natter and walked along together until Walter turned off down Claypath Lane towards Commercial Road.

Claypath Lane was an old pathway, now cobbled, that ran along the side of St. Hilda's Colliery. At this time of night it was deserted – or should have been. Walter came upon a couple under the old bridge – it's gone now. They were too occupied in what they were doing with each other to notice him. It turned out to be the sea captain and the young lady I'd seen earlier. Some Bobbies would have just shifted them on but Walter had been on the receiving end of too many lectures from Mullins about the need to crack down on 'immorality', which in his book encompassed drinking, gambling and fornication. Walter had had to ask me quietly what fornication was, and he now realised that what the couple under the bridge were doing came close enough to what I had described to him, so he arrested them for 'lewd and indecent' conduct in a public place.

They came quietly. The sea captain was a foreigner and didn't say much. The young lady who was clearly attracted to tall men took a shine to Walter. At the station Charlie Nicholls took the charge. The captain was put in the cells and the Matron was called to take care of the female prisoner. She'd have to be searched. While they were waiting, she kept up her conversation with Walter who was enjoying his moment. Charlie Nicholls was listening in. We would all have a laugh at Walter's expense later on as he'd all but agreed to go out with her one night by the time the Matron arrived. She was a very prim and proper maiden lady in her fifties who lived next door to the station.

She took the young woman with a liking for seafarers into the room at the back of the Charge Office to do the search. After a few minutes there was a shriek. The Matron emerged red faced and very flustered. "It's a man!" was all the poor lady could say before she fainted away onto the floor.

Charlie felt responsible. He'd thought he'd recognised the girl but just couldn't place her. It was young Jimmy McNickle, whose parents had a Newsagent's up Laygate Lane, and Charlie had often bought a paper off him. One of the Bobbies was sent to knock up Jimmy's parents to get them to come to the nick and to bring some of his clothes with them. Charlie then bailed him and the captain until Monday.

We were in for a surprise the following night. Who should be standing in the Charge Office talking to Charlie Nicholls but Inspector Mullins. Inspector Tait, one of the old school, had had a nasty fall down Academy Hill that afternoon following a session in the Hop Pole. Mullins had volunteered to cover for him. Well at least you'd never find Mullins drinking to excess in a public house; he was more at home in the lounge of a Temperance Hotel taking a cream soda.

The first thing he wanted to do was to look at our pocket books from last night. He read mine first without comment. Walter knew what was coming.

"Constable Heron, I can't find any reference to the arrest of the sailor so comprehensively detailed in Constable Duncan's book. I'll expect that to be rectified before tomorrow morning. Now, what have we here, a sea captain with an interest in poultry?"

I looked at Walter. He looked back even more bemused than usual.

"You say you could see his cock," Mullins barked.

"Aye, well I could. It was sticking reet oot."

"The correct word, Heron, is penis. You could see his penis. But that's all you say. You don't say what he was doing with it or where it was?"

Walter looked at Mullins as though he was daft.

"Well, it was between his legs."

I was becoming an expert in stifling laughter, and the trouble was that Walter meant no harm. Mullins didn't see the funny side of it, and gave him a ferocious dressing down in front of us all. Walter was on the equivalent of what would be, in these days, a final warning.

Jimmy McNickle was fined two pounds. When the Magistrate asked him if he had anything to say he just smirked and said that he'd been in a frivolous mood. His boyfriend, who did not show up, forfeited his bail and was no doubt away on the high seas.

I stayed on for the appearance of the drunken sailor. Jan Christiansen was with him to act as interpreter. The Chief had been briefed. According to the sailor he had been beaten up and robbed; his anger towards Walter and me was frustration because we could not understand him. He'd been drinking in one of the Holborn pubs when a fellow had come across and asked him if he wanted a girl for five bob. They'd conducted their business partly in sign language and partly in words that sailors can understand in any tongue. The girl had been waiting outside and was a very pretty one. He'd paid the money and he and the girl had gone up an alley to a darkened courtyard. All of a sudden this other man came along, started shouting, gave him a good beating and took his money belt. He could remember him using the word sister. The Norwegian was dealt with leniently.

That night, as I was sitting with Walter in what passed as the Parade Room at Laygate having a smoke before we went on duty, Charlie Nicholls popped his head round the door.

"You're wanted."

We both thought it was Mullins but we were mistaken; standing beside Charlie was the 'Big Fella', Detective Inspector Norman Lamont. He was tall and he was broad with a thick mop of black hair that had still not lost its sheen although he was well into his forties. His deep voice rang out from his barrel chest.

"I need a couple of volunteers for some plain clothes work. Charlie tells me you've only been on nights so far," we nodded, "and you're not known round Holborn?" Again we both nodded. "They'll do, Charlie. I'll speak to Superintendent Burnside about getting you some cover." He turned to us. "Come and see me at Keppel Street tomorrow afternoon after you've had your kip. I'll tell you all about it. Come in plain clothes. You'll be going round the pubs as a couple of sailors on your last night on shore."

I had a problem. Apart from my uniform I only had two shirts and one suit which I wore off duty; most of the time I kept on my uniform trousers and shirt to save wear and tear on my own clothes. I explained this to the Big Fella. Walter wasn't so badly off but he had nothing that would pass for a sailor's rig.

"Don't worry, lads, here's five shillings each. See what you can find in one of the seaman's outfitters on the way up but go for something that's been worn. Let me have a receipt and the change when you see me."

Charlie Nicholls had a word with us after the Inspector had gone. We went to see Jan Christiansen instead. He always had old clothes at his lodging house. We both took some baggy trousers, a loose fitting shirt with no collar, a necktie, a cap and a pair of sea boots. They'd all seen better days and he let us have them for a florin each. If we returned them he'd let us have a bob back. He then took us across the road to Smillie's Outfitters and his good friend Ian Smillie wrote us out a receipt for three and nine pence ha'penny each.

Jan guessed what we would be doing. The Norwegian sailor had not been the only one in recent weeks who'd been led up an alley by a pretty girl.

His guess turned out to be right. The Big Fella had started to become worried and was well aware that not all incidents of this type would be reported. After the last one he'd taken a walk down to the Mill Dam. If you were a mariner looking for a ship, or just looking out for an old shipmate, that's where you'd go. Inspector Lamont was looking for Tommy Ford – Tommy was a note casher. In those days it was common practice for the Agents to give a note as an advance on wages to a seaman who'd signed up for a voyage. It was to help the seaman's family but they would only be cashed 'four days after the ship sailed' with the sailor aboard; if he missed ship – no money. The seamen of course wanted some of the money for themselves. That's where Tommy came in handy. He would cash the notes taking a commission of anything from half a crown to five shillings in the pound. He would then present the note to the Agent and receive its full value after the vessel had left Shields. You could always see him around the Mill Dam or in one of the many Pubs nearby. He wore an old blue suit and a cloth cap. It didn't take long for the Big Fella to find him and they had an interesting chat.

Several of Tommy's customers had been done over after he'd paid them. A seaman about to go on a voyage would have a few drinks before he left and not many would refuse an offer from a pretty young girl when they knew they'd not see another woman for a good few weeks. Tommy was worried – word was beginning to spread that someone was watching for Tommy's customers who'd have money in their pockets and would be easy targets. Tommy had an idea who it might be. He did a fair bit of business just after opening time in the evening in the *Cumberland Arms* at the Mill Dam. He'd noticed that Bobby Doyle had started coming in about that time. The Big Fella didn't need to hear any more. Bobby Doyle and his wife Lizzie were notorious. She was a well known prostitute who worked mainly in Tyne Dock and West Holborn. She'd done time in Durham and so had Bobby for living off her earnings. After her last spell inside she'd retired from the game, so it was more than likely that Bobby had found a new way of making a few coppers, and nothing would be beneath him.

> *"I'll no say men are villains a';*
> *The real, harden'd wicked,*
> *Wha ha nae check but human law,*
> *Are to a few restricted."*

Burns could have had 'Wor Bobby' in mind. Bobby and Lizzie had
three children, Little Bobby, Ellen and Johnny. They'd been dragged
up between the gutter and the workhouse and it would be no
surprise if they ended up like their parents. Lamont was betting that
Bobby was using his daughter as bait and that Little Bobby, who was
a big brawny nowt, was defending his sister's honour by robbing her
customers.

Our job was spelt out by Inspector Lamont as he sat beside his
desk, which took up most of the space at one end of the small CID
room. We would each be given a note from one of the Agents and
we were to go to the *Cumberland Arms* at six o'clock. If Bobby Doyle
was there Tommy would give us the nod. We'd ask him to cash our
notes before we headed off for a night in the boozers.

The first night we went in the *Cumberland* as agreed. Tommy
always drank in the Gents' Buffet. He was the only one there and he
nodded to us. The Big Fella had warned him to look out for a couple
of ugly looking sailors. Bobby Doyle didn't show up. Tommy had a
couple of customers and left at seven.

We thought we might as well work our way through some
of the Holborn pubs on the way back to Laygate. We were at the
Queen's by half past eight. Walter had decided to stick to halves
after his first pint. He did not have much of a head for drink – I had
whisky. The *Queen's* was a lively pub with a long bar and even at that
time it was standing room only for me and Walter. We were not out
of place – a lot of the drinkers were mariners. We were just about
to finish our drinks and make our way out when a young chap got
up from the table where he'd been sitting with some foreign seamen

and went to the bar. He spotted Walter and me and came over. It was Jimmy McNickle.

"I nearly didn't recognise you without your uni..." I grabbed him by the lapels.

"Who you looking at, sonny?" I growled.

Walter hadn't recognised him but took a closer look, put his hand on my arm to restrain me, and said, "Aw, I think I kna' him, Tom."

A few folk had looked round but hadn't taken much notice. I put Jimmy down and whispered to him that we were on plain clothes duty. Jimmy wasn't quite sure what to do.

"Would you like a drink?"

Jimmy was often buying drinks for sailors that he'd just met so no one thought it odd. We took our drinks and moved towards the door where it was a bit quieter.

"You're not in fancy dress tonight then?" I asked.

Jimmy blushed a little. "Na, I usually come out for a drink down Holborn."

"You'll know most of the pubs then."

"Aye, I prefer the *Queen's* and the *Banks O'Tyne*, but I generally have a wander around."

"We're on the lookout for someone who's robbing sailors. He offers them a girl. When the sailor's up a back alley with the girl he gives him a bashing and takes his money."

"Aye, I heard about the Norwegian sailor. He was in the *Banks O'Tyne* that Saturday night. Chrissie Andersen reckons he saw Bobby Doyle in about the same time. He thought he was pimping for Lizzie again."

We finished our drinks and said good night to Jimmy. Walter was looking distinctly the worse for wear by now, so we went and had some fish and chips, and then called it a night.

It was the same the next night, and the night after, but on the Friday we got lucky. We'd just bought our drinks in the *Cumberland* when a shifty looking character walked in. He took his drink to the back of the room. Tommy gave us the nod. After a few minutes we went over to Tommy and I asked if he would cash a note.

"I dain't kna' ye," he grumbled. "I only deal with folk I kna'."

I hadn't expected this. "Come on Mister Ford. I'm sailing on Saturday on the *Jessomene* and I need the cash. I was told by Mrs. Camillieri that you could always rely on Tommy Ford."

He looked up. "You're staying at Mrs. Camillieri's?" I nodded. "All reet then, I'll take a chance. But it'll be five bob in the pound."

"I was told half a crown."

"That's for those I kna'. Take it or leave it."

I took it.

We slowly made our way down Holborn to the *Queen's*. I was pretending to be well away – Walter just acted normal. The bar was packed. We noticed Jimmy sitting in the corner with a couple of rough looking fellows. Walter nudged me. I glanced over my shoulder to see Bobby Doyle who had just come in and was having a good look round. It was not long before he joined us.

"Ye having a good neet?" he asked as he squeezed past a group of fellows standing at the bar.

"Aye, a very good neet." I slurred my words.

"You mariners?"

"Wye aye," was Walter's contribution. "We're sailing the morra'."

Bobby got straight down to business. He had a girl outside who would do anything I wanted for five shillings. I took an example from Tommy and bargained him down to three bob.

"Come on then. After you've finished I'll come back for your mate."

We went outside. Just as we were leaving I heard the sound of a glass breaking and chairs going over, but my attention was elsewhere: just down the road in the doorway of the shop next to the pub stood the girl, and she was bonny all right. I gave Doyle the three bob and then staggered over to her, put my arm round her waist, and with her half holding me up, we walked down the road until she turned me up some steps. There was a street lamp right at the top which gave a faint glimmer of light. We reached a bend in the alley where there was a small courtyard.

"We'll go in there," she said and gently pushed me into the yard. It was dark and it stank. I'd never been with a prostitute before and have never been tempted since. Just as I pushed her against the wall I heard footsteps running up the stairs. A hand grabbed me on the shoulder.

"What 'ye deein' to me sister, ye bastard?" was all I heard as I was spun round. I was ready and I blocked the punch with my forearm. I hit him hard in the stomach with my right fist but he came straight back at me. It was time for Walter. Then the woman grabbed me from behind by my hair and put her foot behind my left knee. The brother took his chance and landed one right on my nose. I then heard Walter's voice. "I'm coming, Tom." The girl and her brother took off up the stairs.

Walter helped me up. Young Jimmy McNickle was with him. When we got down to the street and stood under the street lamp I could see that Jimmy had been in a fight as well. Walter was dabbing my nose with his hanky.

"I'm sorry, Tom. I was just gan' to follow ye oot when these two lads started on Jimmy. They were gan' to bottle him – I had to help him."

"He hit one with a chair and the other took off." Jimmy looked at Walter admiringly.

"Ye pick your friends well," was all I said. Walter asked if I'd got a good look at them.

"I'd recognise the girl again but it was too dark to see much of the fella. He'll have a bruise in his midriff, though, just there." I gave Walter a punch, not quite as hard as the one I'd landed on Bobby but he felt it.

He jumped back. "I said I was sorry, man."

We left Jimmy and went back to Laygate nick to make our report.

"What are we gan' to say, Tom? If Mullins finds oot that I was helping Jimmy instead of keeping close tabs on ye I'll be finished." Walter was right of course.

"We'll just say that when you reached the yard it was so dark you couldn't make out who was fighting and you grabbed me by mistake. The lad and lass ran off and we couldn't catch them."

We called in at Laygate Nick where Charlie rang the news through to CID. The Big Fella was none too pleased and we were told to see him at nine sharp the following morning. I sat down to write up my pocket book; we still had to comply with the formalities. Walter went to make a cup of tea.

"Ye'd better do your book, Walter."

"Aw, it'll wait."

The next morning on the way down to Keppel Street I called in at McNickle's Newsagent's and bought a paper – Jimmy was there and I had a word.

When we went into the CID office the Big Fella was sitting on the chair facing his desk. He had a face like thunder. "Inspector Mullins warned me about you two but I thought that any two able-bodied men could hold on to a prossie and her pimp," and so it went on.

I waited until he'd finished. "Can I make a suggestion, Sir?"

Norman Lamont had a vicious temper, but he was a good Detective and always prepared to listen. He didn't answer straight away but looked at Walter and then at me.

"I don't suppose it can do any more harm."

I outlined my plan. The Inspector asked a few questions then he sat for a while drumming his fingers on the desk.

"We'll give it a try – tonight only. It's your last chance before I hand you back to Inspector Mullins."

At six o'clock that evening Walter and I were back in mufti down the Mill Dam, but it was ordinary plain clothes this time. We were going to keep well clear of Bobby Doyle. Even if he saw us he probably wouldn't recognise us.

About half past six Jimmy McNickle came running over from the *Cumberland*. Tommy had just cashed a note and Bobby Doyle had seen him do it. The sailor was in the *Alnwick Castle*. I had guessed that Bobby would try again as he'd missed out last night and he'd have a good chance on a Saturday. I'd not identified myself as a Police Officer so he should not have been put off by the fact that one of his targets had fought back. We couldn't act as bait again, and we couldn't follow the sailor with money in his pocket or we might put Bobby off. We needed someone who would blend into the background and Jimmy McNickle was just the lad for the job. He was doing it to repay Walter for coming to his rescue. He'd made a condition to his helping us to which I'd agreed, although I'd not told Walter about it yet.

We stayed well back slowly walking down Holborn, having a quiet smoke on a street corner. By half past eight the sailor was unsteady on his feet but had made it to the *Queen's*. Jimmy walked very quickly back to us. We were standing out of sight up Wilson's Stairs.

"Bobby Doyle's just gone in. There's a girl and a big lad waiting across the street."

"Right, you know what to do, Jimmy, as fast as you can."

The Big Fella and two plain clothes polis were drinking in the *Scarborough Bridge* which wasn't too far away. Walter moved off as well taking a short cut up Pratt's Bank. We'd had a scout round that afternoon and found a way to the top of the stairs I'd been led up the other night. We didn't want them escaping again.

It all went to plan. The unfortunate sailor was helped out of the pub by a kindly Bobby and followed the lass up the stairs. Her big brother was not far behind while Bobby Doyle walked casually away down Holborn towards Laygate Street. He was going to be in for a surprise when he walked into the Big Fella. I waited at the bottom of the stairs until I heard shouting and then slowly made my way up. I had to be sure that his money had been taken. I stood quietly by the wall just before the courtyard where the poor devil was being beaten up, then Little Bobby came out, a money belt in his hand. I grabbed him straight away.

"Polis. You're nicked," and a good punch in the kidneys was all that was necessary. The girl legged it up the steps straight into Walter's waiting arms. The two other plain clothes men were right behind us – one gave me a hand with Little Bobby while the other helped the sailor to his feet.

By the time we arrived at Laygate Nick the Black Maria was waiting for us – it was horse drawn in those days. The prisoners were put inside and the sailor went up on the bench with the Big Fella. They were off to Keppel Street.

"Well done, lads," he shouted down to us as he tipped his bowler hat. "Come in tomorrow morning and I'll get started on the paperwork."

We'd arranged to have a drink with Jimmy in the *Banks O'Tyne* to let him know what had happened. I sat down and wrote up my notes, but not Walter – he was too excited.

"I'll do me book the neet. I'll pop roond to the *Banks* and see ye there, Tom." He was off before I could say anything.

We had a good night. It was well after closing time before we left and we hadn't paid for a single drink. I had to help Walter home and put him to bed.

We made it to Keppel Street the next morning. The Big Fella was beaming. The Doyles had coughed – apparently it had all started by accident when Bobby had wanted to put his daughter on the game to make up for the loss of his wife's earnings. Little Bobby had found out and had been furious – he had a soft spot for his sister. He'd gone along with it at first but when she was about to do her first job he couldn't control himself and gave the sailor who was with her a belting. Ellen said that they ought to take some money or their father would go mad – so they found the sailor's money belt and took it all. It was more profitable than whoring.

"I better have your statements though, just in case," said the Big Fella. "It's all right, you won't have to write them yourselves. Give me your notebooks and I'll get them typed up on Monday. I'll have them delivered to Laygate station in time for your night shift."

It was an instruction not a request and Walter and I handed over our books which he put inside his desk. On the way out we bumped into Inspector Mullins.

"You did well but it's back to the beat on Monday. I'll see you on Parade at Laygate before your shift. We'll have a look at your pocket books. They should be interesting reading."

I explained that Inspector Lamont had them.

"Don't worry, Duncan. I'll collect them from him and bring them down to Laygate myself."

Walter was in a state. There wouldn't be anything in his book. He hadn't even written up the first arrest of the drunken Norwegian let alone the two brushes with the Doyles. If Mullins read the pocket book then Walter would be out on his neck.

I didn't know what to do and felt partly responsible. I should have made Walter write up his notes at the same time as I had done mine. Walter was having dinner at his mother's so I left him and had a walk down to the Pier. It was a sunny day, the walk did me good, and I also developed a bit of a thirst. I strolled back towards the Market Place and looked in at the *Mechanics*. Bill Spyles and John Burgess, two of the old timers, were sitting down at a table playing cribbage. I'd done Bill a favour a few weeks before and he always had time for me. John had just won a game so they put the cards down for a minute. They'd heard about the Doyles' arrest.

"You and Walter'll be in the Chief's good books then." John Burgess smiled at me. "Make the most of it."

"I don't think it'll last long, not for Walter. Mullins has had it in for him from the start and now I think he's got him for good."

Bill Spyles looked up, his little piggy eyes showing interest; he didn't care for Mullins. I told them about the note books in Lamont's desk. Bill chuckled to himself.

"Well, I think I can help you out there. What d'ye think, John?"

"Wye of course we can, but it'll cost you a pint."

"Or two," Bill chipped in. I didn't like buying rounds of drinks. It was a costly practice which I tried to avoid, but I had to save Walter's skin. Bill would not say how he was going to help. He was on night shift and so was John Burgess.

"You and Walter come down to Keppel Street at break time tonight. Wait outside the Station until you see me."

It was nearly quarter to two the next morning before we saw Bill. We were huddled in the doorway of the *Havelock*. He waved us over.

"Quick, with me, John's keeping the Sergeant busy."

We went into the Station, down the five stone steps, along the corridor to the CID room, and went inside. Bill still had his lamp and it gave us just enough light. He went over to the desk placing his lamp on the chair. He put his hands under the desk top on his side.

"Right, Tom, take the other side and lift, but careful does it."

The long desk just came up, and lifted off the table top. We took it right off and steadied it against the wall. The Big Fella's papers were all there including the two pocket books. The desk top, which the Inspector always kept locked, had no bottom, and never had, but no one had told the Big Fella. He never knew.

We carefully took out the note books and Walter crouched by the light and wrote down what I told him. It was a shortened version of what I had in mine. Bill kept hurrying us along and it was soon done. The desk top was lifted back on very carefully so that it did not disturb any of the Big Fella's papers. Bill doused his lamp. We looked out of the door. It was quiet and out we went.

Later that evening, at the Laygate nick, Mullins complained about the notes.

"Your handwriting's getting worse, Constable Heron. It looks as though you were writing this in a shithouse in the dark." If only he knew.

Bobby Doyle was sent down for eighteen months. His two children, who had no previous, got six months each.

The *Banks O'Tyne* was a lively place on a Saturday night. Mick Riley played the piano and anyone who wanted to get up to sing could do so. There were some good turns but it was a men-only bar. Jimmy McNickle was one of the stars – dressed up as a woman. That's where he'd met his ship's captain the other night. Jimmy's condition for helping us out was that Walter should come along and help him with a song on a Saturday night. I hadn't told Walter any of this.

We came off nights a week later and I suggested to Walter that we celebrate with an evening out at the Banks. He was more than happy to come along. News had spread, don't ask me how! There was a crowd there – the Big Fellla, Bill Spyles and John Burgess all turned up, a long way from their usual stamping grounds.

We managed to find a table and the drink started flowing. I told Walter that Jimmy would be singing and that he'd asked if he could help him out. Walter didn't seem too worried. "But I cannot sing much, mind," was his only response.

Things changed when Jimmy came out with his glad rags on. Bill and me had to drag Walter up to the piano. It all added to the performance. All Walter had to do was to stand still and look coy. He was a natural. Jimmy was playing the part of a love sick lass singing to her reluctant sweetheart, who happened to be called Walter. I'll give it to Jimmy, he was good, he had all the actions, and every time he moved close to Walter, Walter moved one step away. It couldn't have been scripted better. The crowd liked it so much they had to do it three times.

We stayed behind after closing time in the back room. Chrissie Andersen and Jan Christiansen were there together with a couple of Scandinavian ship's officers. We had all been egging Walter on to walk Jimmy home but there was no need. A tall fair haired Swede took a real shine to the young lady sitting beside him, and Jimmy had an escort for the night.

Market Place

A pair of boots

Poverty and destitution were commonplace in the years after the War, and things would not improve as we moved into the twenties and thirties. I had seen hardship in my home town in Scotland where the Salvation Army provided a 'farthing' breakfast for the needy children – a large slice of bread with margarine and jam and a mug of tea. Things were no better in Shields where we had the Mobile Soup Kitchen in Keppel Street. The poor bairns always had a bowl of something hot at dinner time. There was a Constable on duty when the kitchen was open, but there was rarely any trouble. Mothers would queue with their little ones. Some would take a bowl and have it there and then – others would bring a pudding basin wrapped in a cloth and take the soup home. The women who gave out the soup were good folk.

Perhaps it was because we had the sight and smell of the soup kitchen so close to our HQ that the Chief had set up the Shoeless Children Fund. The Bobbies knew the poor families on their beat, and many a youngster had shoes for the first time thanks to the fund.

The poor were the responsibility of the Board of Guardians. I don't suppose that they were any different from the Guardians in other towns and cities but they weren't over generous. The Receiving Officer would visit poor families, and if he thought it was a genuine case he'd agree to provide help, but it was never enough – it might stop a family from starving but that was all.

Not everybody was happy with this state of affairs and the Labour Party and the Unions would sometimes cause a bit of fuss. Word had reached Police Headquarters that there was to be a march from Jarrow to the Board's Offices in Barrington Street in South Shields. There were about twenty of us standing by in West Keppel Street in case of trouble. It was a peaceful demonstration but quite a large one as the Jarrow marchers had picked up a lot of folk on the way. There were people milling all around and I could see that Inspector Mullins, who was in charge, was becoming jittery. He motioned for us to move forward and we headed towards Barrington Street. One of the old hands, Bill Spyles, went up to Mullins and asked if we should draw truncheons. Mullins hesitated. Bill took silence for acquiescence and drew Gentleman Jim. This was the signal. A deep voice behind me bellowed out, "Draw staves and charge."

It was all we needed, and it is still a mystery to this day who gave the order, but in we went – twenty policemen with heavy wooden truncheons against a crowd of peaceful men, women and children demonstrating against poverty. We dispersed them soon enough and chased them into the surrounding streets and up to the Market Place.

The crowd soon started drifting away. I was with Alec Dorothy and we walked back down King Street keeping an eye out for any trouble. All of a sudden I heard a shout. Just across the road from us a young lad was sprinting off towards the Market. A shopkeeper who was starting after him, glanced round and saw us. "He's away with a pair of byeuts."

There was a large rack of second hand boots and shoes outside the shop. By this time the lad was nearly at the Market. We knew we wouldn't catch him, but we thought we ought to show willing and took off down the street in pursuit. The lad turned left at Crofton's Corner. The mounted officer, McIver, was keeping an eye on things in the Market Place and was seated on Lightning just by the Old Town Hall. McIver was a highland Scot, ex-army, who had seen service in the Boer War. He was a tall wiry man, arrogant and irascible, who rarely smiled, and was not known for the quickness of his thinking. He had seen the lad running with a pair of boots in his hand. Whilst he was reflecting on this he saw me and Alec coming round the same corner and starting to slow up. Something clicked and McIver let out a high pitched cry. "Leave him to me, lads." He spurred Lightning on and was soon into a canter over the cobbles. It was a fearsome sight. The lad looked back and we could see the panic on his face, but he kept on going down past St. Hilda's Church with Lightning in hot pursuit.

We didn't see the arrest but we heard about it. The runner, who had been dodging round the back lanes to try and shake off Lightning to no avail, got as far as Oyston Street, back of the Gas Works. McIver was nearly on him when he tried one last trick – an old one. Many folk left their doors unlocked in those days. If you were being chased you could go in one way, straight through the house and out. McIver's quarry took his chance, he pushed open a back door, ran into the yard and up the stairs – it was an upstairs flat. He thought the horse couldn't follow but McIver had other ideas. He rode straight into the backyard and shouted out that if the lad didn't come back down then he'd take the horse up the stairs. The door at the top opened and the lad came out, held by the arm by a man in shirtsleeves. He would doubtless have let him out by the front stairs but he wasn't going to have a horse running through his home. We met McIver and Lightning as they came back up Waterloo Vale. The young lad was walking in front, boots still in hand, his head hung low in humiliation as Lightning would occasionally nudge him forward. It was the talk of Shields, but many, myself included, thought McIver had gone too far.

The young lad wasn't much more than sixteen – Billy Ruffle from Tyne Dock. He told the Sergeant that the boots were for his brother Geordie, who had asthma and, with the winter coming on, would need some footwear. His father was a docker, but with a family of six his money did not go far. Billy worked in the Docks himself when he could. He'd stand in the line for casual work but never got more than a few days a week. The Sergeant rang down to Tyne Dock and my good friend Walter Heron, who was posted down there, went round to the house and brought the mother up to Keppel Street. Billy was bailed to Court the next day. He was unlucky. The newspapers were full of the march and the 'riots' that had followed, but there had been no arrests apart from Billy – there was no need, no one had done anything wrong apart from standing in the way of twenty charging Bobbies. Billy had been part of the crowd at Barrington Street and had ended up in King Street. He just couldn't resist the chance to get a pair of boots for his brother. The court heard nothing of his circumstances. He had pleaded guilty and when he was asked if he had anything to say he was too scared to speak. It wouldn't have done him any good. The Chairman of the Bench made a speech about lawlessness on the streets of South Shields. For a moment I thought he was going to send him down. Then he said that he needed a lesson that wrongdoing would be punished – three strokes of the birch.

The punishment was administered that afternoon and I was there. I had been asked to assist Bob Jamieson, the Station Sergeant who was to give the birching. Billy was unlucky again – Bob was a straightforward sort, and if the person to be birched was young, then he might not take his arm back the full way, but the Chief Constable had decided that he would attend the birching, which turned out to be the last ever given in Shields, and Bob had to do it by the book. I helped Billy take his shirt and vest off. There were ties on the bar to hold his hands.

"I don't need them," he said. His voice was firm. I looked at Bob.

"It's up to you, Billy, but if you move as I strike I'll have to do it again, and we'll tie you by force if we have to."

Billy nodded. "I won't move."

He didn't move; he didn't make a sound. His back was red after the first stroke, and bleeding after the second, but Billy took his medicine. His knuckles turned white as he gripped the bar. His face was deathly pale as he stood up and turned round after the last stroke.

Bob Jamieson took him gently by the arm and led him to the Police Surgeon who was waiting to inspect the lad's back and dress it. "You took it well, Billy. I hope I won't see you here again," said Bob.

As Billy left the room the Chief came over to me. "Do you believe his story about the boots?"

I nodded. "Aye, I do, Sir. I had a look at them and they'd be two sizes too small for Billy."

He pondered a minute. "Have a word with Sergeant Jamieson when he's finished with the boy. Ask him to get one of the men from Tyne Dock to go round to check on him in a couple of days, and make sure he takes an application for the Shoeless Children Fund."

Bob Jamieson did not need any encouraging. He'd taken a liking to Billy. He'd seen grown men crying like babies after the second or third stroke. He went down to Tyne Dock himself a couple of nights later and took Walter with him to the house. Billy, who was still sore from the beating, wouldn't be lining up at the Docks for a few days. Bob had a long chat with him.

I heard all this from Walter. He couldn't shut up talking about Billy's sister Gertie. He'd seen her the first time he called. She was a bonny lass with lovely fair hair who worked as a waitress in the North of England Café in King Street.

"Did you say much to her then?" I politely enquired.

"Well, not really, but I could tell that she liked me."

Bob Jamieson spent a couple of evenings a week at a boxing club in Holborn. He wanted Billy to join. Billy's mam wasn't very keen but his father supported Bob who agreed to lend Billy a pair of old gloves to get him started. Billy's mother filled in the form for shoes for Geordie with some help from Bob. The upshot of it all was that Geordie had a new pair of shoes and Billy took to boxing. The boxing coach, Stoker Armstrong, who'd been a heavyweight before the War, reckoned that he was a natural – he had strength, timing and could box. It was through Stoker's connections that Billy was taken on as an apprentice blacksmith. Walter was in love, and, for me, it was the start of what would turn out to be a long and sometimes difficult relationship with Archibald McIver.

McIver was Lightning's regular rider. There would always be some fun when we had a new recruit who reckoned himself to be a decent horseman. The Sergeant would ask if he would like to ride

Lightning when McIver was on his rest day. They all jumped at the chance. Lightning was a lovely beast, not like Thunder, who was highly strung and liked nothing more than taking chunks out of the backs of unsuspecting officers loitering in the stables. The rookie would be told to follow the usual route which ended up going along King Street, round the Market and back down to Keppel Street. This is where the trouble would start. McIver had Lightning well trained and he would pull up at each pub where his rider had a drink on the way back to HQ. The horse didn't need any orders, but would stop automatically, leaving his new rider motionless outside the *Mechanics* or the *Douglas*.

Some weeks after the chase down Oyston Street I was working in the Chief's Office. He had noticed from one or two of my reports of crime that I could write in a legible hand, that I could spell correctly, and even compose sentences with subordinate clauses. That was enough for him and I was put in the office for a spell. A Sergeant and two Constables did all the Chief's paperwork with the help of an old typewriter that had seen better days.

You had a good view out of the window and on this afternoon I could see Lightning trotting gently towards the Station on his own. No sign of McIver. Lightning knew his way home and was probably ready for his oats. I took a stroll down to the Yard. Lightning was standing by the stable door so I went across to unbuckle the saddle before walking him to his box, when a nervous looking McIver came into the yard. He had every right to be nervous: Inspector Mullins had seen me going outside, and being suspicious by nature, had followed me out. McIver had taken one too many at the *Douglas* and had missed the stirrup when attempting to mount Lightning – the horse moved off leaving the unfortunate Scot sprawled on the pavement. Mullins was the only one not to see the funny side of it. I was given the job of escorting McIver back to his house. He was no trouble and only needed a steadying hand up the steps. He did have a job fitting his key into the lock though, and the noise brought his daughter to the door. Since I'd been working in the office I'd noticed a lovely looking lass with dark red hair coming and going from the housing block in the Police Buildings. I now knew who she was. She was even prettier close to, but I did not have the chance to introduce myself. She took one look at her forlorn Daddy, one look at me, and let us both have it. She had a sharp tongue.

"Look at the state of him. Me mother'll go mad. He better not be sick like he was last time. And you," she looked at me, her eyes flashing, "you ought to be ashamed of yourself letting him get into that state. You Polis are all the same."

McIver was dragged inside and the door was slammed in my face. That was my Agnes. Well, I thought to myself, the girl's got spirit. I'd have to bide my time. Mullins reported McIver, who was subsequently fined five shillings and given a final warning.

Walter was not having any better luck with Gertie Ruffle. There was a limit to the number of times he could call round to the house to see how Billy was; particularly when the lad was fully recovered, enjoying his work as an apprentice blacksmith, and going down to the Boxing Club two or three evenings a week.

"How'ma gan to see more of her?" he asked me as we were having an ice cream in the Roma in Ocean Road one afternoon. We'd often meet there if we were off duty.

"Why don't you go to the restaurant where she works and have a meal. You can get chatting as she brings you your dinner."

"Wouldn't it look a bit obvious, though?"

"Well, it's a popular place."

"Would you come with us, Tom?"

"In my experience, Walter, courting is best done alone. If it works you can buy me a meal there some other time."

Walter was on nights at the time, so that Saturday he got out of bed earlier than usual and went down to King Street in time for dinner. He told me about it afterwards. As he went in, Gertie and another girl were talking over by the counter. They started giggling as Walter stood in the middle of the dining room, his cap in his hand, not knowing what to do. Gertie walked over to him.

THE FIVE STONE STEPS

"You look different out of your uniform."

Walter just blushed.

"Is it for one?" He nodded. "We're busy on Saturdays so you may have to share a table. Is that all right?"

Well, it wasn't what Walter had in mind but he had no choice. He'd arrived just after twelve when it was quiet, but by quarter past it was nearly full. Walter was joined by a stout, red faced man who was more interested in his food than in making polite conversation. That suited Walter. The man gulped his soup down and even asked for extra bread. Gertie was rushed off her feet, and when she did come to the table she didn't dawdle. The special that day was turkey, and it was very tasty according to Walter. By this time, his dining companion had already had two glasses of beer and was starting to sweat. As soon as the plateful of turkey, stuffing, potatoes and peas, all covered in thick gravy, was placed before him he attacked it as if he hadn't seen food for a week. Walter had never seen anyone cram so much meat onto a fork. The man saw that Walter was looking at him and was about to say something, when his red face seemed to go even redder. He started to cough, he was choking, he got to his feet, and by this time his face was blue. Gertie came running over, slapped the man hard between the shoulder blades and he fell to the ground. There was panic in the Café. The manageress, Miss Booth, ran over and stuck her fingers down the man's throat but could not dislodge the turkey. It was all to no avail and it was clear to all that the man was dead. She shouted to one of the kitchen lads to run down to Barrington Street for a doctor and then draped a tablecloth over the body.

One of the customers, a thin miserable looking woman with a sour face, turned to her husband and said, "I told you that the turkey was tough, and too thick."

Miss Booth was about to say something but Walter jumped in first. "There was nowt wrong with the turkey. It was that fella's own fault. I've nivver seen anyone cram so much into their gob at once before."

That put the woman in her place and won an approving glance from Gertie. The doctor from Barrington Street arrived. He had a quiet word with the manageress who announced that they'd have to close the restaurant for a couple of hours. Walter waited outside until Gertie came out. She was still a bit shaken and agreed to walk down to the Roma for a cup of coffee. Walter was over the moon when he told me all about it at break time that night. "We're gannin' to the flicks one neet when I'm on early shift."

My own attempts to strike up a conversation with Agnes McIver, on the few occasions our paths crossed, had not met with success. McIver himself had not thanked me for helping him home. That, of itself, did not mean anything as McIver was the last person you'd go to looking for thanks. As well as the fine, he'd been suspended from mounted duties for three months. He missed Lightning, but most of all he hated doing night shift. As one of the mounted officers he'd been on day shift for years.

One night in December I was in the Station about half past nine at night having a cup of tea before going on shift. The Fire Bell started ringing. In those days the Police manned the Fire Engine. The crew was mostly made up of old hands housed in the Police Buildings and if the bell rang they responded. They were on an annual retainer of three guineas, and also received a fee for each turn out – three and sixpence if water was used, one and six if not. The Chief Constable was paid one pound eleven and sixpence for each fire even if he did not attend personally. We had a Leyland Tender at that time which had recently replaced the horse-drawn engine. Within minutes of the bells ringing the sirens on the tender went off long and loud. Of course at that time of night the off-duty officers would be in the *Douglas*, the *Mechanics*, the *Hild*, or the *Havelock* – they'd come running. I walked out into the yard where the crew were assembling and doing up their uniforms, while Bob Bruce, the tender's driver, was revving the engine, anxious to get off.

"It's the *Royal* in Albermarle Street," he shouted out as the latecomers jumped on. It was just round the corner from Keppel

Street so I thought I might have a walk over when my shift started. As I was heading back into the Station to pick up my lantern the burly figure of Superintendent Burnside came out into the Yard.

"It's a pub fire, then?"

"Aye. Bob Bruce said it's the *Royal*."

"Bruce's a canny lad; he'll know what to do." By my look, I obviously didn't.

"When there's a pub fire the first thing you do is check with the Publican that he's covered for fire damage." He paused, licking his lips. "There can be a lot of breakages. The next thing to do is to get a barrel out on the pavement for refreshment – fire fighting's thirsty work. Me and the Chief have just finished a meeting with the Buildings Sub-Committee. They'll be coming downstairs presently." He paused. "You're on duty at ten?" I nodded. "Take the motorbike and sidecar and you can keep us up to date on the fire. And bring back a crate or two of the breakages."

When I arrived on the scene there was quite a crowd of onlookers. The upper storey was well ablaze. The Landlady, Mrs. McKeith, was standing on the pavement next to Bob Bruce. She had a shawl round her shoulders and was drinking a brandy for the shock. Two hoses were at work and the brave lads were busy rescuing as much stock from the bars and cellar as possible. Henry Burnside was right. There was a barrel on a trestle just behind the tender and the firemen were making frequent visits to it. An array of bottles and crates was being stacked up next to the barrel. As soon as a bottle was emptied it was put in a crate. They'd be broken in the yard later and the Landlady would claim her breakages. I went over to Bob Bruce and told him that the Super wanted a report. He looked over to the sidecar.

"Henry'll want a few 'breakages' as well. Take back what you can manage. We'll be here a while. Don't let Henry have it all, mind. Take some of the spirits and pour them into a bucket. We'll share them out later and the bottles will come back here. McIver can give you a hand. He was on the spot when we arrived." I'd noticed old

Archie helping out with the 'breakages'.

We filled up the sidecar and McIver jumped on the back as I drove round to the Station Yard. Henry Burnside was waiting. He was a big man who liked his beer and had joined the Force when brawn rather than brain was the main requirement. He picked up a crate in each hand. As he went off with McIver I smuggled as many bottles as I could to the Parade room, and started decanting them into whatever buckets and containers I could find. By the time I returned to the Yard, McIver was back at the bike.

"I'm going back for some more. Henry wants you to help in the Charge Room."

The Chief had brought the Committee men downstairs and the room was full. They were quite merry already. Henry Burnside had brought out all the jugs and pitchers he could put his hands on, and it was my task to pour out the bottles. I had a job keeping up, but had managed to have a few nips myself. Inspector Mullins was in the room but was the only one not partaking. He was a Methodist and had taken the pledge.

I had always believed Mullins to be sanctimonious, but it was only after a conversation that had taken place a few weeks back with Alec Dorothy that I found him out to be a hypocrite as well. Mullins' wife had not settled after the move to Shields. They were a childless couple. She missed her family in Durham and had soon started making regular visits to them, sometimes staying as long as a fortnight. We all knew when she was away – Mullins was more bad-tempered than usual. It was during one of her absences that Alec had seen Mullins one night coming out of the *Stag's Head* in Fowler Street carrying a canvas shopping bag. Alec was on duty and had just turned the corner from Denmark Street.

"I didn't pay much attention at first but there was something about his walk that I recognised. I was ready for a pint anyway so I dodged into the *Stag's*. As soon as I got inside the Jug and Bottle, the Landlord, auld Whisky Willie Callaghan, looked up. 'Not another bloody Polis,' he said as he pulled me a pint. 'At least the other bugger pays for his and takes it yem.' I asked him who it was – Mullins. Whisky Willie had never met him but had seen him once in Court at the Licensing Sessions."

Apparently he was a regular customer. He'd come in for about a week and then Willie wouldn't see him for a while. It all tied in with the times Mullins' wife was away. He normally brought three bottles to be filled up with beer, accompanied every so often with a half of whisky.

Mullins was in conversation with one of the Councillors when we heard a loud bang from outside. I went out straight away with Mullins on my heels. McIver had returned, but he'd misjudged the corner coming into the yard and had driven into the gatepost. No great harm done, although the front wheel of the bike would need straightening out. McIver was more concerned about the bottles in the sidecar – fortunately only one or two had smashed. He looked a mite unsteady on his feet. He'd obviously taken full advantage of his trip back to the *Napier*. Mullins took one look at him. "McIver, have you been drinking?"

It was a stupid question as Mullins was the only one on duty who had not. McIver for once said nowt.

"If you're found to have been drunk while driving that vehicle, action will be taken."

I felt sorry for McIver. I should have kept stumm. "The sidecar was too full, Inspector. When I came back I had McIver on the back as a counterbalance."

"Officer Duncan, this has nothing to do with you, and it's not the first time I've had to speak to you about interrupting me in matters that don't concern you." Mullins never missed a chance.

"The lad's reet." McIver unwisely opened his mouth to speak. The whisky fumes nearly knocked me and Mullins off our feet.

"Duncan, escort Constable McIver to the medical room. Then please ask the Police Surgeon to come to the Station to examine him. I want to know whether he was drunk in charge of a motor vehicle. Let me know when Dr. Roberts arrives."

I took McIver to the examination room. He was in trouble. An infant could have worked out that he was the worse for drink. I sat him down and left him there, locking the door as I went out. I rang Dr. Roberts – he would be about half an hour. In those days it was his responsibility to decide if someone was drunk when in charge of a vehicle – horse drawn or mechanised. Dr. Roberts had one failing – he had no sense of smell.

I made a pot of tea. Mullins was beginning to look out of place without a drink in his hand. He took his tea black and I added a heaped spoonful of sugar together with a good measure of whisky – I took the cup into the Charge Room.

"The Doctor's on his way. I thought you could do with a nice cup of tea."

Mullins gave me a long old fashioned look – there was no love lost between us – but he took the tea. I did not stay to see his reaction as he put the steaming brew to his lips, but he did not call me back. Five minutes later I went in with another cup for him. He was deep in conversation with a Councillor, and merely accepted the fresh one as I took away the old. The third and fourth cups contained more and more whisky and less and less tea.

By the time the Doctor arrived the Charge Room was more like the public bar of the *Havelock* just before closing time. The Doctor looked round the room.

"Now which one is supposed to be drunk?" was all he said. I escorted him along the corridor to where McIver was waiting. Inspector Mullins was not far behind.

When we arrived in the room the Doctor asked for details of the incident. Inspector Mullins provided these, his words nicely slurred.

"Is it right, Doctor," I naively enquired, "that in difficult cases you can sometimes compare the actions of the person accused of drunkenness with those of someone you know to be sober?"

The Doctor looked at me. I think he was beginning to twig. "It would certainly be sound scientifically. You would have to be quite certain that the other person had not touched a drop."

Mullins was listening. "What about you, Duncan?"

"Unfortunately Superintendent Burnside insisted that I had a nip of whisky after I'd returned from the fire." I turned to the Doctor. "The Inspector's teetotal."

"Is that so, Inspector?"

Mullins did not hesitate. He had his reputation to think of. "I took the pledge many years ago. I've had one or two cups of tea this evening though."

"Excellent. Unfortunately I have no sense of smell. Officer Duncan, can you smell the breath of these two men."

I steeled myself.

"There is no marked difference between them," was my honest response.

Then the fun started. The Doctor first asked them to repeat, 'The Leith Police dismisseth us'. Mullins went first and had three attempts. McIver did better. He had the precise articulation of the Highland Scot. The Doctor then took a piece of chalk out of his bag and drew a straight line on the floor. They had to walk along it without falling off. McIver swayed about like a straw in the wind. Mullins had a job even starting but then only put his foot wrong once. The last test was to extend their left arm in front of them, close their eyes, point their index finger, then bring it back to touch the nose. Mullins missed his face completely; McIver nearly poked his own eye out.

The Doctor completed his notes and asked, "You're quite sure you've not touched a drop, Inspector?"

"Quite sure, Doctor, I'm stone cold sober."

"Well, on that basis, I have no option other than to conclude that Constable McIver is in no worse condition than you. If you are sober then so is he. I shall report accordingly."

McIver and Mullins left the room seeing who could say 'the Leith Police' the quicker. The Doctor looked at me. "I've had less entertaining evenings, I must say, and now, Constable, I would like a cup of tea, made in exactly the same way as the one you made the Inspector." I did so. The tea was freshly brewed, two sugars, no milk but a good tot of whisky. I thought I might as well join the Doctor and made a cup for myself.

The Doctor put the cup to his lips. He looked at me. "Very good, Constable, and how many of these do you say the Inspector had?"

"Three or four – four I think, but you'll appreciate that it becomes stronger the longer the tea stands in the pot."

There were no repercussions. The Chief read the report – he was no mug. He had McIver into his office for half an hour. McIver had served under the Chief for nearly twenty years and had a deep respect for him. After that he still enjoyed his pint but he never overstepped the mark again.

Our paths did not cross for a few days. Then McIver came back from his beat a few minutes early.

"Och, Tom." It was the first time he'd called me by my first name. "I came back early to catch ye. I was lucky the other neet." That was the nearest I came to a thank you. "Will ye come round for tea one Sunday? Ye can meet the wife and oor Agnes. She's a dab hand at the piano. She can gie us a few tunes."

I could hardly refuse. It was a few weeks before we were both off duty on a Sunday afternoon but it was worth the wait.

We had winkles for tea and plenty of bread and butter. Mrs. McIver had made a jelly and we had that with some tinned fruit, and some more bread and butter. Then Agnes gave us a tune. Well, I'd expected some Scottish reels, but I was given my first taste of Chopin. I'd admired Agnes as a good looking woman, but as she sat at the piano and played music the like of which I'd never heard before, I fell for her there and then.

Although I was distinctly tongue-tied, I plucked up the courage to ask her if she would like to come for a walk one afternoon along the sea front. She accepted, and so our lengthy courtship commenced. Agnes made it quite clear to me from the outset that she would never marry a Police Constable. She had seen too much of her mother's life with McIver – a Police Sergeant perhaps, but a Constable never. I'd not been particularly ambitious before but now I had a target.

Walter's courtship was destined to be equally long but for quite different reasons. He could never bring himself to ask Gertie to marry him for fear that she'd refuse. His friendship with her came in very useful a couple of years later when her brother Billy started his professional career as a middleweight. He would be given a few complimentary tickets and Walter sometimes benefited. Billy was soon knocking them over at the small halls in Shields. Boxing was a popular sport in those days. We won a few shillings betting on him, but as he became known, the odds on 'Battling' Billy Ruffle shortened. He had not given up his blacksmith's job, and Gertie told Walter that he was having second thoughts about pursuing boxing as a career – he was in love. His girlfriend, Lizzy Simpson, who lived round the corner from the Ruffles, reciprocated his feelings but her family were Salvationists and did not hold with boxing. It seemed that Billy was going to have to choose.

At that time Jack 'Cast Iron' Cassidy from Sunderland was the best middleweight in the North East, and some said in the country. He was as hard as they come, was afraid of nobody, and had never been knocked out or stopped. He was a contender for the British Title and was biding his time. To earn some easy money he embarked on a series of ten-rounders against young boxers from the North East. Billy was one of them. The outcome of the fights was never in doubt and the Bookies would not take money on Cassidy. The betting was all about which round the other fellow would go down in. It was rumoured that Cassidy made more money betting on himself to win in a certain round than in purse money.

The Horsley Hill Stadium was packed. I was there with Walter and Bob Jamieson. Bob had been in to see Billy.

"He reckons he'll do all right. He's confident enough and he's not scared. Many of the young uns Cassidy fights are beaten before they get in the ring. Billy's been saving up his purse money and he's putting a fiver on himself to go the distance."

"What are the odds?" Walter enquired. He liked a bet.

"I've had a look round. Jimmy Crimbone's offering twenty to one."

"Twenty to one," echoed Walter. "Wor Gertie says that if Billy sets his mind on something then he'll do it. D'yees fancy clubbing together and putting a quid on?"

Well a pound was a large bet in those days, but the odds were good. We knew Billy, and I had never forgotten how he had taken the birching. Bob was game – I needed persuading the most. I'm never keen to risk losing my money but the thought of a third share in twenty pounds was tempting. I dug in my pocket and took out six and eightpence. Bob took the money and went off to put the bet on. He waited until the last minute. There was a sudden rush of money on Cassidy to stop Billy in the fourth. One of Cast Iron's friends had been seen putting a large bet on. The other odds lengthened – Bob got twenty five to one against Billy going the distance.

The first three rounds were fairly even. Cassidy hit Billy hard a few times but wasn't pressing him. Billy defended well and seemed to be going more for body shots. In the fourth Cassidy came out for the kill – he was ferocious. He had Billy down three times, but each time Billy took a count of eight and was up on his feet. After the third knock down he seemed more confident. He caught Cassidy on the counter attack with a right cross to the side of the head which caused the Sunderland man to back off for the first time that round. Cast Iron Jack launched a fierce attack in the last seconds of the round but Billy hung on. When the bell rang the Hall was in an uproar. Billy walked unsteadily back to his corner, his face bloodied but his head unbowed. Cassidy had lost his bet and didn't rush out in the fifth. Billy held his own. The crowd was behind him now. He was down again in the sixth when Jack caught him with a three punch combination, but he came back fighting. In the seventh Billy had rattled Cast Iron with a barrage of body punches and the Sunderland man decided he'd had enough. He came forward menacingly and threw a vicious left hook that would have had Billy's head off if it had landed. Billy blocked it with his right, jabbed with his left and then seemed to swivel on his heels and landed a straight right on Cassidy's jaw. It was a peach of a punch; Billy had put all his body into it and Cassidy went down as though he'd been poleaxed. There was pandemonium, everybody was on their feet. No one in Shields had ever seen 'Cast Iron' on the canvas before. Billy was standing over him. The Ref pushed him away before starting his count. His finger moved painfully slowly. I saw him glance at the timekeeper. He reached nine and the bell went. There was nearly a riot. Cassidy's seconds jumped in the ring and pulled him back to his stool in the corner. The towel was flapping like a topsail in a gale.

Cassidy showed why he was called 'Cast Iron' in the eighth. Billy hit him with everything he had. Cassidy just held on – literally. As soon as he came close to Billy he got into a clinch and kept hold for grim death. His experience told. The Ref was slow to part them and Cassidy weathered the storm. The ninth was much the same but Jack fought back a bit more. Billy only had one round to go but 'Cast Iron' had got his second wind. He had his reputation to think of and he knew that the contest must be close. With the Ref only scoring, a good last round might sway the balance. He came out quick and hit Billy hard. It was Billy's turn to hold on. He was tired now and his legs were heavy but he wasn't giving up. They stood in the centre of the ring exchanging punches. When the bell rang they collapsed into each other's arms. There was true sportsmanship in those days.

The Referee took a long time checking his card. All the Shields folk thought that Billy had won. I was not so sure. Cassidy had been on top in the middle rounds and his prospects as a contender would be damaged if he lost to an unknown. The Ref walked to the middle of the ring. The two boxers came to his side. He lifted both their hands in the air. It was a draw!

Bob went straight away to claim the winnings. He was then able to find his way into Billy's dressing room and congratulate the lad.

When he came back we left the Stadium quickly and headed back to town. Bob knew the Landlord of the *Queen's Head* in Cuthbert Street. We'd have a drink there to celebrate and wouldn't need to worry about closing time. Bob told us that Billy was in an awful state. One of his eyes was completely closed and his nose was flattened.

It was Billy's last fight. The next day he proposed to his girlfriend. She said yes but only on condition that he gave up boxing. She didn't hold with it because of her religion. He agreed. He'd made enough money from the bet to be able to buy a pair of flats in Ashley Road and have a bit left over. He had a steady job and they would be better off than a lot of folk – but Shields lost a future British Middleweight champion.

A couple of years later I was in the Market Place one afternoon about half past three. It was a few days before Christmas. The Salvation Army Band was on Crofton's Corner playing some carols and a good few folk were standing watching. I then caught sight of Big Geordie Duff who'd just come out of the *Tram*. He was a tall, well built man and he could spell trouble when he'd had a few. You had to be very careful with Big Geordie – he had a vicious punch and he would throw it very quickly. He was also crafty; he'd make as though he was walking away, and then he'd turn and let you have it.

He went over to where the Salvationists were playing. A young woman who still looked very shapely despite the Army uniform was holding out a can for contributions. Geordie went over to her. He tried to hold her by the hands. "Come on, give us a dance, hinny." I could hear his loud mouth. I was just going to walk over when I noticed that one of the bandsmen had put down his cornet and was going to the aid of his 'sister in war'. I recognised him straight away so I stayed where I was. He was a stocky fellow but he was still dwarfed by Big Geordie. The Salvationist didn't seem intimidated and pushed Geordie away. Geordie looked at him, half turned to go and then let fly. The bandsman had not taken his eyes off the bigger man. He saw the punch, blocked it, feinted with his left, then he seemed to swivel on his heels and landed a straight right on Geordie's jaw. There was a loud smack as knuckle hit bone and the big man went down. It was Billy Ruffle, of course. He may have given up the professional game but he still knew how to punch. The young woman was his wife. They both bent down to see that Big Geordie was all right. He was no Jack Cassidy and it took them a good five minutes to help him to his feet. He stood around for a while a bit unsteadily and then he walked over, stood by the band, and started singing. He had a strong baritone voice. Well, as soon as Mrs. Ruffle took the can round at the end of the carol she was engulfed by people trying to put in their pennies. I was nearly tempted myself but there was more than enough going in as it was.

Pilot's stairs leading up to the Turk's Head

An early call

It was about ten to three on a very hot afternoon in June. I had patrolled along the Long Row, Wapping Street, what was left of Shadwell Street and then walked up the Pilot Stairs to the Military Road. I was sweating profusely in my heavy serge uniform and helmet, and although I was not usually a beer drinker I decided to call in at the *Turk's Head* for a pint. It would soon be chucking out time and as I approached the pub I heard a commotion. Barney Coates, the Landlord, came bursting through the swing doors holding a sailor by the neck.

"You bastard!" he shouted as he threw him into the street. He saw me. "The bugger started a fight and then as soon as he caught a punch puked up all over the bloody floor."

"Fetch me a pint, Barney and I'll take him away for you." The young lad was in no state to look after himself – it was often the case, and we took them in for their own safety. They'd be paid off the ships and head straight for the nearest pub. The young fella starting to crawl over the cobbles had probably been in the bars since the doors had opened, or possibly earlier – some of the Riverside pubs would let the sailors in before opening time.

Barney helped the lad to his feet and gave him his sea bag while I drank my pint down. The young sailor was well away – he was unsteady on his pegs but could manage so long as I kept a hand on his arm. We walked slowly down through the Lawe on to Mile End Road. By the time we reached Keppel Street we were the best of friends. His name was Davey Honeywill and he'd been paid off that morning from the *Majestic,* after nine months at sea. He'd only meant to have a couple of drinks before heading for the Station and back home to Bristol – the old, old story. He was luckier than some – he still had some pay left.

Bob Jamieson booked him in as a drunk. He'd be bailed to the next Court provided he had an address. Bob looked at me and seeing that I was still hot and thirsty said, "Go and have a brew, Tom, and then you can do me a favour."

The job was not onerous. I was to walk along to Smithy Street and tell Dennis Macey that we had a customer for him. Dennis had two rooms above a shop, but the important thing was that he had a rent book. He would take any sailors who'd been put in the cells for drunkenness. They would be bailed to his address – he took them home, cleaned them up, made sure they arrived in court, and no doubt received something from them for his troubles.

He wasn't in when I called but I left a message in the shop and he arrived at the Station about seven. Davey had slept the worst off and went away with Dennis. He was in Court the day after and was fined five bob.

I was surprised to see him a couple of weeks later coming out of the *Scotia* one lunchtime. "You still here, Davey?"

"I like Shields," was his reply, "and me and Mr. Macey get on fine together. He says I can stay as long as I like."

I would see Dennis and him around the town. They were an unlikely pair but they caused no trouble, apart that is from giving Bob Jamieson a few headaches. Dennis wouldn't take any more of our inebriate mariners for the time being, and Bob had either to keep them in the cells or try and find a berth for them in a lodging house with no guarantee that they'd turn up in Court.

Sam Beecroft and I had been on good terms ever since I joined the Force. He had taken me under his wing in my early days on duty in the Market Place. He was a big bluff fellow with a ruddy complexion and a hearty laugh. He'd married a widow woman with property and now lived on the Lawe Top – the better end of Vespasian Street. His wife owned several houses in the area. Sam used to sort out any trouble with the tenants, although in those days the usual remedy for non-payment of rent was a moonlight flit.

He was a regular in the *Turk's* and one morning when we were having a break in the Station he asked me if I was doing anything that night. I wasn't.

"Would you fancy a drink at the *Turk's*? There's a few of us have a game of dominoes on a Wednesday neet but Jackie Wade's bad in bed with his chest."

It was the start of what turned out to be a good few domino sessions at the *Turk's*. We started about half past seven and went on till closing time. Sam drank pints all night; I stuck to whisky. Sam and I played well together and I came out of the evening one and tuppence ha'penny ahead. They were a good crowd. Geordie Smith and Ken Dawson were miners at St. Hilda's, Cuthbert Lawrenson worked in the tallow factory and Nobby Fairless was a boatman. Barney Coates would sit in on a hand in the early evening if it was not too busy.

We were having a rest between games about nine o'clock and the doors opened. In walked Dennis Macey and young Davey. Barney was behind the bar and as soon as he saw Davey he shook his head.

"I'm sorry son. Once you're thrown out of this pub you stay out."

Davey didn't seem perturbed. "I just came to apologise for making a mess the other day. I'm staying in Shields now and I didn't want anyone to think that I was a troublemaker. Mr. Macey will vouch for me."

Barney had known Dennis for years. He used to live in Edith Street and although he was no longer a regular he'd look back in once or twice a week. He nodded to Barney. "He's a good lad. He won't be any trouble."

Barney wasn't one to bear grudges but if he banned Davey he probably wouldn't see Dennis for a while. "All reet then, seeing as he apologised, but if there's any bother, you're both banned."

Davey had noticed me and came over for a quick chat. He was a likeable fellow with a West Country drawl that made a pleasant change from what passed in South Shields for the King's English. We heard a lot of it later that night. Cuthbert Lawrenson started it when he bought some drinks with a ten bob note. You normally only saw one of those on a Saturday night fresh from the pay packet. A few cracks were made.

"Me Missis gave it me. She said, 'Gan on Cuddy, gan and have yourself a pint'."

"You lying sod." Geordie Smith lived just next door to Cuthbert. "Your auld hinny's always hiding her money so you won't get your hands on it."

Cuthbert just smiled but Geordie wasn't daft. "You crafty bugger! You've found oot where she keeps it!"

"Well it wasn't very difficult. It's either under the sitting room carpet or under the mattress."

"You'll be in for it the neet."

"I doubt it," replied Cuthbert. "She probably won't look for it for a couple of weeks if she remembers where she put it."

The others chipped in; their wives were just the same. People didn't have bank accounts and if your husband drank then it was best to hide any spare money. We heard all the hiding places: books, in the china vase and so on. We had a laugh.

I was on night shift the week after. It was lonely on the beat and if you saw anyone else whose job kept them out, you normally stopped and had a chat with them, apart, that is, from the Midnight Mechanics – you stayed as far away as possible. They cleared the privies, loaded the night soil onto carts, and it was taken up the top of Mile End Road. It was put into a hopper and taken out to sea. The stench was horrific, particularly if it was a warm night.

The Knockers-up were more welcome company, and we would often walk alongside them for a while. In those days ordinary folk didn't have watches like they do today and alarm clocks were unheard of. The Knocker-up would do the job for a few pence a week. They'd tap at the window, using a long pole for the upstairs flats. Most of them would wait and see if a light came on. If they saw or heard nowt they'd tap again. People had to be up at all times for shift work and you'd see them from about two or three of the morning till six or seven. Peggy Lampshine did most of the town north of the Market Place and had taken over the round from her aunt who had brought her up. She was a lovely lass, not too bright, but she always had a smile on her face. Peggy had a couple of rooms in Palatine Street.

This particular night I was having a quick smoke in a back doorway off James Mather Street. We weren't supposed to smoke on duty but it was common practice. You needed a quiet corner with a good view. The Inspectors and Sergeants did check the beats but you could see them a mile off with their lanterns. I looked up the hill and saw Peggy coming down. You couldn't miss her – she always wore the same clothes winter or summer: a Sou'wester hat, a long trench coat tied in the middle with a belt and a pair of hobnailed boots. She had a large watch on a chain pinned to her lapel and carried a lantern in one hand and her pole in the other. I was going to cross over and have a word when I saw her stop to look down a back lane. She went slowly forwards holding up her lamp. I stubbed out my tab, put the stub in my pocket – there were a few drags left – and walked quietly across the cobbles. I didn't want to startle her so I stood just behind the end house wall. Peggy was about ten doors down where a fellow had just climbed out of a backyard over the wall. She was talking to him, not very loudly, but she was telling him off. They stood there for a while, then he put his hands on top of the wall and climbed back in. Peggy looked round anxiously, so I moved out of the shadows and walked down the lane.

"Are you all right Peggy?"

"Wy aye, I'm always all reet. But there's something funny gan' on here. I caught someone climbing ower the wall. He said his mate owed him some money. He didn't want to wake him up so he'd gone in the back way and taken it. I telt him he couldn't do that sort of thing. People would think he was a borglar. So he's gone in to put it back."

I didn't expect to see him again – he'd be over a few back-yard walls, in the rear and out the front of one of the houses further down – but I was wrong. A few minutes later we heard a scuffing noise and who should come clambering over the wall but young Davey Honeywill. When he saw the uniform his face fell but when he realised it was me he gave me a broad smile.

"Hello, Constable Duncan. Has the young lady told you that I was just putting some money back?" Peggy's face lit up – she'd probably never been called a lady before.

"She did, but I'd better search you anyway. Turn out your pockets."

He only had a few pennyworth of change, a penknife and a very small lantern case with a stub of candle inside. Peggy had obviously taken a shine to him and they were chatting away as I went through his pockets. I'd intended to arrest him, but I couldn't see a charge of going equipped for theft standing up, and he'd obviously put back whatever he'd taken in the first place. In those days you had to make your own decisions there and then.

"I'll let you off this time, Davey, but if there are any reports of theft I'll be straight round to your place. You still living at Dennis Macey's?" He nodded. "Well you can keep Peggy company for a while."

"I'll keep me eye on him." Peggy was serious now. I left them walking down the street together. She let him carry the pole but held on to the lamp herself. There were no reports the next morning of any thefts on the Lawe Top, but there'd been another break in at Winchester Street, where once again it was mainly jewellery that had been taken. The head of CID was worried – it was the fifth burglary in recent weeks and he had no clues. It couldn't have been Davey as he had been with Peggy.

The next night I saw her again and who should be at her side but Davey Honeywill. I said hello and asked her if Davey had stayed with her all night. He had and had even walked her home. I learned later that Davey met up with her each night that week. By the Thursday he was having breakfast in Peggy's flat in Palatine Street, and on the Saturday he wasn't seen coming out until the afternoon.

The source of my information was Sam Beecroft. Peggy was one of his wife's tenants.

I saw Sam about a week later on a Saturday night. He had been on the two till ten shift and I was taking over. We always doubled up on a Saturday in the market and John Burgess was with me. Sam stopped to have a natter.

"You off to the *Turk's*?" I asked.

He looked a bit embarrassed. "Not the neet."

John Burgess laughed. "You'll be seeing Mrs. Hankey home then?"

Mrs. Hankey worked on the pie stall. She knew all the Bobbies and would often let you have a piece of pie if you stood by the stall looking hungry. It was rumoured that some got more than pie.

"Well her husband's at sea and I divvent like to see her walking home on her own. Anyway I'm off noo."

John Burgess looked at me. "He'll be back to the Station, out of his uniform, he'll have a couple of pints in the *Havelock* and then he'll be back here. You'll see him hanging round the pie stall, and then he'll take her yem."

"He likes his pie hot?" was all I could think to say.

John laughed. "You could say that. I hope his missis doesn't find out though." Our conversation was cut short when a young lad came running up. "There's ganna be a fight outside the chip shop, ye'd better come. There's a little fella who's ganna be murdered."

We crossed the Market as quickly as we could but by the time we arrived it was all over. There was always a good queue for fish and chips on a Saturday night, and this big fellow had apparently pushed in. Only one man in the shop had had the nerve to ask him to go to the back of the queue – Teddy Denby, a pitman, a Deputy at St. Hilda's who was out with his wife. He was a small man, not much over five foot tall, but he was broad shouldered and strong and in those days you didn't become a Deputy if you couldn't handle trouble. The queue jumper had suggested that they should step outside. Teddy's wife had tried to stop him but he'd made his

mind up. When John and I came on the scene the other man was
sitting on the cobbles, blood pouring from his nose. I bent down
to see that he was all right and saw that it was Little Bobby Doyle.
His nickname had nothing to do with his size – he was nearly six
foot and well built. He was called 'Little' because he was the son of
another Bobby Doyle, a real villain, who was doing time in Durham.
Little Bobby had also been involved but had only been sent down for
six months.

"You're out now then, Bobby?" I asked. He looked at me but
said nowt. There was no love lost between us.

"You working?" He shook his head. "Well you seem to have
plenty of money for beer and fish and chips." We sent him on his
way. When Teddy and his wife went back into the shop there was a
spontaneous round of applause and they let them go to the front of
the queue.

We took a walk round the Market Place. "Do you get in the
Turk's then, Tom?" John Burgess asked.

"Aye, I sometimes play dominoes with Sam on a Wednesday
night."

"I was in there the other afternoon. Barney Coates wasn't very
happy. A couple of the regulars had stopped coming in. They'd been
talking one night about where their wives hid their money. Well,
apparently some of the notes their women had put under the carpet
had gone. Their wives had said they'd taken the money to go out
drinking. Knowing who it was it wouldn't have surprised me but
Barney says they swore blind they hadn't."

It had made no difference. Their wives had taken extra from
their pay packets and they hadn't been able to pay for their beer.
Barney had given them a slate but he wasn't very happy.

The next afternoon I was having a walk round town and I called
at Dennis Macey's to have a word with Davey. It was a good job I
did. Dennis had the younger man up against the wall outside the
house. Davey's sea bag was on the cobbles. I was not in uniform and
when I went to separate them I was invited to bugger off by an irate

Dennis who had not recognised me. Davey put him right.

"After all I've done for him; I took him in; I've looked after him; and he's leaving just so he can have it off with some tart. No decent woman would have him, the bastard."

I didn't want to become involved. Davey went over to pick up his bag. "You can't stop me, and Peggy isn't a tart," was all he said. The doors were starting to open – a barney on a Sunday afternoon after the pubs had closed was not unusual. A fellow whose face seemed vaguely familiar was coming down Smithy Street towards us. He had the gait of a sailor and white hair poked out from under his cap. He stopped to ask Dennis if everything was all right. "Aye, come on in." They went in and up the stairs as Davey and I walked off.

"He seemed upset at you leaving?"

"I stayed with him because I needed a billet and I didn't want to go back home, but he's no right to talk about Peggy like that."

We said no more about it. When I thought that he'd calmed down I brought up the subject of money disappearing from hiding places under the carpets of houses not too far away from the *Turk's Head*.

"I know you've done it once because I was there."

"It was me, but I only did two houses in Fort Street the night before you and Peggy caught me. I only intended it as a loan. I thought they wouldn't miss the money for a while and I'd have time to put it back. Those houses are easy enough to get in if you've got a pen knife. Most of the windows are loose and the catches push back easy. There's hardly any risk once folk are abed, and I can get just enough light with my little lamp. When I heard that the money was under the carpet, that's the first place I looked. I'll put it back tonight. Peggy'll lend me the cash. As well as moving in I'm going to work with her full time. Tommy Dick's suffering with the rheumatics at the moment and Peggy's going to take some of his customers. With the two of us it'll be easy enough."

I said goodbye to him at the bottom of the Mile End Road. I never found out why Dennis Macey was so angry with Davey but there was no doubt that he was jealous of Peggy. He showed a nasty side and started going to the pubs near Palatine Street spreading gossip. He nearly got thumped a couple of times because people knew Peggy and although she was a bit eccentric she'd never harmed anyone. He started telling her customers that she wouldn't be reliable now she was living in sin with a sailor. He was given short shrift, but some of the muck he spread stuck and the gossip reached the ears of Mrs. Beecroft. She was a Churchgoer and like many at the time believed that abstinence from anything that brought you pleasure was the path to salvation.

The next time I saw Sam he was not very happy. "I've just been round to Peggy's. That young sailor's still there – he seems well settled in and works with Peggy now. Peggy's happy and the lad's harmless enough, but me wife said that I had to give her notice as she's not having anyone living in sin in one of her properties. Peggy got so upset when I said she'd have to leave the flat that I told her not to worry for a while, I'd talk to the Missis. She's not gan' to like it, though."

I didn't think much of Sam's problems for a few days. There'd been more break-ins. The last house to be done had been in Bent House Lane. They were big, high houses and the thief had got in through an attic window. The Detective Inspector had no leads so he had decided to put a few of us into plain clothes to keep a look out. I was to team up with John Burgess and we were to dress in working clothes, with a knapsack, so that we'd pass unnoticed. There was always somebody on the streets walking to, or back from, work at nearly every hour of the night. The Big Fella, Detective Inspector Norman Lamont, gave us a briefing before our first watch.

"I reckon there'll be two of them – one on the watch outside and one who does the breaking in. They never take anything heavy so I can't see the need for anyone else. But if you see anything, wait until they're both on the ground. The one who broke into the house on Bents Road has no fear of heights."

Two nights later John Burgess and myself, wearing workmen's

clothes, walked up and down the streets of Shields – along Winchester Street, down Bent House Lane up Fowler Street and along Erskine Road. We saw nowt.

The next night happened to be a Wednesday so I thought I'd look in to the *Turk's* for a game of dominoes. I mentioned it to John and he said he'd join me. I had another reason for going in as I wanted to see if any of the missing money under the carpet had turned up. I was just settling into a game when Nobby Fairless walked in, a broad smile on his face. Barney Coates looked up.

"Well you're a sight for sore eyes. I thought I'd seen the last of ye."

"It's me auld hinny's fault. She swore blind I'd been under the carpet for her money. Well the neet, when I came in, she was as nice as ninepence. 'Sit doon, Nobby and hev your tea. I've done an extra herring for you.' Then she telt me. She'd gone to put a ten shilling note under the carpet till the end of the week and she'd felt something. She put her hand under and there was the note she thowt she'd lost. All crumpled up but further in than usual."

We had a good laugh. Ken Dawson who'd been sitting in the corner sipping a half got up and went out. Ten minutes later he was back. "I asked her where she thowt she'd put the ten bob I was supposed to have nicked. We rolled the carpet back and there it was – a good foot in and all crumpled."

They were both in the money and a good night was had. I only had a couple of nips but John drank his pints down as usual. I could see that we'd be stopping in several back lanes as the night wore on. We went into Keppel Street to get changed and have a brew before setting out. There wasn't much point in going on the watch until well after twelve.

It turned out much as I suspected: every half an hour or so John Burgess needed to pop down a back lane to relieve himself. At about half past two John suggested that we stop for a cup of tea. He'd put a flask of tea and a couple of sandwiches in his knapsack. We went down a back lane off South Woodbine Street. John very quietly

opened one of the doors and we stood inside a backyard doorway.
You didn't see workmen eating their bait in the street. After we'd
finished we headed off down Broughton Road. John decided he
needed to have another piss and he went off down a back lane. I
heard him say something and then he came back.

"You stay here, Tom, I'm off doon the other end. I was just
getting started when I saw someone in the shadows two doors down
from me. He pretended he was doing the same as me. I asked him if
he was all right and he said that beer went straight through him. He
was quite a size and he sounded like Little Bobby Doyle."

"The lookout?"

"I'd bet on it."

Off John went down the Road to come into the back lane from
the other end. I stood behind the wall of the end house and every
now and again took a quick look up the lane. I was well away from
the street lamp so there was little chance of the lookout seeing me.
We didn't have to wait long. I heard a scuffing noise and then the
sound of voices – very quiet. I stood out from the wall and looked
down the lane. There were two men. As they saw me they took off.
I put my whistle to my lips, blew hard, and ran after them. It was
pitch dark so they didn't see the burly figure of John Burgess until
the last minute. He caught the bigger of the two in full flight and
they both went down.

"Hold on to him, John, I'll catch the other bugger."

It was only by chance that I did. He was fast even with a sack in
his hand. He'd cut through to Bent House Lane and was running up
towards the Marine Park. He had the legs on me all right, and if he
reached there before me I'd never catch him. As I looked up I saw
Peggy Lampshine and Davey Honeywill coming round the corner
of Wouldhave Street.

"Stop thief!" was all I could shout as I was breathing heavily –
I've never been one for running up hills. I thought they were going
to let him pass, then, just as he was nearing them Davey dropped the
pole, caught his legs and the fellow went crop over creels. Davey was

onto him in a flash and held on until I arrived.

He was no trouble but I cuffed him just in case. I recognised him as the fellow I'd seen in Smithy Street going into Dennis Macey's and I realised why the face had seemed familiar – it was Eric Molls. A few years ago he had rescued a young lad who had climbed up one of the derelict buildings in Shadwell Street and couldn't get down. The wall the lad was sitting on looked as though it could crumble at any minute and there was no time to wait for the Fire Engine with its long ladder. Eric Molls had shinned up the drain pipe – he had been one of the best tops'l men in the business in the days of the sail ships, and had no fear of heights.

Reinforcements arrived and he was taken off to the Station with his accomplice.

"You're a bit out of your way, aren't you?" I asked Peggy.

"Aye, I'm doing a couple of three o'clock calls for Tommy Dick. His chest's still bad. We'll have to be off soon, back up the Lawe Top for the four o'clockers. We start getting busy then."

"Sam told me about the trouble you're having with your Landlord."

"We thought we'd sorted it out. Me and Davey are getting married, but when Sam told his wife she said it didn't make any difference. We'd been living in sin and she didn't want that sort in one of her hooses."

There was no pleasing some people.

"I'll have a word with Sam. When's the happy day?"

"Three weeks' time when the Banns have been read. It'll be at St. Stephens; there'll only be us."

The Big Fella was pleased with the arrests but he was not very happy when Eric and Little Bobby would only confess to the one job. They swore blind that they had nothing to do with the other break-ins and there was no evidence to connect them. CID searched their homes and found nothing. The DI tried to persuade the Chief to charge them anyway arguing that the *modus operandi* of all the recent break-ins was the same. Two weeks later another burglary took place when Eric and Little Bobby were on remand in Durham. Inspector Lamont could only charge them with the one offence and they got six months each with hard labour. He reckoned that there was a fence behind it all who was putting others up to do the burglaries but he couldn't prove his theory and none of the stolen property was turning up in Shields.

I'd thought hard about Peggy and her problems with Mrs. Beecroft. There was only one way to solve them. I had some compunction about blackmailing Sam but I had never liked hypocrites, even very good natured ones like Sam Beecroft. I caught him early one morning as he came off night shift. If all the rumours I'd heard were true he'd have paid a midnight call on Mrs. Hankey, whose husband was still away at sea.

"Sam, you're going to have to persuade your wife to let Peggy and Davey stay on at Palatine Street after they're married."

"I wish I could but her mind's made up."

"I'm sure you'll find a way."

He looked at me.

"You wouldn't want your wife to find out that you've been walking Mrs. Hankey back home from the pie stall on Saturday nights."

"You wouldn't dare."

"You'll be evicting two young people for fornication outside of wedlock when you're doing the same thing yourself."

He hit me. I wasn't expecting it and I went down. He didn't wait for me to get up and stalked off. 'Well,' I thought to myself as I rubbed my jaw, 'that's the end of my Wednesday night domino sessions.'

My words had their effect though. I saw Peggy and Davey a few days later in the middle of the night. Sam had been round to say that his wife had had second thoughts. Sam had asked the Vicar to call to see her and he had talked to her about forgiveness. She'd reluctantly agreed to let them stay but on condition that there were no more complaints. They were over the moon. I was just about to go on my way when Davey stopped me.

"Peggy wants me to ask you to do us a favour. Would you be my best man? I don't know anyone else."

I was going to decline until I caught the look in Peggy's eye and said yes. It would mean swapping a shift, but you could always find someone to help out provided you'd return the favour.

The wedding was on a Saturday morning. Peggy and Davey could not afford to pay the organist so it would be a short service. The Vicar had squeezed them in at half past eleven before a midday wedding. I'd picked Davey up from Peggy's flat at five to eleven sharp. He hadn't been up long, was nervous, and looked as white as a sheet so I took him into the Palatine Hotel for a glass of whisky. We were waiting outside the Church at twenty past when Dennis Macey came up the street. He walked straight up to Davey and me and spat his words out.

"Getting married, are you? Well I'm gan' to object, you little bastard."

He didn't say any more. I'm normally a mild mannered chap but I'd taken a dislike to Macey. I'd begun to have my suspicions about why he had been so keen to look after the young sailor, but he wasn't going to spoil his wedding day. I hit him hard on the shoulder, and as he span round I grabbed his collar with one hand, his belt with the other, ran a few steps with him, and then sent him flying over the cobbles. As he struggled to his feet I kicked him hard in the backside. He didn't look back and ran off down Mile End Road. It was just in time. Peggy came up the road with Tommy Dick and his wife. Tommy was going to give her away.

Word had got round and there were a few folk there, mainly neighbours and one or two of Peggy's clients. John Burgess and Bill Spyles who were on night shift had come along. They had known Peggy's aunt before she'd passed on. It was all over in ten minutes and Peggy asked us back to her flat – she'd made some sandwiches.

John and Bill walked down to Turnbull's Brewery and arrived in Palatine Street each carrying a two gallon bucket of beer; some of the neighbours brought some pies and cakes they had made. We were crammed into the two rooms and spilling out on to the street. It was a lovely do and we left them to it at about five o'clock that evening. They'd asked to be married on a Saturday as it was the only night they had off. Only a handful of people worked on a Sunday and Tommy would cover for them.

Just four weeks later Davey Honeywill was arrested for bigamy. The Bristol Police had been in touch with DI Lamont. A Mrs. Honeywill had called in at the Bridewell and made a complaint. Her husband was a sailor and she'd not heard of him for over a year. She'd learned that he had recently married a Peggy Lampshine at St. Stephen's Church in South Shields. The Big Fella had checked with the Vicar of St Stephen's and had then asked the Bristol Police to send him Mrs. Honeywill's statement and her marriage certificate. I'd been called in to see him but couldn't say much. He mainly wanted to know whether I thought Peggy knew. If she did then she was liable for prosecution as an accomplice. I was sure she didn't.

Davey didn't deny it; there was little point. He just said that they'd had to get married or they would have been out on the street. It was no defence – bigamy was a serious crime. Davey was remanded in custody to Durham Jail and would be sentenced at the Quarter Sessions. Prisoners who were to be sent to Durham were taken in the horse-drawn Black Maria to the Station and then put on the train with an escort. I'd drawn the short straw and was to accompany Davey. Of course everybody knew that I'd been the best man. It was Inspector Mullins' idea of a little joke to see me and Davey handcuffed together on a trip to Durham Jail.

I think it was because he knew me that Davey told me what he did. Inspector Lamont had told Davey who had shopped him. It was recorded in the Police statement from Bristol that a Mr. Dennis Macey had visited the City, found Mrs. Honeywill and told her about

her husband's 'marriage'. It was no great surprise but Davey had
been hurt. Macey had looked after him and Davey had been grateful
to him. As we were on the way to Durham Davey asked if the Chief
might put a word in for him with the Judge if he was to help us nail
a villain. It wasn't unusual so I said I would mention it to the DI. I
thought it was going to be some small thing until he started telling
me about Dennis Macey's little sideline. He was a fence but he'd
recently branched out and was behind the recent spate of burglaries
in Shields. He had a half share in a little pawnbroker's shop on the
Scotswood Road in Newcastle and as soon as he had any loot he was
on the shilling ferry up the Tyne. No wonder we'd never found any
trace of the stolen valuables in Shields.

When I arrived back in Keppel Street I went straight to the Big
Fella. I left him a happy man. He was on the train the next day to
Durham and had a long talk with Davey.

Although it took some planning, the arrest of Dennis Macey and
his accomplices was achieved without a hitch. We knew that he left
his house as early as possible with the proceeds of any robbery and
went straight to the ferry landing. My good friend Walter Heron
was sent down there to stand amongst the workmen waiting for the
ferry. He had on a cap and work clothes. With Dennis coming to the
Station so often to take away his drunken sailors he knew most of
the Bobbies by sight, but Walter had been working in Laygate for a
while and looked no different from any other working man going
up by river to Newcastle. A uniformed officer would walk past the
landing now and again which was not unusual. They were there for
three days before Dennis turned up one morning. This time Walter
actually got on the ferry. The uniformed Constable carried on his
beat. He had the motorbike parked just round the corner and was
straight off to the Station. CID telephoned Newcastle Police who
would have plain clothes officers waiting at the other end. Dennis
Macey was followed up the Scotswood Road into the pawnshop and
then arrested. The loot in his bag was not reported missing until
later that day. The Newcastle Police found a lot of other stuff of

interest to both Forces.

Davey Honeywill received three years. Had it not been for Inspector Lamont's efforts on his behalf he would have been sent down for at least five.

Peggy came to see me afterwards and asked if I could help her to pen a letter to Davey in prison. She could barely write herself so I put down a few words for her which she signed, and I sent it to the Prison Chaplain with a covering note from myself. In those days there was no routine visiting for prisoners, and any contact with them had to be arranged with the Chaplain who was responsible for the moral welfare of the prisoners. I received a short letter back enclosing Peggy's letter. The Chaplain had no intention of encouraging prisoner Honeywill's immoral liaison with Miss Lampshine and would not permit any contact between them. He had been trying to persuade Honeywill to become reconciled with his wife, and had requested the Prison Authorities to transfer the prisoner to Horfield Prison in Bristol, so that he would be able to receive visits from his wife. We heard afterwards that she had only visited Davey once, had spat in his face, and left.

Peggy heard nothing from Davey for three years, then one morning she found him sitting on her doorstep when she came back from her rounds. He had walked all the way from Bristol to Shields. He moved back in with her and they lived together as Mr. and Mrs. Honeywill – they had to move of course as their landlady put her foot down this time. Davey helped Peggy on her rounds and took over when she became pregnant with the first of their three children. They eventually married in 1959 after Davey's first wife died. Davey and Peggy were grandparents by then. It was a very quiet affair in St. Stephen's one Wednesday afternoon. I was best man again. Peggy thought it only right.

Cuthbert Street

A sure thing

I was one of the team that raided Jack Conway's in Adelaide Street in 1922. At that time, in the Laygate area, there was a bookies' runner down every back lane, and most of them worked for Jack Conway. Folk nowadays, who just walk into betting shops to put a bet on, don't realise that up until the 1960s street betting was illegal, but it still went on and enforcement was not easy. For every bookie you nicked there were still dozens more happily taking bets, and in the 1920s there was no shortage of punters.

Bill Spyles nearly had Dick Burke, the bookie, one day but Dick went into a back lane and vanished. He'd gone into one of the backyards, straight up the stairs, his wooden leg knocking on the steps forewarning the householders, and out the front. He had an advantage over Bill: he knew which folk left their doors open for the bookies – it was the talk of Shields.

Inspector Mullins had made the decision to carry out the raid. Councillor Turnbull had complained to the Chief about the number of bookies' runners in the streets and Mullins had been asked to do something about it. Mullins was the man for the job, a teetotal Methodist, who was down on any of the things in life that brought pleasure, gambling being one of them. As those of you who have read previous pages in these memoirs will know, I did not have a high regard for Inspector Mullins and I've no doubt he felt the same way about me, but he planned the operation against Jack Conway meticulously.

He made sure that only officers working out of Keppel Street would be involved. His thinking was that those from Tyne Dock and Laygate were more than likely to put bets on with Jack and might tip him off. That was the trouble with Mullins – he always thought the worst of people. It caused a lot of ill feeling when it became known and was to have repercussions.

The main difficulty in raiding a bookie's house was to ensure they were not warned off in advance. Although a single Bobby

THE FIVE STONE STEPS

walking down the street was a common sight, a group of them heading anywhere near a bookie's premises would set the alarm bells ringing. Jack had lookouts and runners on nearly every street corner around Adelaide Street. As soon as they saw anything untoward they'd beat it back to Jack's and the takings and betting slips would disappear. Mullins also wanted to be sure that Jack would be in the house when it was raided.

Mullins put the word out and it didn't take long for Bill Spyles to finger Titch Foster – a pathetic specimen who'd been in and out of Durham and who'd do anything for money but work for it. He wasn't a regular snout but he was one of those who Bill would lean on to get information. He was taking bets for Jack Conway so Bill had a quiet word – it didn't take much – Titch didn't want to go back inside and Bill could be very persuasive.

According to Titch, Jack liked to go out and about and talk to the other bookies and tipsters. He frequented most of the Pubs in the Laygate area, taking bets himself and collecting slips that the Landlords had taken for him. He always returned to the fold between half past three and four o'clock when he'd sort out the day's winning bets with his clerk, Wilf Geff.

Mullins decided that the best time for the raid would be just after four in the afternoon. He wanted to hit Conway hard when there was certain to be a lot of money on the table. He was not a betting man himself so he had a quiet word with Superintendent Henry Burnside. Henry liked his beer and in Mullins' book those who drank were also likely to gamble. It was early September and Henry suggested that Mullins might try St. Leger Day. In those days the St. Leger, like the Oaks and the Two Thousand Guineas, was every bit as popular as the Derby and the Grand National. Everyone who liked a flutter would have something on, and those who didn't bet regularly would be tempted.

At about four o'clock on St. Leger afternoon I was sauntering along Victoria Road with John Burgess. We were dressed as workmen, but this time, to make it more realistic, we even had a good bit of coal dust rubbed on our faces. Miners coming off shift were a common sight on the streets. We'd already taken care of two of Jack's runners on the corners of Green Street and Cuthbert Street. The horse-drawn Black Maria was stationed in Claypath Lane where we had handed the culprits over to a couple of uniformed officers. Sam Beecroft and Bill Spyles were doing the same in Laygate Lane. When there was no sign of any other suspicious looking characters we walked down the back lane of Adelaide Street – we were to cover the bookie's back door. Mullins and the uniformed Bobbies would come in the front. It worked like clockwork. As soon as we heard the whistle we went in. A couple of Jack's men tried to make a run for it but we sent them back.

Mrs. Conway was in the scullery cleaning some herrings for Jack's tea.

"A'm sorry lads, we divvent take bets at the hoose."

"It's all right, hinny, we're the Polis; we're after your man."

"Well ye divvent look like Polis to me," she said and went back to her herrings.

Jack and Wilf Geff had stayed where they were, sitting at the big table which filled Jack's sitting room. It was full of smoke. Wilf was reckoned to smoke a hundred a day – his fingertips and his nostrils were yellow with the nicotine. The betting slips were laid out in neat little piles, all over one side of the table. No ledgers were kept. All the slips were arranged by order of the first race on the slip. If the horse won then the slip would be moved over to the payout pile or, if it was an accumulator, moved down to the next race. Wilf would mark in pencil on the slip how much was to be carried over. He could work out odds at a glance. The only paperwork he kept apart from the slips was a note of the takings so far and of the winning bets. It was usually scribbled on the back of an old envelope or some other scrap of paper. We didn't see it of course – as soon as he heard the police whistle Wilf just crumpled it up and tossed it onto the open fire.

Jack Conway was a large man with a big round face and a

balding head. He greeted Mullins with a sigh.

"Can you not let an honest businessman alone, Officer?"

Mullins' only response was to arrest him. Sergeant Ernie Leadbitter had brought the bags to collect up the evidence. The takings came to £850 15s 3d. They were counted into the bag in the presence of Wilf and Jack. None of us had ever seen so much money before. Ernie scooped up the betting slips into another bag.

"You'll be careful with them now." Jack didn't want any slips going missing or any new slips being put in the bag later on by an unscrupulous Bobby. He didn't know Mullins.

"It's nowt to do with you now, Mr. Conway. And it'll be the last you see of them. We're going to confiscate the lot this time."

"Not the slips. You can't do that. I won't be able to pay oot – and it's St. Leger Day."

Mullins turned his back on the angry bookie and made sure that everything was taken. Jack and Wilf were escorted out of the house to the Black Maria that was now waiting out front. We were to walk back to Keppel Street. I was not much of a betting man, and I had been intrigued by Mullins' comment about the betting slips. I asked the others if he was right. It was Bill who replied.

"The takings are confiscated. No question. With the slips it's up to the Magistrates, but it all depends on whether the Chief asks for a confiscation order. He got his fingers burnt back in 1904 – he'd not been Chief Constable very long. I'd just joined the Force myself. He raided Horace Blackman's in Cone Street and he applied for the slips to be confiscated. It was the first time it had been done in Shields. Horace said he wasn't paying out, he'd return the stake money to regulars but that was all. Even so he reckoned afterwards that what the regulars claimed was more than double his normal takings. There was hell to pay. We nearly had a riot when Peggy Chambers went to demand her winnings. She'd had a threepenny accumulator come up and reckoned she was owed thirteen pounds twelve and fourpence." He smiled. "I can remember it now. Peggy was banging on the door and yelling like the devil. They reckon that they heard her over on the fish quay in North Shields. If Horace had paid out, half of Shields would have been round claiming big wins. He came out to reason with her but Peggy wouldn't listen. She got hold of him by his beard and would have had his head off if I'd not gone in. We made four arrests and had two officers injured. The Chief learnt his lesson. After that he left betting raids to his Inspectors. He won't apply to confiscate the slips unless the arresting officer requests it."

When Jack was booked in Mullins made it clear that that's just what he intended to do. "It's the only thing that'll punish them." Word soon got round.

Bill Spyles was not the sort of man you would call a hypocrite, at least not to his face – you'd likely end up on your back seeing stars. He was one of the few Constables in Shields who relished chasing after street bookies, but he was also one of those who was always having a bet, and it caused a few problems for him. Any bookie who saw him coming didn't stand around long enough to find out whether Bill was going to hand him a betting slip or walk him back to Keppel Street. Bill had to ask others to put bets on for him. He'd usually catch the young Bobbies. At the time of the Jack Conway raid Bill had organised a little betting syndicate – there was him, John Burgess, Henry Milburn and Sam Beecroft. They each put in thre'pence and Bill would work out a treble, cross doubles or an accumulator. They would make a bet about twice a week. The morning of the raid my very good friend Walter Heron had called into Keppel Street to see me. He was off duty himself but he would often pop in for a chat. Walter was on the way to see his girlfriend, Gertie Ruffle, who worked in the North of England Café in King Street. We were having a cup of tea before we readied ourselves for the afternoon's business. Bill caught Walter just as he was getting up to go.

"You're heading towards the Market, Walter?"

"Aye."

"Can you put a bet on for me?"

"Aw, not again Bill. Can't you get someone else?"

"Well if I could I wouldn't ask you now, would I? If we win I'll give you something. Mind you put it on in the Market Place with Freddie Sheppard." Walter had done this many times before.

"All reet man, divvent fash yersel'." And Walter was off.

On the way back from the raid in Adelaide Street Bill had stopped to buy a Shields Gazette. He checked the racing results – the latest ones were printed in red ink as late news on the back page.

"We've got five horses up." He could hardly contain himself. "It's all on Wild Oats in the last race at Catterick. It'll be on the radio news at six o'clock." There was a wireless in the Charge Room and Bob Jamieson let us in to listen. Wild Oats came in at 7 to 1.

"How much have we won?" asked Henry Milburn.

"There's some difficult odds." Arithmetic was not Bill's strong point. "But it must be over twenty pounds."

I had an idea. "Why not ask Wilf Geff? He'll work it out for you in two seconds. They'll be releasing him on bail soon, won't they, Sarge?"

"Aye, they will. Hang about, Bill, and I'll catch him when he's being bailed." Bill stayed handy for the Charge Room while the rest of us made ourselves scarce. I heard what happened afterwards; we all did.

After Jack Conway and Wilf Geff had signed the bail form, Bob asked Wilf if he could stay behind a minute.

"I'll wait for you outside." Jack didn't like the inside of a nick. Sergeant Jamieson gave a shout and Bill came in and handed Wilf the copy of the bet.

"They all came in. Can you tell us how much we'll win?"

Wilf didn't comment on the irony of the situation. Working out odds was just business to him and he hardly glanced at the piece of paper.

"Twenty One Pounds Eleven and Eight pence, plus your stake money – you won't be paid out till after the Court case, and if your

Inspector confiscates the slips you'll be lucky if you get your stake back."

"It's all right; we didn't put the bet on with Jack. It was with Freddie Sheppard."

Wilf, who had started on his way up the five stone steps, stopped. "Well someone put exactly the same bet on with us. There'd been four winners up by the time of the raid." Wilf had a photographic memory for bets and he'd looked at this at least three times. "Titch Foster took the bet. The pseudonym was Curly three crosses." Wilf went on his way.

Bill was not a happy man – Curly XXX was his pseudonym and had been for years. He decided to see Walter that evening. I thought I'd better go with Bill. We had a drink in the Tyne Dock first and were waiting for Walter outside the nick just as he came on duty for night shift. His surprise at seeing us turned to panic as Bill grabbed him by the throat and held him against the wall. I won't set down here exactly what Bill said for fear of offending the blasphemy laws.

I tried to calm Bill down but it was not easy. His cheeks were flushed and his little piggy eyes were nearly sticking out of his head. He had to take a breather sometime though and Walter managed to get a word in.

"I'm sorry Bill. Wor Gertie was sent for a message to the Market and I walked along with her. Ye kna' what her family are like. They're strict Methodist. If she saw me putting a bet on she'd have had a fit. I walked back to Laygate and saw Titch Foster on the corner of Cuthbert Street. He gave me a funny look and said he was surprised I was having a bet. I said it was for someone else. Anyway I can't see why you're so excited about it. Jack Conway always pays up, doesn't he?"

"We raided Jack Conway's this afternoon and Mullins says he's going to confiscate the betting slips."

"Bloody hell, Tom, he's not, is he?" The look on our faces gave him the answer.

"Well you should have telt us. I wouldn't have gone near any of

Jack's runners if I'd known."

Walter was right of course. I told Bill on the way back on the tram.

"Aye, I suppose so. It's all Mullins' fault, but I'm not giving up. We'll have to find a way to persuade him to change his mind."

"You mean you'll have to find a way, Bill. It's nowt to do with me. I only came along tonight to make sure you didn't hurt Walter."

He wasn't too pleased. I left him outside the *Mechanics* – it was past closing time but Bill knew the Landlord.

I had been going out with Agnes McIver for a couple of years. It was hardly a lightning romance. She would occasionally let me hold her hand but that was all I'd managed. Archibald McIver, her father, was none too happy that she was seeing another Police Officer, but I'd helped him out once and he did not cause any problems. Agnes had not got over her first love, Captain Herbert Jaggers, who had been everything I was not – tall, dark and handsome. She'd known him since Sunday School. He was the son of Charlie Jaggers, Foreman at Turnbull's brewery. He'd joined up as soon as he was eighteen in 1916. He was a brave lad, became Sergeant in nine months, and was given a field Commission just before he was killed in action in the Somme in 1918 – he was awarded the Military Cross posthumously. Agnes had taken his death badly, had suffered a breakdown, and had subsequent bouts of neurasthenia. She was an excitable woman and could be unpredictable. I persevered but I felt that any passion in our relationship was on my side only.

I was a little surprised to see her waiting for me in the Station Yard one afternoon just as I was coming in at two o'clock. She asked if she could meet me after the shift and we could have a cup of coffee in the Roma. I said yes and wondered all afternoon whether my luck was changing – a ten o'clock coffee with Agnes. As soon as we were settled in the Roma with our foaming cups she said she needed my help. She went straight to the point; she always did.

Agnes gave piano lessons and because she wasn't allowed to give them from the Police house she went to the pupil's home. She was highly thought of and had customers in the best parts of Shields.

One of her clients, Mrs. Barrowclough, lived in Mowbray Road. She had a fifteen year old daughter who took the lessons two mornings a week. Mrs. Barrowclough liked a bet. One of Jack Conway's runners called round every morning, 'Dapper' Digby Johnson. I knew him of old – he was a nice looking lad, with wavy brown hair and dark brown eyes. He was always dressed to kill and wore his cap at a jaunty angle – in the summer he'd sport a boater. He took most of Jack's bets in the Westoe area and was very popular with the ladies. He'd met Agnes once as she had finished her lesson, and after that he always seemed to time his visits so that he'd see her either coming in or leaving.

"I think he liked me but I told him I was engaged." She caught my worried glance. "Well, I had to tell him something. He asked if I liked a bet. I said that I knew nothing about horses and that my Dad had always told me that it was a mug's game. He said he knew a sure thing for that afternoon that would come in at ten to one. If I wanted he'd put thre'pence on for me. I needn't give him any money; he'd take the stake out of the winnings."

He must have thought she'd just come over. I had a premonition about what was coming.

"And it won?"

"Yes. I won two and six. Every time after that he had a tip and I couldn't see any harm in it. But for the last few weeks they've been losing. I hadn't been paying him as I had no winnings. He wanted his money back, or something else in return. Oh, he was very smarmy about it. 'You could come round to my room one evening. We'd soon work something out.' I told him I wasn't that sort. Well the other day I heard Mrs. Barrowclough talking to him. She was putting a bet on a horse in the St. Leger – her husband had had a tip from an ex-jockey who knew the trainer – so I decided to put a bet on. The horse was called 'Royal Lancer'. I'd stopped trusting Digby so I wrote my own slip out, and I gave him the money for the bet, five shillings."

I nearly choked on my coffee.

"You put five shillings on!"

"Well I needed a big win to pay Digby off."

"How much do you owe him? I'll give you the money." I regretted saying it as soon as the words were out of my mouth.

"Two pounds, twelve and six."

I swallowed hard. I didn't like going back on my word but that was a lot of money. Even though I loved Agnes I was going to have to let her down.

"It's all right, Tom, you needn't worry. Royal Lancer came in at thirty-three to one, but Digby won't pay out. I just wanted you to have a word with him and to get my winnings."

I felt like having a word with Dapper Digby and if I did he might not look so dapper afterwards.

"He can't pay out. You must know. We raided Jack Conway's on St. Leger day and Inspector Mullins is going to confiscate the betting slips. If he does then you'll be lucky if you get your five bob back."

"Well, you'll have to persuade Mr. Mullins to change his mind." She drank her coffee down. "You can walk me home now."

I spent the next few days pondering what to do. Jack and Wilf had appeared in Court. The case had been adjourned for seven days so that Jack's barrister, C.B. Fenwick QC, could be present. Jack could afford it. Mr. Fenwick's eloquence would keep Jack's fine down to what would be a pittance for him. He would do well though to persuade the Magistrates not to make a confiscation order for the betting slips if the Chief asked for one.

I'd been in Court one morning and was leaving the Station when an angry looking fellow came marching up the steps.

"Excuse me, Officer, where do I gan to make a complaint."

"What's the trouble?"

"It's nowt to do with ye, son, I want someone in authority."

"Well, you can see Sergeant Jamieson, but if you're wasting his time you'll be straight back out down the steps."

"I'll tek me chances."

"What's your name?"

"Tom Hankey."

I took him along to the Charge Office. Sergeant Bob Jamieson was not pleased.

"We don't want time wasters in here. Now what do you want and be quick about it."

Mr. Hankey was not put off.

"I want to complain about Constable Beecroft."

I'd been making myself scarce, but stopped to listen when I heard Sam's name.

"Me brother's away at sea and this Officer Beecroft's gannin' roond to his hoose when his wife's on her own. At neet as well."

"She's probably a bit scared being by herself."

"Gettaway man, Elsie Hankey's scared of nowt."

It all fell into place. Sam had been seen walking Mrs. Hankey home from the pie stall where she worked on a Saturday. I'd fallen out badly with him about it.

The Sergeant was not interested. "What someone does in their private life's nothing to do with me. Now bugger off."

That's how we dealt with complaints in those days, and that's where it should have ended had not Inspector Mullins come down the corridor at that precise moment.

"Is this man causing trouble, Sergeant?"

"I'm just trying to stop one of your Police Officers seeing me brother's wife. He's at sea."

Mullins was always ready to believe the worst of folk, particularly his officers. Bob Jamieson did his best to keep Mullins out of it.

"I've explained to him that we can't interfere with what a Policeman does in his private life."

"But he's in with me brother's wife when he should be on the beat. The neighbours'll tell you."

Mullins looked at me for the first time.

"Have you got nothing better to do than skulk around corridors, Duncan?"

"Yes, Sir." I was off but not before I heard Mullins tell Bob that they both should listen to what Mr. Hankey had to say.

I made a point of seeing Sergeant Jamieson as I came off shift. "What was that all about?"

"Aye, I thought you were listening. The rumours about Sam and Mrs. Hankey seem to be true. Tom Hankey reckons that when Sam's on night shift he calls in most nights about half past twelve.

"You can imagine Mullins' reaction. Adultery's a sin, and he's not having a Constable in this Force getting away with it on duty. I shouldn't be telling you any of this by the way. He told Tom Hankey that he'd look into it but that he shouldn't mention it to anyone. He made it clear to me that if Sam was forewarned he'd know where it came from."

"Is he going to speak to Sam?"

"He wouldn't say. I've a funny idea that he's going to try to catch him red-handed."

That would be Mullins all right.

"When's Sam on night shift?"

"Mullins asked me the same question. He starts back on nights next Monday."

I thought to myself that if I were Mullins I'd bank on Sam calling in on Mrs. Hankey on that Monday. If he'd been missing his nightly cups of cocoa with the seaman's wife he'd want to make up for lost time. My suspicions were confirmed from an unexpected source. I'd meet up with Walter two or three times a week, shifts permitting. We'd have a drink or go to the pictures. I saw him a couple of days after Tom Hankey's complaint about Sam. Walter was full of himself.

"Ye kna' I divvent think auld Mullins is as bad as they say." This surprised me coming from Walter. Mullins had been the bane of his life and was the main reason Walter had asked to stay on at the Tyne

Dock nick when he could have moved back to Keppel Street.

"He came doon the Dock the other day and asked Sergeant Bowhill if he could spare me next Monday neet for a special operation. He wouldn't say what it was but I've to meet him at Keppel Street at midnight. I think he's realised at last that I've got potential."

It was typical Mullins. Anybody else would have wanted to know what the job was and the old hands would have had nothing to do with it, or they would have made sure that Sam knew.

It was a casual remark that Bill Spyles made the next day that gave me an idea. We were going out on duty and I asked Bill if he'd come up with any scheme to stop the betting slips being confiscated.

"I've thought of nowt else. The only way is to nobble Mullins, but to do that we'd have to have something on him, and he does nowt that you could have him for."

"What about a spot of adultery while on night shift?" I innocently enquired.

Bill's little piggy eyes lit up. "You wouldn't be joking?"

I'd found out the hard way that it was best not to joke with Bill. "No, I'm not, but it will take some planning. I'll see you at break time."

The next Monday night I finished my shift at ten o'clock. After I'd changed and had something to eat I went round to Tom Hankey's house. He was expecting me. We waited until midnight and then made our way to Fort Street where Elsie Hankey lived. It was cold and had started to drizzle. We were in a back lane just off the Mile End Road and had a good view. About half past midnight we saw a Bobby's lantern coming along the pavement. The dark figure stopped outside Elsie Hankey's door, the lantern swinging to light up both sides of the street. The Policeman didn't knock on the door – he just pushed it open and in he went. Tom Hankey wanted to rush over straight away.

"Hold your horses a minute. If you want to catch him red-handed you need to give him a chance to get his jacket off."

Just then we saw another figure coming along the street, another officer of the law. He too stopped at Elsie's, pushed the door open and went in.

"There's two of them, the buggers."

I had to hold him by the arm to stop him running on in. "Bide your time."

I couldn't keep him back for long. We crossed the cobbles and reached the front door; it had been left ajar.

"In you go. And don't forget: don't mention my name or I'm for it." Tom thought I was getting back at Sam. I didn't wait round and made my way quickly to Mile End Road where Bill Spyles was on the corner.

"You're on, Bill," was all I said.

I went home and waited for Walter. He'd agreed to let me know what happened as soon as things had settled down. It was nearly half past six before he turned up and he was in a very merry state. Not as drunk as a Lord but near enough.

The plan had worked like clockwork. Mullins had not told our Walter much. He'd waited until they'd reached the top of Baring Street before he said anything.

"I think one of our Constables is up to no good, Heron. He's paying nocturnal visits to a married woman in Fort Street."

"What, at neet?" was Walter's only contribution. They stood just round the corner of Trajan Street and had a clear view up the hill. As soon as they saw the Bobby's lantern coming down past the Roman Fort they pulled back. The dark figure turned into Fort Street.

"Right, lad. You go down the back lane. It's number twenty four. I'm going in the front. If Constable Beecroft comes out, you stop him and wait for me."

Walter did as he was told. After about two minutes the back door of number twenty four opened. Out walked John Burgess who was nearly the same build as Sam.

"Evening, Walter."

"Evening, John."

John walked off to resume his beat. He'd swapped for the night with Sam.

Walter waited a while and then went into the backyard. He'd been told by Mullins that if Constable Beecroft had not come out in five minutes he was to let himself in by the back door if it was open. John Burgess had left it ajar for Walter who went in by the back at the same time as Bill Spyles came in the front. They met in the living room. Tom Hankey was giving poor Mullins a real tongue-lashing. Mrs. Hankey had been happy to welcome Mullins into her home. She'd denied any knowledge of a visit by Constable Beecroft and had invited the Inspector to check the bedroom. Tom Hankey had come in just as Mullins and Mrs. Hankey were standing in the bedroom doorway. She started in shock when she saw the brother in law and put her arms round Mullins. Tom Hankey could only draw one conclusion.

"You conniving devil. You thought you were on to a sure thing after I'd telt you aboot Beecroft, and it looks as though you were reet. Tomorrow morning I'm gan to see the Chief Constable."

Bill stepped in. He didn't want to give Mullins any time to disillusion Tom Hankey.

"Right, you, out of here you miserable little bugger. You're not talking to an Inspector like that."

An embarrassed Mullins was left with Walter and Mrs. Hankey. Mulins asked Walter why he had not apprehended Sam Beecroft – Walter said that Constable Beecroft had not come out the back way. Mrs. Hankey brewed them both a cup of tea and they then made their way back to the Station. Mullins did not say a word.

Constable Spyles was waiting for them.

"I think I've sorted things out for you, Sir."

"How do you mean, Constable?"

"I managed to calm old Hankey down a bit. I told him what a fine officer you were, like, how you'd led the raid on Jack Conway's. He was interested in that. He asked if it was true that you were going to ask for the confiscation of the betting slips. I told him it was, so far as I knew, but that you could always change your mind. Well…" Bill paused for effect, "apparently he backed the winner of the Leger – with Jack Conway." Bill stopped talking; he looked flustered. Mullins was no fool.

"And if I do change my mind about the slips?"

"He said he'd forget about the night."

"Of course, if he makes a complaint the whole business of Constable Beecroft's behaviour would have to be looked at again. That could have a damaging effect on morale."

"Definitely." Bill could hardly contain himself as Mullins agonised.

"Well, I don't think I'll have any option. Mind you, it will be up to the Chief. He'll want a good reason for my change of heart."

"I'll tell Hankey not to bother to come in tomorrow then?"

"Aye. It's a good thing you were passing, Constable. Weren't you a little off your beat?"

"I was in the Mile End Road. This fellow said he'd seen someone suspicious looking going into number twenty four."

"Good work, Spyles."

Of course Bill had made it all up. He'd threatened Hankey with a good hiding if he dared whisper a word to anyone about what he'd seen, but he assured him that Sam Beecroft would not be going round to Mrs. Hankey's in the future. We'd all agreed that Mullins should not have an inkling that we were behind the little plot. Tom Hankey had come in very useful.

Bill Spyles asked Walter to hang around and meet them at the Railway Station in Mile End Road at five o'clock. They were going to have a breakfast to celebrate. It was something the old hands did from time to time. When Walter arrived Sam Beecroft had just come back from Robertson's kipper factory; he had five pairs of kippers wrapped in newspaper. John Burgess was not far behind with two large loaves from Robson's the baker's. They stopped in at Turnbull's brewery on the way back to Keppel Street. The night foreman brought them a two gallon bucket of freshly brewed beer and a half pint glass. The drill was simple: you dipped the glass in the bucket, drank it straight down and passed it on to the next man. They then went back to the nick and demolished the bread and kippers. The Sergeant said nowt. He had his pair of kippers to take home with him.

I'd have liked to have been a fly on the wall when Mullins went to see the Chief to tell him that he had changed his mind over the confiscation of the betting slips. When Jack Conway and Wilf Geff appeared in Court the Chief outlined the facts. He asked that the takings be confiscated but made no application in respect of the betting slips. Mr. Fenwick Q.C. made an emotional plea on behalf of the two accused. Result: a fifty pound fine for Jack and ten pounds for Wilf.

"You'll be paying cash?" asked the Clerk of the Court. Jack stepped forward and counted out twelve fivers. It was all part of the job for him.

Bill sent Walter to fetch his winnings the next day. Agnes got hers two days later at her next piano lesson at Mrs. Barrowclough's. She paid Digby off and still had a good sum left over. She foreswore gambling after that – or at least that's what she told me.

The only one who lost out was Sam Beecroft. When Bill Spyles had tipped him off about Mullins' plans to catch him out he'd made it a condition of our helping Sam that he'd put an end to his dalliance with Mrs. Hankey. Bill wasn't making a point about the morals of the situation, he just wanted to be sure that Tom Hankey didn't have any cause to complain again. Sam wasn't too upset. Elsie's old man was due in at Liverpool on the *Girl of the Period* in ten days' time and he'd have to make himself scarce anyway. Bill made sure that Sam knew of my part in things. Sam wasn't one for speeches. One afternoon he just asked me if I fancied a game of dominoes at the *Turk's* that night and we were back to normal.

One of East Holborn's narrow streets in which can be seen the Hop Pole inn and Mrs Camillieri's Lodging House

A pair of blue eyes

I'd been back in the Chief's Office for about two months and I'd
had enough. He'd specifically asked for me as I knew my ABC and
could write plain English – not all Policemen of that time could say
the same. The Office was run by a Sergeant who had the help of
two Constables, and together they did all the Chief's paperwork.
There was one typewriter which was an antique even then. We had
to make up our own shorthand when the Chief dictated a letter,
and it did not always come out as intended. The Sergeant, Ernie
Leadbitter, was a nice enough fellow who was nearing retirement –
a desk job was all that he wanted. My work was much appreciated.
The Chief had complimented me on two separate occasions – it
was not a good sign. I wanted to go back on the beat – that was real
Police work. The Chief was keen for me to stay in the office.

I was busy typing out a statement for Court – one finger at a
time – when I heard voices raised in the Chief's Office. Ernie had
not been in long. There was then a thwack as a file of papers hit the
glass panel on the Chief's door. Minutes later Sergeant Leadbitter
came out looking very flustered with the papers all awry. The Chief
was normally a mild mannered man, but something had set him off.
It was usually poorly written reports or sloppiness that irritated him.

Ernie looked round at us sheepishly. "It's Albert again." He
didn't need to say any more.

Charlie Nicholls, who had been the Officer in Charge at Laygate
nick for a good few years, had finally retired. The usual practice
was for the Bobby next in line for retirement to take over, so Albert
Hedley had stepped into Charlie's shoes. Officer in Charge sounds
a grand title but there wasn't much to the job. You manned the
Station and made sure that any paperwork was sent up to Head
Quarters. The Officer in Charge would accept any charges but they
all had to be confirmed by the Station Sergeant back at HQ. It was
these administrative burdens that were beyond Albert. He was one
of the old timers and he had definitely not been recruited for his

brains. Albert was a cheerful cove who seldom lost his temper but could always be relied upon in a barney. He was a stout, well built man whose muscle had mostly turned to fat. Straggly fair hair, now mostly grey, topped a large fleshy face. He didn't smoke cigarettes or a pipe, but was very fond of snuff.

"Is he going to put him back on the beat?" I asked quietly.

"He'd like to but Albert's only got a year left and it would upset the lads. Albert's a popular bugger."

I thought things over and then had another word with Ernie Leadbitter who went in to see the Chief – it was fixed up in minutes. I was to go back on the beat but would be transferred temporarily to Laygate. I'd do as normal a shift as possible, but I'd agree my hours with Albert so that I was always in the Station when the paperwork was done at the end or beginning of the day. The original intention was that I should just cast my eye over what Albert had produced. After a few days I realised why the Chief had thrown the file against the door – the man was barely literate. Albert had been non-committal about my help but he'd soon accepted me. He knew that it was either that or go back on the beat, and he didn't want another winter walking round Holborn in the dead of night in his greatcoat. When I suggested that I should do all the paperwork for him he was not too happy, but he knew his limitations and reluctantly agreed. In a couple of weeks we were bosom pals. He had started to become quite morose as he had worried about the form filling and the constant complaints from HQ. Once I'd proved that I could do the job, and wasn't looking to undermine his position, he relaxed and became more like his old self.

I was sitting at the table in what passed for the Charge Room one Friday morning. There'd been a drunk and disorderly last night and I was sending the charge sheet to be confirmed by HQ. Albert took a pinch of snuff, passed me the box and I took a small pinch. Albert liked a strong snuff which would send me sneezing for hours afterwards if I took too much.

"Will you do me a favour this morning, Tom? Instead of your

usual beat will you call on the Arab lodging houses to check that everything's all right? I've heard that there was some trouble when the *Margerita* signed on."

Jack Fleck, one of the Laygate Bobbies, had been up the Mill Dam the day before. The Mill Dam was the place where all mariners would congregate. You went there if you were looking for a ship or if you wanted to meet your old mates. The Bobby on duty there was Big Andra; he was never called anything else, and was known the world over. Andra had told Jack that the Master of the *Margerita* had agreed with Abdul Said to take eight of his lodgers as firemen and trimmers. The Union then got involved and the Master went back on his word. There was a bit of a scuffle as the English crew went to sign on.

Albert seemed very thoughtful. "Lucky for us Mohammed Hassan was there and calmed the Arabs down, but Big Andra reckons there's something going on. Just have a quiet word and see if you can find anything out. If there's trouble brewing I'd like to know. I don't want a repeat of the 1919 riots; nobody does." There had been a serious riot in the streets around the Mill Dam when the Union had stopped a number of Arabs from signing on despite the fact that they had just paid up their backlog of Union dues. One of the Arabs had had a scuffle with the Union Official and the Shields men had set upon the Arabs, chasing them down Holborn. The Chief had gone to the scene himself to take charge and had called out the Royal Navy Bluejackets and a unit from the Durham Light Infantry before order was restored. Things had settled down since then.

They were a sociable lot at Laygate but Jack Fleck was the odd man out. He kept himself to himself, did his job but that was it. He was tall, wiry, very intense and could never keep still. He was only a couple of years older than me and had spent three years in the trenches. That could have affected him. He and his wife lived in one of the houses near to Laygate nick. Mrs. Fleck was different altogether from her husband; she was a lovely looking lass with blonde hair and a willing smile. Mind, it didn't do to smile back if Jack was near – he was a jealous man.

There had been Arab seamen in Shields for many a year and by the 1920s they were becoming a settled part of the community. Like other foreign seafarers they mostly lived in the lodging houses in Holborn but some were marrying local lasses and were beginning to move out into the Laygate area and up to Maxwell Street. I made my way through Holborn's narrow streets and alleys, and called in on Mohammed Hussain. The Arab Boarding House Masters were much more than just that: back in the Yemen they would have been important tribesmen and they were the leaders of their community; they would look after the men who stayed with them; they'd take their money and act as bankers for them; they'd find them berths on ships. I would come to know them all. Mohammed Hussain had been in Shields probably as long as any of the Arabs. He seemed pleased to see me and offered me a coffee. The Arab variety was not to my taste and I politely declined. Some of my colleagues had acquired a liking for it. Albert was always trying to find an excuse to pop into one of the coffee shops for a free brew. After a while I asked him about the trouble at the Mill Dam.

"Trouble?" he asked. "There's never any serious trouble these days."

"We heard that there was some problem over the crew for the *Margerita*."

"It was all a bit of a misunderstanding. Abdul Said had agreed with Captain Neilsen that eight of his men would sign on. Then Mr. Sibson, the Union man, saw the Captain. I don't know what he said but Captain Neilsen agreed that he'd take only four of Abdul's men and four Union men. Our people were not happy. I'd just agreed that morning to provide a crew for the *Lydia*, and I said I'd find places for the four of Abdul's men who couldn't go on the *Margerita*."

"Who did you say the Union man was?"

"He's new, Sibson… Kenny Sibson, I think."

I knew Kenny Sibson all right. We used to have him in for drunk and disorderly after each voyage. I hadn't seen him for a while but I couldn't understand how he'd become a Union Representative; mind, he had a big mouth which might have helped. He'd be up to something.

"Do you know why he got involved? I thought that things had settled down after the 1919 riots."

"I think you better have a word with Abdul Said. He might know more than me."

I thought I'd visit some of the other lodging houses first. Abdul Said could be a tricky customer. I was not told anything directly but I gained the impression that none of the other Boarding House Masters expected any problems. They all said the same as Mohammed Hussain, that I should have a word with Abdul Said. He greeted me very politely but could not help. As I was on the point of leaving he asked me if I knew Mr. Sibson.

"Aye, I've had the pleasure."

"I have heard of him myself, and was most surprised that the Union should choose someone of such low character to be their representative. I know the other Union men and we only had trouble with them the once. Jack McGlashem and Tommy Short were very good men. You could trust them."

That was all he said. There was definitely something going on between Said and Kenny Sibson and until it was sorted out there could well be trouble. I'd need to keep my ear to the ground.

I was walking back down Academy Hill when I saw young Geordie Hussain and his barrow. As usual he had a crowd of women waiting to buy his fruit and veg. Fred Riddle with his coal lorry was trying to pass but Geordie took no notice.

"Have an apple, Officer?" he shouted in his broad Geordie accent, and without waiting for my reply he tossed one over. I caught it with my left hand and put it in my pocket for my bait, shouting back my thanks.

He turned to his customers. "As recommended by the Polis, ye can have two pounds for thre'pence ha'penny."

He was one of the characters in Holborn. He would have been about eighteen, with light tan skin, shiny black hair, and beautiful blue eyes. He had been selling fruit and veg off his barrow for a couple of years and had a good little business. He played on his good looks and would flirt with the ladies. When he was round Laygate Street he'd often pop into the nick with a bag of fruit. He had a soft spot for Albert and the feeling was reciprocated.

A couple of days later I was called to a fight up Johnson's Hill. A barefoot lad had been sent to run for a Policeman. I didn't have far to go but by the time I got there it was all over. Geordie Hussain was lying on the ground curled up, his hands holding his groin; his nose was bloody, his barrow turned over and his produce all over the place. A couple of Geordie's customers managed to get him to a sitting position. He was still holding his private parts. His attackers had punched him to the ground and had then started kicking him in the balls. One of them had shouted to Geordie that he'd cut them off next time if he did not leave his wife alone

"Did you know them?" I asked Geordie.

"I'd never seen them before in my life. I wouldn't go near a married woman. I think they must have mistaken me for someone else."

I looked at him. "Do you know any other blue eyed Arabs who push a barrow?" He said nowt. The few people around had righted his cart and were picking up his scattered produce. There were people there who had next to nothing, but they would never think of taking any of Geordie's fruit or veg. He'd remember those who'd helped, and they would always get a bit extra to the pound. There was not a lot more that I could do. The only description I had was two rough looking fellows in working clothes. Geordie didn't want to make any more of it.

I'd noticed a little old man in a cloth cap and muffler standing in the doorway of a tobacconist's. He waited until I'd set off down the hill and then he started to follow me. He waited until I'd turned the corner into East Holborn before catching up.

"I saw who did it, Constable, but I divvent want anyone to kna' it was me that telt ye. It was the Boyle brothers. They live up Nelson's Bank." He then crossed the road and was off. That's often how it worked. No one liked to have a reputation as a Copper's nark but some folk liked to help.

I waited until noon before heading up Nelson's Bank. If they had been out and about mid morning they'd either be out of work or on shifts. Either way they would be more likely to be home for dinner. Nelson's Bank was not the best address in Shields; they were old houses with lots of tenants. In those days people often stood or sat on their doorstep to see what was going on. I asked about the Boyles and was soon heading down a dark alleyway between two houses into a back court. The Boyles' doorway was on the right, down a corridor – they had the two back rooms. I knocked on the door and went in.

There was only a small back window, and were it not for the light of the open fire it would have been dark as night inside. The family was having dinner – soup. I could see lumps of potato in the yellow broth. The mother was holding a baby in her arms. She was a small black haired woman with two recent shiners to match. Three other children sat on boxes around the table and two men were on the only chairs. There was one bed against the wall with extra mattresses piled on top. Before I could say anything the bigger of the two men stood up and came round the table towards me.

"Has that bloody Arab shopped us already? He's not lost much time." He had an Irish accent.

"Are you the Boyles?"

"Aye," he sighed, "I'm Jimmy and this is my brother Michael."

"I was given your name by someone who witnessed the attack. Geordie Hussain had no idea who it was that hit him, but he says that the last thing he would do was to go near any married woman."

I looked at Boyle's wife and then back at him. "Have you been thumping your wife as well?" I started to become annoyed. I did not like men who hit their women although it was a common thing in Shields. He must have sensed my anger and moved back to his seat.

"That's nothin' to do with you. She denied it. But it must be true, it was written down. I got this letter. I'm not so good with writing so I asked Mr. Hayes at the shop on the corner to read it. He started to say it out loud but then he stopped and took me into the back room so no one else would hear it. "

"It's not true," shouted Mrs.Boyle, "and where do you think I'd find the time to see Geordie Hussain, with the children and your brother to look after?" There was some spirit left in Mrs. Boyle.

"But it was written down. Words aren't lies."

Boyle had a problem: he couldn't read himself and he took the written word as gospel.

"Have you got the letter?" I asked.

"I have not. I threw it in the fire."

"That's a pity. We might have found out who sent it. I believe Geordie and your wife – it's probably someone who has a grudge against Geordie. I can't see why – he's a popular lad."

"You mean it wasn't true, the writing?"

Michael Boyle then spoke up for the first time. He had gingery hair and a hang dog expression.

"It's the poison pen." He spat the words out. There was a silence. Jimmy Boyle looked worried.

"You could call it that, but it's no defence. I'm going to have to arrest you both for assault."

"It's the poison pen." Michael Boyle repeated his words with even greater venom.

"You can't arrest them." Mrs. Boyle was close to tears. "They've been queuing up at the Docks every morning now for months and they're starting to get regular work. They're hard workers. There was nothing this morning, but Jimmy thinks there's a chance of a place on one of the regular gangs. If you arrest them how am I going to feed the little ones? If you tell Geordie that it's the poison pen he'll know that Jimmy made a mistake. I'll make Jimmy apologise to him, so I will."

"Ye will not. I'm not apologising to an Arab."

"You will, so you will."

A half hour later I was walking down Holborn with Jimmy and Michael looking for Geordie and his barrow. We found him just round the corner of Nile Street. When he caught sight of the Boyle brothers he nearly took off but he saw me. He still moved to the far side of the barrow as we came up to him.

"It's all right, Geordie. This is Jimmy Boyle and his brother Michael. They've come to apologise."

Geordie said nothing – Jimmy looked at his boots for a couple of minutes then he stuck out his big right paw. "I'm sorry. It won't happen again."

Geordie took the hand and they shook. Michael did the same, muttering, "It was the poison pen. We didn't know it was the poison pen."

Geordie looked puzzled so I helped out.

"Someone wrote Mr. Boyle a letter saying you were after his wife."

"It said a bit more than that," Jimmy chimed in. "Have you upset anyone that they should say such things?"

"I divvent think so. But if they write to all me customers' husbands I'm going to have to watch oot!" Geordie paused. "Is your wife the dark haired woman from Nelson's Bank? She's always got two or three bairns round her skirts." Jimmy nodded.

"Aye, the accent's the syem. I expected to see her this morning. She normally buys her tetties for the weekend on a Friday."

"We haven't had a lot of work this week."

"Here," Geordie reached down and picked up a near empty sack and put it on the scales, "there's about a stone in there. I'll let you have them for a tanner. I dain't normally give tick but as you're with the Polis I'll make an exception."

143

THE FIVE STONE STEPS

Jimmy didn't know what to say. He picked up the sack and put it over his shoulder. "I'll pay you back, so I will, don't you worry about that. Thank you, Mister."

"Bring the sack back as well, mind."

As the Boyles walked off I told Geordie that I wouldn't be charging them. Geordie wasn't put out. "There's nae point. Anyone would have done the syem. It's the letter writer that needs a good hidin'."

Later that afternoon I had a quiet word with Albert. I thought he'd be interested as he had a soft spot for Geordie. He opened his snuff box, took a large pinch and passed the tin to me. "Geordie's a good lad. You know he's Mohammed Hussain's son?" I nodded.

"And have you ever thought why he's got such lovely blue eyes?"

"It had crossed my mind."

"I'll tell you the story of Geordie's birth but keep it to yourself; it's not commonly known. You know what it's like on the beat – you have to make your own mind up on what's best." Just then Jack Fleck came in with a drunk.

"Couldn't you have taken him home, Jack? There's never a bloody quiet moment here." He looked at me. "Do you fancy a drink tonight, Tom? The *Adam and Eve*?"

Later that evening in the *Adam and Eve*, Albert told me all about Geordie. Albert had been a young Bobby on the beat in the years before the War, when Arab seamen had just started shipping out of Shields – Mohammed Hussain had been one of the first to set up his own lodging house. Albert was on night shift and had been checking the back gates of the *Hop Pole Inn*. An Arab seaman came running up Academy Hill looking for Albert. "Come quickly, please, come quickly." He didn't have much English but he was obviously worried about something so Albert went along with him. As the man had mentioned Mohammed Hussain's name Albert knew he did not have far to go. When they arrived he was taken straight through to the private rooms where Mohammed and his wife lived. Mrs. Hussain was holding a baby in her arms with Mohammed and several seamen lodgers gathered round.

"Thank you for coming, Officer. We have a problem. Ali brought us a baby a half an hour ago. My wife says it's newly born, and hungry. She's still feeding our own baby and could take this one to her breast, but says she doesn't want to become attached to it if it's going to be taken away. She says we must tell the Police. I'm glad it's you, Officer Hedley."

Albert had a look at the baby. It was a boy, wrapped in a clean sheet. He seemed healthy enough – he was dark skinned but had blue eyes and a healthy pair of lungs.

"Do you think it's an Arab baby?" Albert asked.

"Not just Arab. It looks to me as though he has an Arab father and a white mother." There were no Arab women in Shields at that time apart from Mohammed's wife. When he had set up his lodging house he had arranged for her to travel to Shields with her brother who was a seaman. The other Arab seafarers who had wives and children in the Yemen sent their money home, and would eventually return there. Others had married Shields lasses and settled in the town.

"Where did Ali find it?" Albert asked.

"It was in a pub doorway up Payne's Bank. Ali saw the white sheet. As soon as he realised it was a baby he brought it to me. We didn't know it had Arab blood until we had a good look at it."

Abandoned babies were usually taken to the Work House. If they were lucky they'd be adopted but not many people wanted an extra mouth to feed. A half-caste child had little chance – it was most likely a git – a prostitute's child. Albert looked at Mohammed.

"If I take him from you he'll end up in the Workhouse. I doubt if his mother will come back for him."

"Show him the note, Ali."

Ali handed over to Albert a piece of paper that had been placed inside the sheet. It was well written and he could remember the words by heart: *'Please look after this poor child. He has done no harm to anyone but the colour of his skin would bring shame on his wretched mother who must abandon him.'*

Albert asked Mohammed if he would look after the child and bring him up.

"That is what we want but only if we know that we can keep him. We would not want him taken away."

Even at that time Albert did not like paperwork. Had he taken the child back to Laygate nick he would have had to make a report and then go and see the Board of Guardians. "Does anybody else know about the baby?" No one did. Albert told Mohammed that he could keep the baby so long as he told anyone who asked that the child was his.

"But what about the blue eyes?" Mohammed asked.

"Don't you have Arabs with blue eyes?"

Albert laughed as he told of the lengthy discussion that followed. Each of the seamen swore that they had seen an Arab with blue eyes; they gave descriptions of the place and of the relatives who knew the man. Albert couldn't understand a word that was said but he got the gist. The baby's cries were starting to upset Albert so he suggested that Mrs. Hussain should feed him. She took the baby into a back room and in a few moments the crying stopped. Albert accepted a cup of coffee. Mohammed Hussain seemed thoughtful.

"I shall bring him up as though he were my own son. I shall give him an Arab name, Ali, after the one who found him but I shall also give him an English name. Can I call him Albert after you, Constable Hedley?"

Albert was not pleased. If word ever got round that the foundling had been given his name the gossips of Shields would soon be having him as the bairn's father. Albert, who hailed from Cumberland, thanked Mohammed but said that what the child wanted was a good Shields name and he suggested George.

Albert told the Officer in Charge who agreed to keep things between themselves. Albert had kept the note – he took it home and put it in a drawer. No one reported a lost baby.

Albert called in regularly to ask after the little one. In no time at all he was running round the streets with the other children. Mohammed had made sure that the lad spoke English as well as Arabic and he became Geordie to all his mates. Mohammed's wife never really settled in Shields and died of pneumonia when Geordie was still a toddler. Not long after his wife's death Mohammed married again to one of the young women who worked in the lodging house. She was a Shields girl and took good care of Geordie and his older brother Said.

I asked Albert how Geordie had started in the greengrocery business. The lad had been helping his father in the lodging house one day when Ted Bates came round with his cart to deliver the regular order of fruit and vegetables. He was late. His lad had not turned up that morning and he was on his own. Mohammed asked Geordie to help Ted unload. After they had finished Ted asked Mohammed if Geordie could help him out with the rest of the deliveries – Geordie was more than happy to do so. Ted called round later that night. He had found out that his lad had had an argument with his old man and was going away to sea. He wondered whether Geordie would like the job on a regular basis. Ted was no fool: Geordie was a hard worker but he was also an Arab. There was a lot of competition between the greengrocers supplying the boarding houses. With Geordie, who could speak Arabic, helping him, Ted thought he would have an edge and so it proved. After they had finished the deliveries, Geordie helped out in the shop with Ted's daughter, Alice. She was only a couple of years older than Geordie. They got on well together – too well. Ted wasn't having any of it. He liked Geordie but he wasn't prepared for an Arab to go out with his daughter. Then Ted's son Nobby came out of the Army and Ted took him on in the shop. There was no need for Geordie. Ted didn't want Geordie going to a competitor and Nobby wasn't one for getting out of bed early in the morning. He'd had enough of that in the Army. So Ted kept Geordie on for the early morning deliveries.

He also agreed to let Geordie use an old barrow that was rotting away in the yard. He'd let Geordie have the produce and they would share the profits. It worked out well. Geordie had soon earned enough to buy a new barrow and Ted agreed to let him keep more of the profits.

A week later there was more trouble at the Dam. A Ship's master had refused to honour a deal he'd struck with Abdul Said and took on a white stokehold crew instead. Sibson was at the bottom of it. Albert was worried. He had been present at the 1919 riots and had seen enough. He didn't want any repeats and decided to go and see Abdul Said himself. He asked Jack Fleck to look after the station and took me along with him. This time Abdul Said invited us in to his private office just off the main room. It could have been a retired sea captain's study. There was a large mahogany desk and paintings of sailing ships hung on the walls. Pride of place on a small side table was a ship's chronometer mounted on a heavy block of wood.

We sat in two comfortable chairs and one of Abdul's housemaids brought in three cups of coffee. Albert licked his lips – I drank mine out of politeness. It was as black as pitch and was only just made palatable by several heaped spoonfuls of sugar. Abdul was friendly but was not giving anything away. He was clearly angry at Sibson's tactics and asked Albert if he could use his contacts with the Seamen's Union top brass to stop what he felt was victimisation. As we were about to leave Albert took a good look at the chronometer.

"That's a lovely piece. They don't make them like that anymore." As he bent over to look more closely he let out a low whistle. "It's engraved. *Presented to Thomas Sibson, First Mate on the Highland Lass, on his retirement after thirty years' service with the North Eastern Sailing Ship Company, 1898.*'"

Albert looked at me and we both looked at Abdul. He replied perfectly calmly.

"The chronometer was handed to me as surety for a debt of ten pounds. When the debt was not paid it became my property."

"The debtor wouldn't by any chance be Kenny Sibson?"

"As a matter of fact it was. One of the seamen staying here introduced him to me. He asked me to lend him some money. As it was a large amount I asked for a pledge. He offered the chronometer that is engraved with his Grandfather's name. When he couldn't pay back in time I gave Mr. Sibson one extension of time, then another. When he didn't pay after that, I kept the pledge. Now he has the money and wants it back. He is using his position to force me into parting with it."

There was little more to say. We now knew why Sibson was singling out Abdul Said but there was nothing we could do about it. Things got worse the following day. There were several scuffles between the Arabs and other seamen trying to sign on. Albert received a telephone call from HQ – Big Andra had heard a whisper. The Master and Officers of the *Alberta* would be at the Dam tomorrow afternoon. They usually took Abdul Said's men as firemen and trimmers, but Kenny Sibson had been heard bragging in the *Alnwick Castle* that Shields men would get first look in. It had all the makings of a repeat of 1919.

Albert told us that morning that we would be needed in the afternoon. The Chief wanted a large Police presence to stop any trouble before it started. I walked up through Holborn with Albert and Jack Fleck. Albert had closed the nick at Laygate. About twelve Bobbies from Keppel Street were already there and I recognised Bill Spyles and John Burgess. Bob Jamieson was in charge. You did not often see him out of Keppel Street, but the Chief had obviously decided that he wanted someone he could trust. They had their truncheons ready and it was easy to see why. There were a lot of Arab seamen there and most of the other Lodging House Masters had come to lend moral support to Abdul Said. Mohammed Hussain was there with Geordie by his side.

Albert thought that he'd go over and have a word with Mohammed. Jack and I were following behind and just then a shout went up. The *Alberta's* Master accompanied by the Shipping

Company's Agent had come round the corner and was walking towards the Shipping Office. An Arab seaman was jostled and pushed by a rough looking character. I went across and stood between them. It was then that I heard a shout.

"He's got a knife." It was Jack Fleck – his truncheon swished through the air and hit Geordie's arm hard. There was a crack followed by a screech of pain as Geordie fell to the ground clutching his arm. I then saw Albert move quickly. He might have been overweight but he could shift. His hand went out and caught Jack Fleck's wrist. I saw something shiny fall on to the cobbles. Albert bent down, picked it up and put it into his pocket. He said something to Jack. Jack looked hard at him and then backed off. Albert and Mohammed Hussain were bending over Geordie. The Arab seamen were becoming restless. Albert looked at Mohammed.

"Tell them it was a mistake. We'll have to get Geordie to the Hospital. His arm's broken."

"You're not arresting him?" Mohammed Hussain was worried.

"He's done nowt. Jack just saw a flash. He must have thought it was a knife."

The lodging house keeper spoke quickly in Arabic to his men and word soon spread round. My attention was distracted by the sound of a voice. It was the Agent – Big Andra had hoisted him up onto a beer crate in front of the Federation Offices. The Agent shouted out that he was taking on half a dozen of Abdul Said's men as stokehold crew for the *Alberta*. He was also looking for firemen and trimmers for the *Ulysses* and deck hands for the *Fair Wind;* any one could come forward. I learned later that on his way down to the Mill Dam Sergeant Jamieson had called in at the Thrift Street Offices of the Shipping Company. He'd averted a riot.

Albert had told Bob about the chronometer. Bob didn't want things flaring up again, but you never knew with the likes of Kenny Sibson. After he left the Dam that afternoon Sergeant Jamieson went on a little tour of the Pawnshops. He found what he was looking for in the Pawnshop Dock – Gompertz' in Thrift Street.

The next day he would go to see Abdul Said in the company of Jack McGlashem who was now the Northern Regional Secretary of the Seamen's Union. He'd done Kenny Sibson's job for years and was well respected. They called in at Laygate nick after the visit and told Albert all about it. Abdul Said had been pleased to see them, invited them into his office and coffee was brought in. Jack had unwrapped the brown paper parcel he had been carrying. It contained a ship's chronometer in sparkling condition, a real collector's piece.

"We know there's been a few problems lately, but we hope that this will help soothe things over."

Abdul took the chronometer in his hands. "It's a beautiful piece. There's an engraving as well." It had the name of one of the Bristol clippers etched on its side. "They will make a lovely pair."

Bob coughed. "We were actually thinking that you might have no need of the other one."

Abdul did not need any further explanation.

"There'll be no further trouble with the Union, of course." Jack McGlashem had seen though Kenny Sibson.

Abdul made the exchange.

I knew nothing of Bob Jamieson's doings on that afternoon at the Mill Dam, although I would find out in time. Albert and I had more pressing concerns. Bob Jamieson had made it clear to Albert that the Chief would expect a prompt report on the incident involving Jack Fleck and Geordie. As I would have to write any report Albert took me with him back to Laygate nick. Jack wasn't there so we walked to his house. His wife answered the door. She had two black eyes and she looked as though she'd been crying.

"He's in the kitchen."

He was sitting in one of the two stuffed chairs by the open fire – a bottle of whisky and a glass were on the small card table beside him. He looked up as we entered the room but said nowt. It was the first time that I had seen Jack sitting still.

"I'm not sorry for what I did."

Albert took an army knife from his pocket. "This is yours, Jack, isn't it? The one you were going to throw down beside young Geordie after you'd broken his arm."

"Aye, well, what if it is?"

Albert had told me that after Jack had hit Geordie he had seen something in his hand, which had looked like a knife. Jack was going to plant it beside Geordie, who would have been in big trouble. Albert's quick thinking had saved the young lad.

"Why did you do it, Jack?"

Jack reached down for another drink. He said nowt.

I looked at his wife who was sitting by the table looking as though she was going to start to cry again. The memory of Mrs. Boyle came back to me.

"You haven't been sent a letter about your wife and Geordie Hussain, have you?" I asked Jack. The look in his eyes gave the answer.

"How do ye kna'?" Jack snarled.

"Geordie was beaten up last week by an angry Irishman who received a poison pen letter. It was all lies."

Mrs. Fleck finally broke down, the tears flooding down her cheeks. "I told him it was lies, but he knew better; he said he was going to fix Geordie good and proper. It was him who told Geordie that there might be trouble and that he better go with his Dad to the Dam this afternoon. And if you raise your hand to me ever again, Jack, I'll leave you."

"Have you got the letter?" Albert asked.

Jack reached into his jacket pocket and handed it over. It was in a dog eared white envelope. Albert took out the letter and handed it to me. It said much the same as the letter to Jimmy Boyle. The handwriting was clear but quite distinctive – the letters were larger than normal and slanted backwards.

"Jimmy Boyle burnt his but he remembered it word for word," I said. "It's from the same person. Someone's got it in for Geordie."

"We'll keep this, Jack. The sooner we find out who's been sending these the better, or we might find Geordie dead down a back alley." Albert paused. "You ought to be up on a charge of assault, and if the Chief finds out you were trying to plant evidence you'll be out on your ear."

Jack had turned deathly white. He looked at his wife and then at Albert.

"Is young Geordie all right?" I thought he was going to break down but he controlled himself. "I dain't kna' what to say."

"He's in the Ingham Infirmary with a broken arm. It's a clean break so it should mend soon."

We paid a visit to Geordie whose arm was in a cast, and then returned to the nick to write the report. 'An honest mistake on the part of Constable Fleck who thought he saw a glint of something in the young Arab's hand. It was a snuff box and he was about to offer a pinch to his Dad. Constable Fleck has been overwrought of late as his wife has been ill.' The snuff box was Albert's idea. Geordie had been reluctant to go along with it this time, but Albert had promised him that he'd find out who was writing the letters. The young Arab was more concerned about how he was going to push his barrow with one hand. An idea came to me as I left the hospital, and I called in on the Boyles later that evening. I'd noticed a young lad of about twelve on my last visit and when I mentioned Geordie's problem, Jimmy got the drift straight away. Little Peter Boyle took a few weeks out of school and helped Geordie. He'd load up the barrow, push it, and help Geordie serve the customers. Geordie did what he could and would use his good arm on the barrow when they went up any of the hills. Peter was given a few pence and a piece of fruit for himself but every couple of days the barrow would go round to Nelson's Bank loaded up with potatoes and any leftover vegetables – Mrs. Boyle made good use of them.

Albert went in to see the Chief with Bob Jamieson. The Chief read

Albert's report. He was no fool – his only comment was that he had never seen an Arab take snuff before.

It was action stations for me and Albert. He'd had a word with Arthur Amos, the Postman. No one liked poison pen letters and Arthur agreed to help. Whoever was writing the letters almost certainly lived in Holborn. When Arthur collected the post from the boxes he'd drop the bag off at the nick. He'd tip out the contents on to the table we'd put in one of the cells, as we didn't want anyone seeing what we were doing. Arthur would leave us to it and we'd look at each envelope to find a match. Albert had brought in a paraffin boiler and kept the kettle going. We carefully steamed open any suspect envelopes. We didn't have much luck for the first couple of days. Arthur was starting to become worried as his gaffer had noticed that he was late on his rounds. Then we got lucky. We had found two envelopes which both looked identical to the one Jack had received, and they had the same backward slanting writing. One letter was to an address in Holborn, the other was to Scotland. Albert steamed open the first one, then handed the letter to me.

"It's to Charlie Allen."

"What, the fat barman at the *Old George and Dragon*?"

"Aye, and it tells him to watch his wife, who's been meeting Geordie Hussain secretly."

"If Charlie gets his hands on it he'll kill Geordie."

There was rarely any trouble in the *Old George*. Charlie was big and he could be very nasty if he wanted to. I put the letter to one side. "Let's have the other one, Albert."

"We don't need to, now we've found one."

"We still need to know who sent it and the writing looks identical."

Albert, who was becoming quite an expert, held the envelope over the steaming kettle, opened it carefully with a knife and passed the letter to me.

"It's from a Minnie Mensforth of 5 Plesant Place, to her sister in Scotland. The writing's identical to the letter to Charlie. Do you know her?"

"Minnie Mensforth? Her husband's a cobbler, works at Wilson's. She's Scottish. When she first came to Shields she was a Bible preacher – they called themselves missionaries. She and her sister used to hang around the Arab lodging houses trying to convert the seamen. I don't think they had any luck – her sister went back to Scotland but Minnie stayed. She married Jack Mensforth who played the organ at the Chapel up Johnson's Hill – still does so far as I know. You've probably seen her, Tom. She has her hair done up in a bun, she wears glasses and she always has on a long trench coat, down to her ankles, summer or winter. I wouldn't have thought she'd have done a thing like this."

We put the letter to her sister back in the envelope. When Arthur returned we told him we'd found the writer.

"Thank God for that. I've been pushing me luck. Ye gan' to prosecute?"

"I doubt it," Albert replied. "We'd have to say how we found the letter. Me and Tom'll go to see her and make sure she stops."

Plesant Place no doubt once lived up to its name. Now it was like most of Holborn, run down and looking its age. The houses were in a courtyard at the back of Cone Street. Minnie Mensforth was a stern looking woman who very reluctantly invited us in. We were taken into the front room. It was spotless and looked as though it had never been used. The floorboards were polished and there was a black mat in front of the fireplace. As Albert walked into the room Minnie stepped over quickly and took his arm. "Would ye mind not stepping on the mat, it leaves awfu' marks."

We sat down on a couple of straight back wooden chairs. Albert came straight to the point.

"There's been someone sending poison pen letters, Mrs. Mensforth. They've been written to husbands of decent women saying they're being unfaithful with Geordie Hussain."

"That doesn't surprise me. He's shameless and so are some of his customers. Weel, ye know what they say about the Arab men,

too hot blooded and they just canna' resist the white women. I
wouldn't be surprised if he was working for the white slavers."

Albert handed her the letter. "We have reason to believe that you
wrote this letter, Mrs. Mensforth."

She said nothing but went very quiet. "And where did you find
this?"

"Some letters from the Cone Street box were damaged,
including this one and one of yours to your sister. In view of the
contents it was passed on to us. The letter to your sister's been sent
on."

"Well, someone had to do something." She was angry and not a
little upset.

Albert gave her a real talking to. He had worked Minnie
Mensforth out. She was not a remorseful woman but she could not
face the prospect of being publicly shamed. She and her husband
were regular attenders at Chapel and Minnie in particular let
everyone know. By the time Albert had finished she was pleading
with him not to prosecute. He put on that he needed some
persuading, but eventually agreed on her promise to write no more
letters.

The only person we told was Geordie. We thought he had the right
and he was not the sort to go looking for trouble.

"Aye, I kna' who ye mean. When I first started the barrow she
was as nice as ninepence. Then one day when it was quiet she
came up reet close to me and asked if I wanted to come roond to
her hoose one afternoon for a cup of tea. It was obvious what she
wanted, and her auld enough to be me mother. I telt her to bugger
off, I'm not like that. She never came back to buy owt but I'd see
her walking past looking. I'd start flirting with women customers,
especially if they were young and pretty."

"Ye mean like Mrs. Boyle and Jane Fleck?"

Geordie looked a bit embarrassed. "I never meant any harm.
Anyway I wouldn't want to upset wor Alice. Her Dad's dead against

us going out together as it is. Ye won't tell him aboot this, will ye?"

We gave our word. Geordie would eventually marry Alice after Ted's death, and he would help her and Nobby run the family business. They moved up to Frederick Street and are still doing well.

It was about two weeks later when all the dust had settled that Albert came into Laygate nick one afternoon. It had been quiet and so he'd popped home for his dinner and I'd covered for him.

"Tom." He was out of breath and excited. "Me wife was tidying out some drawers and she found this. It was under an old pack of cards." He held out to me a crumpled piece of paper. "It's the note that was left on young Geordie when he was abandoned."

Albert had said that he'd bring the note in if he found it, but I'd thought he should stop living in the past. I'd heard most of the old stories twice all ready. I expected to hear the tale of the abandoned baby once again. My lack of enthusiasm must have shown.

"Look at the writing, man."

I looked. I went over to the desk and opened the drawer. I'd put the letter to Jack Fleck inside in case things started up again. I put them side by side on the desk top.

"Identical."

Albert leant over. "I thought they were."

We said nowt for a while, then Albert looked at me. "Minnie Mensforth's Geordie's mother? I can't believe it."

"Well it looks that way. But how would she have met an Arab?"

"Don't ye remember? I told you when she first came to Shields she was a missionary. She used to go to the Arab lodging houses and coffee shops."

"She must have made a convert," was my only reply.

"Will we have to tell them?"

"Definitely not. I can't see that it would bring either of them any happiness." I took Jack Fleck's letter and threw it in the stove. "We don't need this anymore. I suggest you take your piece of paper and put it back in the drawer, Albert."

As Albert was folding up the piece of paper before putting it back into his wallet, he looked over to me.

"You know, when Minnie Mensforth was doing her missionary work she wasn't what you'd call attractive, but she caught the attention of most of the menfolk round here. She had the most beautiful pair of blue eyes you'd ever seen."

Comical Corner showing the Burton House – the Ha'penny Dodger Ferry Pontoon is shown in the bottom right corner

A tale of two caps

I was standing at the corner of Erskine Road by the railway bridge.
It was a bright October day but freezing cold, a nor'easter was
blowing and I was glad of my overcoat. I saw a black car coming
at speed up Fowler Street – I was thinking of flagging it down and
asking the driver to slow up when I realised that it was the Chief's
car. Bob Bruce was driving and Norman Lamont, the Head of CID,
was in the back. They saw me and the car skidded to a halt a good
fifty yards up the road.

The Big Fella poked his head out of the window.

"Come on, Constable, there's been a break-in at Westgarth."
It was on my beat, one of the big houses in Westoe Village. I ran
towards the car and jumped on the running board as we set off.

The Chief had had a call from Major Hardistie. He was a war
hero who had lost part of his face and one of his arms at Wipers.
He had married the daughter of a rich colliery owning family before
war broke out and on his return had settled in the family home
at Westoe. He had taken an interest in civic affairs and was on the
Police Committee where he was well thought of. He had, of course,
rung the Chief Constable personally to report the burglary.

"The Chief wants it solved, and quick – it's jewellery, expensive
stuff." The Detective Inspector was shouting in my ear as I clung on.
I'd seen Chicago gangsters riding on the running boards in the silent
movies but they had not had Bob Bruce to contend with – he was
the Fire Tender driver.

"Will you tell Bob we're not going to a fire," I shouted out but it
had no effect.

Bob only slowed down as we went through the stone gate posts
and up the gravelled drive. Westgarth was a handsome building – it's
now gone, of course, along with Westoe Hall and other big houses.
It's a shame, they were fine buildings and all very well looked after.

Major Hardistie himself opened the door and ushered us in.
We walked through the stone flagged hall to the sitting room. I

had never before seen such luxury, although I had heard this room described to me in every detail. A grand piano was at one end of the room where my Agnes gave lessons to the Hardisties' twelve year old daughter, Emily.

Cecelia Hardistie came into the room and went to stand by her husband. The Major, who was in his early thirties, had probably been a good looking chap before the War. The patch over his right eye and the glazed and scarred red skin on that side of his face had ended all that. His wife looked a few years older than him. She might have been plain were it not for the bright sparkle in her eye.

They explained that she had gone to her jewellery box earlier that morning as they had been intending to go out for the evening. The box which had an expensive Chubb lock had been specially made for her. The key had been in the usual place and when Mrs. Hardistie had opened the box it was empty. The jewellery must have been taken the night before as she had opened the box the previous day.

"I'll take a look if I may." Inspector Lamont was keen to make progress.

The Major looked in my direction. "I appreciate that you have to do your job, Inspector, but it is in my wife's bedroom."

"Of course, Major. Constable Duncan, can you have a look round outside?"

I walked along the gravel path round the house. There was not much to see, but then I noticed a gardener up a ladder pruning an old apple tree. I walked across and as I drew closer I recognised him – it was Mickey Jobling. He couldn't have been more than eighteen but he'd already done time for burglary. A couple of years ago an officer would be round at the Joblings' after every house breaking. I'd heard that Mickey had been released from Borstal a couple of months back.

"Hello, Mickey, are you the gardener here?"

Mickey smiled back. He did not seem worried at my presence as it was not unusual for the Chief to call at Westgarth on Police

Committee business.

"Aye, I'm under gardener; auld Tommy Cruickshank's head gardener. He spends most of his time on the vegetable plot."

"Does Major Hardistie know you're just out?"

"Wye aye. He wanted to give an ex con a chance. Sergeant Jamieson recommended me. Mind I had to promise him I'd gan straight."

I looked back at the house. The Big Fella was on the front steps waving his hand; he wanted me back.

"What's Mr. Lamont doing here? I saw the car come. I thought it was the Chief Constable – I've seen him before."

"There's been a break-in. Some jewellery's gone."

I left him to his pruning as the Detective Inspector came to meet me.

"It's an inside job all right. I reckon they got in last night through one of the windows; the one on the hallway was unlatched. No one had thought to check it as it was never usually opened. A stairway from the kitchen leads right up there so anyone could have sneaked up to undo the latch the day before they planned to break in."

He looked across at Mickey. "They'd need a ladder. Is that who I think it is?"

"Aye, Mickey Jobling. He says he promised to go straight."

"Don't they all. The Major mentioned he'd taken on an ex con to give him a chance, said he felt it was his duty, being on the Police Committee. He said there's a hut round the back where the gardeners keep their things."

We walked back to the tree. "Come on down, Mickey. We're going to have a look in the shed."

Mickey came down. He had a hangdog expression. "I promised Sergeant Jamieson that I wasn't gan' to get into any more trouble." He blushed. "I'm gan' out with Peggy Surtees but she won't marry me unless I can prove that I can gan straight."

"Big John Surtees' daughter?" Mickey nodded. The Big Fella knew the Surtees clan. They were a large family and some of them were villains, but not Big John. He was no angel, mind; a waterman, and as hard as they come.

"Well, if you want to marry his Peggy you better keep your nose clean. If you've done nowt you've nothing to worry about."

The shed was in a corner of the garden at the back of the house. Mickey showed us where he kept his things; he had an old army bag for his bait. I picked it up and looked inside. There was something shiny at the bottom – a single earring. I held it up and it sparkled in the light of the weak autumn sun.

"Now what's a diamond earring doing in a gardener's bait bag? Arrest him, Constable Duncan."

Mickey just took off and he was fast. I could shift a bit myself in those days, but I was no lightweight and fifty yards was about my limit at top speed. I was nearly onto him as he headed down one of the paths between the beds. There was a four foot high privet hedge which enclosed the garden and he hurdled it like a professional, left leg straight, right leg following bent high at the knee. I knew how it should be done but you can't go hurdling in a Constable's greatcoat. By the time I'd forced my way through the hedge he'd reached the wall and was away. I could hear someone shouting behind me – it was Tommy Cruickshank. "What've you done to me bloody hedge!"

It was not my day. The Big Fella sent me off with a flea in my ear while he went back to the big house to ask the Major to identify the earring. When I got back to the Station everybody knew about it. The first thing that Inspector Mullins said, as I came down the five stone steps, was that he'd heard I'd arrested a privet hedge. "You'd do better to grab the villains, Duncan." There was no love lost between us but I'd rather see him with a smile on his face, even if it was at my expense, than the usual sneer.

Bob Jamieson was more sympathetic. "Mickey Jobling came to our athletics club after he'd been let out of Borstal. He's a canny runner – the quarter mile's his best event – I've no wonder he left you standing."

"You should put him in for the hurdles, Bob; he's a natural. You should have seen him go over that hedge. It didn't slow him down a second."

"Well even if you're right I won't get the chance now. I still can't believe it. He seemed so keen to join the club and to go straight. That was one of the reasons I recommended him to the Major."

"You asked the Major to give him a job?"

"Well, not exactly. He popped his head round the Charge Office door one day, on his way out from seeing the Chief upstairs. He said he needed an under gardener, and he was prepared to give someone a chance."

"You mean he asked for an ex con?"

"I suppose he did."

The Joblings lived down Wapping Street in the oldest part of Shields down by the River. The streets were cobbled and narrow – there were lots of Quays and Courts where some of the old Shields families still lived. Alleys led down to the Tyne, and, on the other side of the street, narrow steps led up the bank. There were many old pubs and some buildings were said to date back to Tudor times. On the quays you'd find sheds, small factories and warehouses – tallow, rope, timber, netting – anything to do with ships. A lot of them were empty now as the trade moved more towards Tyne Dock. The Shadwell Street end was either demolished or derelict and in a few years it would all go. The area still had its character and its characters; there was a strong sense of community – the folk down there were called the Townenders and they stuck together.

The Big Fella asked Mullins to take a few Bobbies down to see if they could find Mickey. He wasn't at the Joblings' but they'd already heard what had happened. Dolly Jobling stood on her front step, a scarf round her head and a clay pipe sticking out of the corner of her mouth; her arms were folded over her ample bosom.

"Wor Mickey didn't do it; he's learnt his lesson. You gan and ask Sergeant Jamieson, and if he had done it he wouldn't have left anything in the first place ye'd look. He's not ower clever but he's not daft."

Mullins' attitude didn't help. So far as he was concerned Mickey was an ex con and was guilty. He said as much and he soon had everybody's back up. They looked in all the obvious places but Mickey was nowhere to be found. Mullins went round to the Surtees' in Hopper's Quay. Big John was on the river – it was a good job – Mullins threatened little Peggy Surtees with prosecution when she tried to stop him searching a derelict boat shed at the end of the Quay. By the time they called it a day Mullins and his team had upset most of the folk who might otherwise have helped us.

Henry Milburn was the beat Constable. He was a big man, about six foot tall and fourteen stone but didn't carry much fat. He'd been down the mines before the War. He'd served in Palestine under Allenby and had come back a Corporal. He'd realised that there could be more to life than slaving away at the coal face, and had joined the Shields Police. Having been brought up in Heron Street, he knew the area from the Long Row to Pilot Street like the back of his hand. I was having a cup of tea in the Parade Room as he came off shift the day after Mullins' raid. He joined me for a brew.

"He's stirred up a reet hornet's nest doon there. Why didn't they just ask me to caal roond? If someone wants to gan missing in Auld Shields ye're never gan' to find them by storming in with the troops. I'll tell ye, Tom, I felt scared a couple of times today. There were gangs of fellas ootside the boozers having a right go at me. 'Mickey Jobling's innocent.' Everybody believes it. I'm gan' to see Bob Jamieson. I think we'll have to double up on the beat till things gan quiet."

"Well, the Chief wanted it solved quickly. Major Hardistie's on the Police Committee."

"Aye and daint ye think they divvent kna' it? They're saying there's two laws. One for the rich and one for the poor and Big John Surtees is stirring it up for all it's worth."

Big John was a member of the Labour Party, some said a communist.

"There's only one way to find Mickey. That's for someone

to keep an eye out and watch Mickey's mother or his girlfriend. Wherever he is he'll need food and drink."

"You mean sending in someone in plain clothes?"

"Are ye daft, man? Any stranger turning up noo, poking their noses anywhere near the Joblings' would be spotted a mile off, and found beaten half to death doon an alley. Naa, we need someone to give us a tip off."

"I thought you said everybody thinks that Mickey's innocent."

"Mebbe they do, but most of the Joblings are villains and there'll be someone happy to settle a score." He finished his tea and went off to find Sergeant Jamieson.

The outcome was a revised duty rota with all beats in the Wapping Street area doubled up. I was one of those chosen and, to my surprise, so was my very good friend Walter Heron who temporarily transferred from Tyne Dock. It did mean, however, a change in my shift pattern over the coming week. I had agreed to take Agnes to the Theatre on the Wednesday but I would now be on duty that evening.

I called at the McIvers' house to break the news. To my surprise Agnes was not too upset – she'd see if she could find someone else to go with. As it was just after two in the afternoon, she asked if I would like to take her for a coffee at the Roma. I agreed – it was one of the few times Agnes had ever asked me out anywhere. She would normally agree to my suggestions for an outing, but more with resignation than any great pleasure. As we settled down to our coffees it soon became clear why – she wanted to find out what I knew about the break-in at Westgarth.

"I gave young Emily her lesson yesterday. They were all talking about it. I always have a cup of tea in the scullery afterwards with Jane Laidler. She's a maid; her brother served in the trenches under my Herbert."

Agnes' fiancé, Captain Herbert Jaggers, had been killed in the last stages of the War. She had been badly affected by his death and never missed a chance to remind me of him.

"Of course had Herbert not been taken from us, I would no doubt have been a social acquaintance of the Hardisties rather than their daughter's piano tutor. Well, Jane said that Mr. Cruickshank was adamant that Mickey couldn't have done it. He said he'd put the ladder away himself the night before, and he'd put his gardening cap on the third step up as he always did. It was there the next morning. If anyone had come in the dark for the ladder they would never have seen the cap and it would have ended up on the floor."

"Has he told the Detective Inspector?"

"Jane said that he'd told the Major who said that Tommy shouldn't stick up for the likes of Mickey Jobling, and that he didn't want his employees running off to the Police."

It was food for thought. "Has Mrs. Hardistie said anything?"

Agnes had a vivid imagination which sometimes verged on the hysteric. The goings on at the Hardistie household had enthralled her.

"She's saying less than ever. Did you know that they sleep in separate bedrooms?" I didn't. "When the Major came back from the War with his face in such a state and with no arm, she wouldn't let him back into her bed. The first time she saw him she nearly fainted and couldn't bear to look him in the eye. The one eye he had left, that is. He's a gentleman of course so he didn't try to force her, but they say at the Hall that when he goes up to Newcastle or to London he's never short of a fancy woman." Agnes was getting carried away and her voice was rising. "They say he pays for it. Well, he'd have to with a face like that." The other customers were looking round so I shushed Agnes. She leant closer to tell me the rest. I was even able to hold her hand on the table without her pulling away.

"Jane says that a couple of months before the break-in, they had a big row. The Major had an investment he wanted to make and had asked his wife if he could have the jewellery as security for a loan. The jewellery's hers, they're heirlooms. Well she refused point blank. She said that she was going to give them to the bank to keep safe but he wouldn't let her. He said they were well insured and he wasn't going to go running to the bank every time she wanted to wear them." She paused to take a sip of her nearly cold coffee; I'd finished mine minutes ago. "She hasn't spoken to him since the robbery. Mind, he hasn't been there much – he was off to London on the train the day after."

As she finished her drink I told her about the problems down Wapping Street. "You'll never find him. The folk down there stick together."

The Shields Gazette had reported the burglary and the fruitless search for the suspect; the Police efforts were described as heavy handed; the claims of Mickey's innocence were quoted. There was even a Leader warning that the Police should not be seen to be always siding with the wealthy against the less fortunate. Big John Surtees had used his contacts in the Labour Party to good effect, and a public meeting was held in the Market Place to protest against the Police action.

Major Hardistie had returned from his business affairs and was making himself unpopular with the Chief Constable. He was unhappy with the lack of progress and was not pleased that the Labour movement was becoming involved – they were communists and agitators and ought to be put in their place.

It may have been a coincidence but two days later the Chief was informed that Hedley Davies was coming to Shields to speak in the Congregation Hall off Ocean Road. Davies was a right wing agitator. He would come to prominence during the National Strike when his gangs would attack picket lines, and in later years he teamed up with Moseley and the Fascists. He'd already made a name for himself in the North and was supported by some of the local Members of Parliament who were opposed to the Labour movement.

We were expecting trouble. It would be a public meeting and John Surtees had already said that he was going to be there. All during the day of the meeting gangs of rough looking customers started arriving, wearing brown armbands to mark them out as supporters of Hedley Davies. They were little more than thugs. Major Hardistie had been invited to attend and called in on the Chief – the organisers wished him to make clear to the Chief Constable that, whilst they did not expect any trouble, they had employed a large number of stewards and would look after any problems inside the Hall themselves. They would not wish a Police presence and would regard them as trespassers if they entered the premises uninvited. The Chief passed the message on to Sergeant Jamieson who was on duty that evening. He spoke to Bob personally making it clear that he was happy to leave any decisions on the night to Bob, as Duty Sergeant. "It's very important that we're not seen as being involved on one side or the other. We keep the peace. Inspector Mullins will be on call if you need him."

"I shouldn't think so," was Bob's response. Bob had been passed over when Mullins was appointed and there was no love lost between them. Bob Jamieson was one of the old school; for him the job of the Bobby was to keep order. He knew the ropes as well – there was a lot of toing and froing that afternoon; all the old hands were contacted. Bob asked Walter to stay in the Charge Room with him.

The meeting at the Congregation Hall started at eight. At about half past the motorbike rider, who had been posted outside the Hall, drew up at Keppel Street nick with a screech of brakes and ran down the five stone steps to the Charge Room. Bob and Walter were ready. Bob got in the sidecar and Walter sat behind the driver. They were at the Hall in minutes. They could hear the sounds of fighting as they pulled up at the kerb. There was a rough looking character on the door. Bob went over; Walter was just behind. His instructions were clear: he was there to watch Bob's back.

The thug spoke. "You can't go in. It's a private meeting."

"Get out of my way or I'll knock you senseless." Bob drew his truncheon. Walter did likewise. The fellow backed off into the Hall and ran to his masters. Bob went in. There was pandemonium – Big John Surtees with about a dozen of his mates had tried to storm the platform and had been set upon by the Stewards. It was a real scrap. Bob did not go very far into the Hall. Hedley Davies was on his feet watching the melée. As soon as he caught sight of the Police uniforms he shouted out to his men. "The Police are not welcome here. They are trespassing. Evict them."

The Stewards, the lowest of the low, did not need any invitation. Most of them had cudgels and those that hadn't had armed themselves with chairs. They left off their attack on Big John and came towards Bob and Walter. The Sergeant whispered to a terrified Constable, "I'm going to back out slowly. You stay behind me and watch my back." They did just that. The mob of Hedley's men followed them out of the Hall, cudgels at the ready. They were cowards – two Policemen were going to be easy game. Once outside, Bob and Walter ran towards the motorbike. Hedley Davies' hooligans came running. As soon as they were on the street half a dozen Shields Bobbies came out of the shadows, truncheons in hand. It was a massacre. I was there along with Bill Spyles and John Burgess. We laid in hard. Bob and Walter turned quickly to join in the fun – it was over in minutes. John Surtees and his friends came out; they'd taken the chance to escape. They saw the bully boys lying on the ground or holding onto a wall clutching their arms and legs. They said nowt; there was no need. We made no arrests but justice had been done. The Chief had a full report. He heard nothing from Major Hardistie; what could he have said? The Sergeant had left the Hall when called on to do so. The other Police Officers who had been passing by had acted purely in self defence. We had a good night in the *Havelock* after time.

Word got round and the folk down Wapping Street became a little more friendly, but there was still no sight of Mickey Jobling. I was on the beat there one morning with Walter. We were standing at the bottom of Cat Leap Stairs when I saw a familiar figure coming along the pavement. It was Hughie Ross, hobbling along with his crutch, mumbling away to himself. He stopped as he saw me. We'd got to know each other when I first came to Shields and he would always say hello – in his own style.

"Ye got nowt better to do, ye lazy bugger."

"And what brings you down Wapping Street, Hughie?"

"I was born doon here, man. I often take a wark alang to Shadwell Street, not that there's much left noo."

"We're looking out for Mickey Jobling." Walter joined the conversation.

"I'm not bloody daft. All Shields is talkin' aboot him. Well so far as I'm concerned, I hope you catch the little sod. I hate the Joblings. They should all be locked up in Durham Jail where they belong."

"Folk round here say he didn't do it."

"I couldn't care less. He still should be locked up. Any son of Jack Jobling should be put away on sight."

Henry Milburn was right: the Joblings did have enemies and Hughie Ross was one of them.

"Walter," I said, "give Mr. Ross a tanner for a drink. You'll need a pint after walking all this way, Hughie." Walter gave me a look. "It's all right, Walter. You'll get it back." Well, he might if things went as I planned. Walter reluctantly handed over the coin to Hughie.

"Hughie, you'll keep your eyes and ears open for us. If you hear anything about Mickey you'll let us know."

"I'm not a nark."

"I thought you wanted to see him locked up? There'll be a few bob in it for you."

Hughie's eyes lit up. "Well, the Joblings have had it coming for years."

"Mickey's going out with Peggy Surtees. She'll know where he is."

"She'll be well shot of him. I'll be doing the lass a favour." He stomped off. Nobody would notice Hughie hanging around.

Walter looked at me. "What did you mean 'you'll get it back' – the money?"

"If Hughie turns up trumps then you'll be able to claim it back off the Big Fella – expenses." It didn't always work but I didn't tell Walter.

I was seeing Agnes quite regularly; she couldn't wait to find out the latest on Mickey Jobling and the Hardisties. There was not a lot to tell but one afternoon as we went for a walk in the South Park she told me something that worried me.

"I was giving a lesson the other day at Mrs. Barrowclough's. She said that Digby was saying some nasty things about you." Dapper Digby was a bookies' runner. He'd tried to lure Agnes from the straight and narrow and had nearly succeeded. She didn't speak to him now or so she said.

"He told her that you had planted the jewellery that was found in Mickey Jobling's bag."

I didn't overreact; I'd had worse things than that said about me. "And where did he get that idea?"

"He heard it from Tommy Cruikshank in the *Westoe*. Tommy's been telling everybody. He says he's got proof."

It was interesting to say the least. I thought I'd better pay Tommy a visit – these things had a habit of getting round and before you knew it, it would be in the Shields Gazette. Tommy was always in the *Westoe* after nine o'clock in the evening. I was on morning shift that week so I asked Walter to come for a drink with me. We found Tommy in the Gents' Buffet; he was sitting with his cronies in the corner. I asked Walter to get the drinks in and went over. He recognised me.

"Have you come to compensate me for my privet hedge?"

The others laughed. I sat down facing him.

"You remember the morning of the burglary?"

"I'm not likely to forget it."

"Five minutes before we arrived at the House I was standing on the corner of Erskine Road."

"Aye, well what of it?"

"When we arrived at the House, I went inside with the Inspector while he talked to the Major. I then came out and was talking to

Mickey until the Inspector asked me to search the shed."

"I'm listening."

"Well can you tell me when I could have put my hands on the piece of jewellery that was found in Mickey's bag?" I raised my voice. "I'll not have you spreading lies, Tommy Cruickshank, or I'll put you through your bloody hedge head first."

Walter arrived with the drinks. "Hey, calm doon, Tom. I'm sure Mr. Cruickshank can explain."

Tommy had gone quiet. "I nivver said any such thing."

"Others have heard different from Dapper Digby."

"It's him you want to put through a hedge. I was talking to him the other neet. I'll tell you what I said – I told him that Mickey couldn't have done it. The ladder wasn't moved that neet. I have an old gardening cap but the auld hinny won't let it in the hoose. I always leave it on the third step up on the ladder because it's sometimes dark in the shed when I get there in the morning. It hadn't moved; if anyone had come in the neet they would have knocked it off."

"Aye. My Agnes told me."

"The piano teacher?" I nodded. "She's a bonny lass." He paused to take a drink. "So Digby said how did the jewellery get into Mickey's bag. I told him that I didn't kna'. I said it couldn't have been there before the Police arrived because I'd seen the Major in the shed having a look round earlier that morning. He must have thought the worst of Mickey from the start. I divvent kna' why he took him on in the first place if he didn't trust him. Mind he's a good worker. It was Digby who said that it must have been you."

I took a long swig of my whisky. I could imagine Digby taking pleasure in running me down. We had an enjoyable evening. Tommy Cruickshank was a likeable fellow and we ended up playing 'fives and threes'. The next morning I went back to Keppel Street half way through my shift. After I'd had my brew I went in to see the Detective Inspector. He was sitting at his desk in the CID office. I first of all explained what my Agnes had said about the Hardisties.

"Have you nothing better to do than to spread gossip? That's what it's like in these big houses. The servants are always yapping to each other about something."

I carried on and told him of my conversation with Tommy Cruickshank.

"You're saying that before we got there the Major had been poking around in the shed?"

I nodded.

"Ye bugger. The Major wants to borrow money on the jewels. His wife won't let him. He then asks Bob Jamieson to recommend an ex convict to work in the house. There's a break-in. The Major goes to the shed just before the Police arrive, and when they do, they see Mickey Jobling, well known local burglar, up a ladder; they search his bag in the shed and surprise, surprise, find one very small piece of the missing jewellery. The next day the Major's off to London on business."

He looked at me and sighed. "I'll speak to the Chief. But we still need to find Mickey and hear what he has to say for himself."

Walter and I continued our patrols along Long Row and Wapping Street. We must have looked in every old shed and disused building there was. A couple of days after I'd seen the Big Fella we were walking along Wapping Street and nearly bumped into Hughie Ross as he came out of 'Split Raisins', an old grocery shop. A former owner had been so mean that he would split a raisin to keep to the correct weight.

"Can't ye watch where you're bloddy gannin'. I've been looking for you all morning. I'm not talkin' to ye in the street. I'm just off to the *Burton Hoose*." He hobbled off on his crutch still mumbling to himself.

There was a bitter north wind coming off the river as we turned down Comical Corner. Hughie was waiting for us by the side entrance where it was sheltered.

"Ye better give me that beer money you were talkin' aboot."

Hughie's whisper would have carried to North Shields on a clear day. "I kna' where he is. I tell ye, youse lot are hopeless."

I elbowed Walter and he handed over a florin.

"Ye'll nivver guess in a month of Sundas, and he's been reet under your nebs. You're a laughing stock roond here."

"Just tell us where he is, Hughie and you can bugger off for your drink."

"I followed Peggy Surtees the other dinner time. She had a pudding basin in a cloth."

It was a common sight. If the man was working close to home one of the children would be sent to carry him a hot dinner.

"She caught the Ha'penny Dodger." The Dodger was the direct ferry between North and South Shields for foot passengers. The landing was at the bottom of Comical Corner not twenty yards from where we were.

"Well, I didn't kna' what to dee so I hung aboot. She came strite back on the ferry carrying an empty basin. The next day I got doon early. She came alang at the syem time so I got on the Dodger with her."

Hughie paused for effect. "You're nivver gan to believe this, you stupid buggers. As soon as the Dodger pulled away she went ower to the boiler house door. There was a lad there with an oily cap and a pair of dungarees. Weel, I thowt he was one of the crew. Then she gives him the bowl. I got a good look at him. He's got a beard noo but it's Mickey Jobling all reet." Hughie cackled to himself. "Reet under yer nebs. You're the laughin' stock roond here." He pocketed his money and went into the pub. Walter and I just looked at each other.

"Do you fancy a trip on the Dodger, Walter?"

We walked over to the Ferry Landing. The Dodger was just leaving North Shields. We stood behind one of the cabins on the pontoon. I didn't want Mickey jumping into the Tyne if he saw us; it was too cold for swimming. We waited until the ferry had tied up and the passengers had disembarked. We moved forward quickly and Walter held back the handful of passengers who were waiting to cross as I stepped on to the gangplank. Percy Robson, the Ferry Captain, was waiting for me. Percy was a character, noted for the greasy black cap he always wore. It was rumoured that he even kept it on when he slept. He wasn't wearing it today – he had a brand new navy blue one.

"I hear you've got a stowaway, Percy."

"What if I hev'?" He snarled back. "I've known Mickey for years. If he says he didn't do it, then he didn't do it."

"We only want to ask him a few questions."

An unshaven fellow wearing a greasy black cap and a pair of dungarees came out of the boiler house. It was Mickey. I thought for a minute that he was going to jump over the side.

"Don't be daft now, Mickey. If you go overboard you'll have to come out somewhere, and you won't last long in the water today. We just want to ask you a few questions. We think we know who stole the jewels but we need to speak to everybody who worked at the house."

"You're not arresting me, then?"

"Not unless you refuse to come to the station."

Mickey looked at Percy. He took off his cap and handed it back to him. "Thanks Poice, ye can have your cap back noo."

Percy put it on and handed the new one to Mickey.

"Thank Christ for that. People were beginning to talk." He looked at Mickey and at me. "It was my idea. Mickey came running aboard saying the Polis were after him for something he'd nivver done. He was going to head north. I telt him he was stupid, he'd be better off among friends. So I gave him me cap and a pair of dungarees for disguise and telt him to stay on the ferry. He slept on it at neet. I didn't think anyone would give him away."

"They didn't, Percy." I wanted to protect Hughie. "There were so many rumours going around about your cap, I thought I'd better take a look."

As we led Mickey up through Comical Corner I saw Peggy

Surtees coming down from Wapping Street with a pudding basin tied in a cloth. She took one look and turned back. I knew what to expect; we'd not got far down the street when Big John Surtees and a couple of big strapping fellows came running up towards us. We stood our ground. I'd already had a quiet word with Mickey.

Big John stood and faced us. I could hear Walter's knees knocking together.

"It's Mr. Surtees, isn't it?"

"Aye."

"I thought I recognised you from the Congregation Hall."

He looked at Walter. "Were ye the lad with the Sergeant?"

"Aye."

"You're a brave lad."

Walter blushed.

"I was just telling Mickey that we've found some new evidence. We don't think he did the burglary at Westgarth, but the Detective Inspector needs to talk to him as soon as possible to hear what he was doing the night of the robbery."

John Surtees said nowt. He only had on a shirt with no collar or tie, the sleeves rolled up. I was feeling the cold in my overcoat.

"I don't think the Inspector will want him in the Station in the state he is. I was taking him home so that he could have a shave, clean himself up and have some dinner. We were going to stay with him."

"There's no need, Constable. If the Polis had asked politely last time instead of swarming doon here Mickey would have come in. I'll see that he gets there."

"About half past one?"

"Aye, we'll be there."

We left them to it. Peggy Surtees came running over and held Mickey's hand as they walked on.

Walter and I had gone straight back to the Station. They were taking bets as to whether Mickey would turn up. He did. The Big Fella took him into the CID office; he was in there for about half an hour. Big John and Peggy waited in the corridor. Mickey came out looking happy enough.

"I'm free to gan. But they divvent want me to de any mair ferry work. I'm to stay yem from noo on."

Bob Jamieson was hanging about. "I'll see you at the club in the spring then, Mickey."

"Aye, ye will, Mr. Jamieson."

The Detective Inspector called me and Walter in.

"You did well, lads. We're almost certain that the Major did it himself to sell the jewels and claim the insurance. The Chief has been on to his contacts in the Met. They promised to get back to him this afternoon. The Chief is planning to see the Major tomorrow morning. We might need a couple of Constables, so you two be ready.

"Mickey was a big help. I showed him the earring that was planted in his bag. He looked twice at it and asked if he could have it for a minute. He put it in his mouth, bit on one of the stones, not very hard, mind, and just said 'Paste'. He's been taught from an early age to tell fake jewellery from the real thing. I hadn't thought to have it checked."

As we were leaving Walter piped up. "Detective Inspector, we had to give our informant a bit of money to find out where Mickey was. I was wondering what the procedure was for getting it back, like."

Norman Lamont laughed. "You're probably out of luck, Constable Heron. If Mickey Jobling's innocent you'll get nowt. You'd only get your money if it resulted in an arrest."

I left quickly.

The Detective Inspector had a quick word with Walter and me the next morning. The Met had made enquiries of the usual outlets for high class stolen jewellery. Nothing had been sold but two of the jewellers had mentioned a character who'd tried to sell some paste jewellery as the real thing, and who had been genuinely surprised, if not shocked, when told that it was fake. He'd been described as a man with a military air about him, but having a badly disfigured face and only one arm. It was the Major all right. Either the Hardisties had been robbed some time ago by someone with enough inside knowledge to be able to swap the originals with fakes or Mrs. Hardistie had had copies made without telling her husband. The Chief had decided that he only needed the DI and one Constable so I went along. Walter was still trying to have a word about the money he'd given to Hughie Ross so I was not put out to be parted from him.

The Major seemed surprised to see us as we were ushered into the drawing room. The first words he spoke told us quite clearly the truth of what had happened and that it was not a robbery. "I was going to ring you as a matter of fact. We want to drop all charges against the Jobling fellow. I hadn't realised that my wife had sent the jewellery to be repaired. She'd forgotten all about it and it was only yesterday that she suddenly remembered."

The Chief Constable was an imposing figure, nearly six foot tall, straight as a ramrod. He looked directly at Hardistie.

"I'm sorry, Major Hardistie. I will need to interview both you and your wife," he paused, "formally. We have information that leads us to believe that a serious deception has taken place."

Hardistie went pale on the one side of his face that showed changes and raised his voice. "Are you doubting the word of a gentleman?"

"I have met many gentlemen in my time, Major, but never one who employed an ex convict with the sole intention of having him sent back to jail for a crime he never committed. We have a witness who saw you go into the shed where the earring was found and we have a description of a man trying to sell jewellery in London. The man thought it was genuine but it was not."

The silence was broken by Mrs. Hardistie who was standing in the drawing room door. She did not look at her husband.

"Chief Constable, I feel that I have caused you a lot of trouble.

I had the jewellery placed at the bank some weeks ago and a good quality copy made of the important pieces. I did not tell my husband as he had expressly forbidden me to move the jewels to a bank. When they were apparently stolen, I did not say anything as I assumed that you would catch the culprit and that they would be returned. I never suspected for a moment that my husband had taken them. When he told me on his return from London I was shocked. I wished I'd told you earlier but I dreaded to think of the scandal. I want to put matters right. I wonder whether you and I could have a private word. I'll arrange for the maid to bring some tea for your officers."

The Chief could not refuse.

I never found out what was said in Mrs. Hardistie's private sitting room but the upshot was that only the Major accompanied us back to the Station. He was made to feel very uncomfortable spending an afternoon in the cells but no charges were brought. He went to live in London and was given an allowance by his wife. Bob Jamieson was called in by the Chief and then went out down to Wapping Street to see Mickey Jobling. Mickey was asked to report for work as usual and would be paid in full for the time he had been absent. He was given a small increase in salary and was told that when he married he would be allowed to occupy one of the cottages at the back of the House.

I felt guilty for a long time about Walter. I knew that in my heart of hearts I should have at least gone halves with him on the money he'd given to Hughie Ross, but I was only on a Constable's wage. I managed to pay him back about nine months later and it eased my conscience. The Ingham Infirmary Sports were one of the highlights of the year. The Force usually did well, particularly in the Cumberland wrestling where we had two world champions. Walter and I were in the tug of war team.

We saw Mickey Jobling. He had been as good as his word and was running for Bob Jamieson's athletic club. He was entered in the quarter mile and came a disappointing fourth. I was chatting to

Bob later on – he was a bit put out. One of his best hopes in the 440 yards hurdles had been fooling around and twisted his ankle.

"He can't walk let alone run. Well, there's nowt I can do about it. We'll just have to scratch him and give the race to the Harriers."

"Why don't you give Mickey a chance?"

"Mickey Jobling?"

"Aye, I told you he was a natural hurdler."

"But he only came fourth in the quarter mile."

"I wouldn't worry about that. Give him a chance, if he's willing."

Mickey Jobling was more than happy to have another run and so he was put in as a late replacement.

There was always a bookie around at the Sports and you could normally place a bet on most races. I found Walter and asked if he fancied a flutter. He was always game so we had a look round and who should we see but Dapper Digby. He knew me and wouldn't do me any favours, so I asked Walter to put the bet on. He walked up to Digby and asked what the odds would be on Mickey Jobling in the hurdles.

"Ye've got the wrong race, man; he was in the 440 yards and he lost."

"Well, I've been told that he's in the hurdles as a late replacement for someone who's injured."

"Had on a sec." Digby walked off and had a word with one of the starters.

"Aye, you're right. Well, if he was fourth on the flat, I can't see him doing any better over the sticks."

"Aye I kna' but he's a mate of mine."

Walter was gullible and he looked it, but he was learning that it could sometimes be an advantage.

"Twenty to one."

"Ten shillings to win." It was a big bet but Digby just took the money; he didn't even bother to lay it off.

Mickey was in the inside lane. As the gun went he shot out of the blocks and nearly came a cropper over the first hurdle. He knocked it flying and lost a few yards on the rest of the field, but he soon recovered and started concentrating. He ran at a steady pace and at the next hurdle his left foot shot straight up over the hurdle with his right knee bent nicely as he sailed over with inches to spare. It was not a fluke. The next hurdle was cleared in the same way and although Mickey was still the back marker he was starting to make headway. Bob Jamieson was standing beside me. "You were right, Tom – he's a natural."

Mickey was now in his stride and working his way through the field. By the back straight he was in third place and closing. He flew over the last hurdle and using all his speed made it first to the tape. There was a huge whoop from just behind us where Walter was standing.

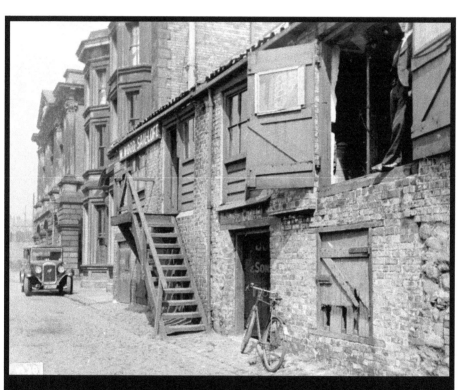

Corporation Quay, Mill Dam

A cross to bear

I was on duty one evening in the Market Place. It had been a fine spring afternoon and although there was a chill north wind blowing it was still pleasant enough. My thoughts were interrupted by a booming voice coming from the St. Hilda's end of the Market Square.

Public Meetings had to be licensed but you often found individuals spouting off on a soap box. I walked across and as I got closer I saw a tall, well-built man with a shock of chestnut hair holding a Bible clasped in both hands as he addressed a small crowd. I stopped and listened; he was a natural preacher and he then struck up with a hymn, 'When Jesus of Nazareth passeth by'. He sang unaccompanied but his baritone voice carried well over the Market cobbles and the crowd stilled.

After the last verse he announced that any who wanted to be saved should attend his meeting at seven o'clock at his Mission Hall at the back of Denmark Street. I then twigged who it was; I had heard of him – Pastor Stevens. He had not been in the town long but his reputation was spreading. The crowd drifted away and quite a few headed off down King Street following the Pastor, singing 'We Shall Gather at the River'.

I was to come off shift at eight to attend the compulsory night classes that the Chief had ordered which were held every Tuesday and Thursday at Police Headquarters. His unhappiness at the standard of written reports had increased as he grew older and as his patience diminished. All new recruits and those who had joined the Force over the last five years were obliged to attend. I was not particularly looking forward to the prospect but a couple of hours later I was in a class of ten taking dictation from Beaky Thomas. He was a teacher from the Commercial School and all right in his own way. I always sat with my very good friend Walter Heron – neither of us were star pupils – in Walter's case it was deserved. He had his good qualities but Readin' 'Ritin' and 'Rithmetic were not among them. I got poor marks for a different reason. Beaky liked a drink or two and it was more or less obligatory to follow him round to the *Wheatsheaf* after the class had ended. The first time I went along I made the mistake of reaching the bar before the others.

"Well that's very kind of you, Duncan. I'll have a pint." I said nowt. I just turned my back on him as though I'd not heard, ordered my whisky, took it and sat down. Walter was not so lucky and ended up buying a drink for Beaky and one or two others. Since that day it seemed to me that I received low marks whilst the ones that regularly drank with Beaky did better. Walter and I would avoid the *Wheatsheaf* and usually had a drink in the *Albermarle*. This particular night Walter twisted my arm. He needed some better marks and as it was unlikely that he'd achieve anything off his own bat he had decided to buy Beaky a drink or two to improve his chances. I went along. Fraser Thompson was with us. He was from Scotland, like me, but as he had been posted to Tyne Dock on arrival at Shields I'd not had a lot to do with him. I was beginning to know him better now that he was working out of Keppel Street. As fellow Scots we should have had something in common but I never took to him. He hailed from Ayr – as the great poet says:

> *"Auld Ayr, wham ne'er a town surpasses*
> *For honest men and bonnie lasses."*

If Fraser was anything to go by then Burns must have meant to refer to those who stayed put in Ayr. The man was two-faced and ambitious. Not many would see through him, but I was naturally suspicious of those who were over-friendly on first acquaintance, but always ready to run down the last fellow they had been talking to. He was also unique in the Shields Force in that he would step forward if volunteers were called for. We had known for some time that Bob Jamieson, the Station Sergeant, was due to retire, and I knew that I would get no further with my Agnes unless I managed to take the Sergeant's stripes. Fraser made no secret of the fact that he hoped to be considered, and went out of his way to please his superiors. As those who have read previous pages of these memoirs will know, I was not highly thought of by a certain Inspector Mullins. Fraser Thompson, on the other hand, was his blue-eyed boy and could do no wrong. He was also one of Beaky's star pupils – he always drank at the *Wheatsheaf* after the class.

As we supped our drinks I mentioned that I'd heard the new Pastor in the Market Place.

"Aw, divvent mention him to me," Walter replied.

"It's all wor Gertie can talk aboot. Her brother Billy and his wife gan to the meetings and they say he's saving hundreds of souls. She wants me to gan alang with her one neet."

"Well, you should go." Fraser had a mischievous smile on his face. "You could take her for a walk in the Marine Park beforehand. If you have a bit of luck with your Gertie you might need saving yoursel'."

"Aw, hadaway man, she's not like that." Whilst another man might have taken against Fraser, Walter was just embarrassed. I was to find that it was just the sort of crack that the Scot would make. He was always eyeing up the barmaids in the *Wheatsheaf*, and he was not after a long engagement. I couldn't blame him given the lack of progress I had made towards any sort of physical contact with my Agnes, and if Fraser did become Sergeant then I might never get beyond the holding hands stage.

Beaky was hovering with a near empty glass. "Did I hear you mention Pastor Stevens? From what I've heard your workload is going to increase if he gets his way." He paused for effect, drained his glass and held it out. "Now, whose round is it and then I'll tell you more."

Walter did the honours.

"Pastor Stevens believes in sin and redemption, the most deadly of sins being carnal." As a good teacher he could tell by the look on Walter's face that the lad had not understood. "Of the flesh, Constable Heron, of the flesh, and prostitutes are amongst the worst of the sinners. Pastor Stevens will generate such a religious fervour amongst the good folk of Shields that you Bobbies will spend all your time chasing the street walkers down back lanes and raiding disorderly houses at night."

Beaky took a good swig; he only talked in short bursts so as not to slow down his drinking time. "He will then receive any of the unfortunate women into his mission hall with open arms."

"I thowt ye said he didn't like them?" Walter was a straightforward fellow.

"He loves them, Constable Heron – any Christian worth his salt loves a sinner. He will redeem them and grant them forgiveness for their sins so long as they repent."

Time was called and we finished our drinks. We made to move off but Fraser was talking to one of the barmaids. He seemed in no hurry to come with us, so we left him to it.

Beaky turned out to be right and Walter ended up going to one of Pastor Stevens' meetings. Who should he see there but Inspector Mullins and his sour-faced wife. Mullins had gone up to Walter at the end of the meeting; he was beaming. "I'm pleased to see you here, Walter. I had no idea you were a devout man, like myself." Well neither had Walter. "I only wish we had more like you in the Force."

In those days Shields was one of the busiest sea ports in the country. Sailors are much the same the world over, and where there are men coming off ships after a long voyage with money in their belts, there'll always be prostitutes. The women would find their customers in the many pubs where sailors congregated. We enforced the law and if we came across a woman soliciting we'd arrest her. We knew the regulars: Broken Arse, Ginger C***** and Mary C*****, Queen of Tyne Dock, to name a few.

Brothels, or disorderly houses as they were known, would spring up from time to time. We took particular pleasure in raiding these at night, if we could. Night shift could be very tedious and a raid on a disorderly house was always a lot of fun; you'd see the girls and their clients half undressed and there'd always be someone who'd try to make a run for it. We relied on tip offs – most law abiding souls did not like a house of pleasure on their doorstep.

Not long after our discussion in the *Wheatsheaf* we were given new orders: prostitution was to be stamped out in Shields once and for all. If we arrested a prostitute she was to be given a caution only, on condition that she was sent down to the Mission to see the Pastor. As it turned out most were happy to agree. It was no trouble – there was a guest house in Ocean Road which we called the Stables. All the girls who had nowhere else to sleep bedded down there – it was only a five minute walk to the Mission Hall.

A couple of days later I bumped into Fraser Thompson. We were both walking down Waterloo Vale heading back to the nick.

"Do you know Teddy Denby, Tom?"

"Aye, he's handy with his fists." I'd seen him flatten Little Bobby Doyle after an argument about queuing in the Fish and Chip shop.

"He is that. I've just come back from his house in Wilson Sreet. He's given his missus a real belting and pushed her down the back stairs. I was patrolling in Claypath Lane and one of the neighbours saw me; she thought he'd murdered her. The ambulance has just taken her away to the Ingham."

Mrs. Denby would only say that she slipped and fell down the stairs. She was lucky there was nothing broken but she'd take a while to mend. Fraser found Teddy Denby in the *Queen's Head*. Teddy admitted nowt and said he wasn't having her back. He gave her more than enough for the housekeeping but she couldn't resist a bet. He had a Union Meeting that night and had gone to put his suit on. It wasn't there – his wife had pawned it. She needed the money as she'd lost the housekeeping on the horses. She was always betting and she had to walk miles to get her groceries as she'd run up so much tick in the local shops. He'd warned her the last time a shopkeeper had come knocking on the door. When he'd found that his suit was in pawn it was the last straw. He'd taken their son, little Teddy, to his mother who would look after him until things were sorted out.

Fraser seemed preoccupied after that. I learned from Alec Dorothy that he'd been to see Mrs. Denby after she'd been bandaged up. Alice Denby had gone to her sister's in Maxwell Street for a few days; it was on Alec's beat. He'd seen Fraser and had gone along with him. Mrs. Denby was an attractive woman; she had lovely dark brown hair and deep brown eyes to go with it. Alec reckoned that Fraser fancied his chances. Since his marriage had broken up Alec and I had not been the closest of friends, but it didn't stop us from passing the time of day.

"Do you think Fraser's got any chance with her?"

"Well her husband's thrown her out so she'll have no money and she might need comforting."

"You mean she's easy meat?"

I didn't answer. I should have known Alec Dorothy better. Alec had a flaw in his otherwise good character – envy: he always wanted what someone else had.

Meanwhile as Beaky had predicted, we became very busy. So many arrests for prostitution were being made that Bob Jamieson had asked me to help him in the Charge Office. I did so gladly. One afternoon Walter came in with an inebriated woman on his arm.

"Soliciting in a public place, and you could throw in drunk and disorderly if you want, Sarge."

"Is it her first time?" Bob asked.

"Aye, and I've not seen her before."

"Put her in the cells for the time being until she sobers up then we'll caution her and send her down the Mission Hall. Let's book her in."

As I took her particulars for the charge book, I asked her name – Alice Denby. I asked her address – she started crying. Her husband had thrown her out and her sister's husband had said he didn't want her sort in the house. 'No fixed abode' went into the book.

It was later that afternoon that the trouble broke out between Fraser and Alec. They both came in for a brew at about five o'clock. Walter was there and told them that Alice Denby was in the cells for soliciting. Fraser said that as he knew her he'd see that she was found a lodging house for the night. Alec butted in.

"It's all reet, Fraser, I'll look after her. She might appreciate a shoulder to cry on."

"It's nowt to do with you. I've been to see her a couple of times."

"Well, if you're not getting anywhere yoursel', you might as well let someone else try his chances." Alec was a little bit too obvious and Fraser went for him. Walter and me had to get between them. For once it was Walter who took charge of things. His sessions at the Mission Hall were taking effect.

"You ought to be ashamed o' yoursels. We're here to protect these poor women, not prey on them. I arrested her and I'm taking her doon to the Mission Hall." Alec and Fraser looked daggers at each other but both went on their way.

I went along with Walter. The door to the Mission Hall was open. It was just after six in the evening and there seemed to be no one about. Walter shouted out a loud 'Hullo'. A deep voice replied from the back of the Hall. "Just a minute, I'm coming."

"That's the Pastor," said Walter. We heard a door opening and Pastor Stevens came out from a corridor at the far side. He looked a little flushed and his normally immaculate hair was a bit ruffled.

"It's you, Walter, and you've bought another soul to be saved. I was just trying to comfort a poor lass who's just come in off the streets." A shabbily dressed but quite pretty young woman was just behind him. "Now you just sit there, pet, and I'll take you along to Mrs. Coutts in a minute."

He came over to us and shook Walter's hand warmly. I was introduced and he held out his hand to me as well. He had a firm handshake and looked me straight in the eye. "Officers of the law are always welcome in the house of the Lord. But I hope next time you will be out of uniform. You must come to one of our meetings."

I said nowt. Walter explained that Alice Denby had been cautioned and that she had nowhere to live.

The Pastor held out both hands to Alice and looked deeply into her eyes. She seemed completely overawed. He then raised his eyes to the ceiling. "Lord, we have another sinner come to repent." He looked back to Alice. "Sister, your troubles are over; the Lord welcomes you. Go over there and sit with young Florrie; I'll be over in a minute." Alice seemed loath to let go of his hands but at last she did and slowly went to where the other girl was sitting.

"I'll have them taken over to Mrs. Coutts. She has a large house in Winchester Street. She'll give them a room, and a rent book, and she'll find them work, but all on condition that they come regularly to the Mission. Will I see you at our meeting tonight, Walter?"

"Aye, me and Gertie are coming."

He looked at me. "I've another commitment, Pastor."

I was with Walter the next day when Sergeant Jamieson asked about Alice Denby. Walter told him that she would be lodging with a Mrs. Coutts. Bob looked thoughtful. "In Winchester Street?"

"Aye, d'ye kna her?"

"Aye. Daisy Coutts is a widow; her husband, John Coutts, was a Sergeant in the River Police. He'd been paying a courtesy call on a skipper new to the Tyne. He missed his footing on the ladder and fell between the ship and the cutter. He went straight down. They never recovered his body. Apparently it wasn't the first call he'd made that night and sea captains are very generous with their whisky when the River Police come aboard. She moved to Winchester Street after her husband's death. CID raided her about a year and a half ago. She was done for keeping a disorderly house."

We were all silent for a moment.

"Well, she's probably seen the light," Walter conjectured.

I had a more jaundiced view of human nature. "Or the work she's finding for them isn't exactly what Pastor Stevens had in mind."

JOHN ORTON wait

Bob nodded in agreement. "If they have their own rooms and a rent book we'd have a job pinning anything on Daisy Coutts. Winchester Street's on Alec's beat. I'll ask him to keep an eye out."

Alec Dorothy was not the most subtle of Bobbies. To him, keeping an eye out meant planting himself outside Daisy Coutts' house and standing there on the pavement for an hour at a time. Any gentlemen callers who might have been heading in that direction crossed to the other side of the street and walked on. Daisy was not one to be intimidated. After the third day she came out and asked him to move. Alec said he'd do no such thing. Voices were raised and Alec threatened to arrest her for disturbing the peace. She went indoors, put on her coat and came straight down to Keppel Street where she saw Bob Jamieson. He said he knew nowt about it but that he had every confidence in Constable Dorothy; besides, if nothing was going on in her property she had nothing to worry about. She went away and came back two hours later with Pastor Stevens who asked to see Inspector Mullins.

Mullins of course was thick with the Pastor. He also knew Mrs. Coutts from the Mission and so far as he was concerned she was doing good work. He said that he'd look into it and make sure that Mrs. Coutts was not troubled any more. He then went and had a word with Bob Jamieson. Things had not been easy between them ever since Mullins had been appointed Inspector over Bob's head. They'd had differences but had always managed to avoid a confrontation. Mullins took a hard line this time. He wanted Alec Dorothy up before the Chief – Bob was having none of it. Their voices were raised and one or two of us who had just come out of the Parade Room were standing outside trying to listen in. The noise must have alerted the Big Fella, Detective Inspector Lamont, who came out of his office, strode down the corridor and as he walked past us, paused and asked, "What's going on?"

I quickly put him in the picture.

"Right. Bugger off you lot and get out on the beat." He pushed open the Charge Office door and went in.

The outcome was known soon enough. Walter and Alec were called in to see the Sergeant. Alec was to be sent down to Tyne Dock and Walter was to take over his beat. It suited everybody, apart from Alec and Walter, that is, but they got over it. The Pastor and Mrs. Coutts knew Walter from the Mission and felt they had gained an ally. Mullins was not unhappy.

Apparently Bob had been about to explode at his suggestion when the Big Fella had given him a large wink and he'd said nowt. Norman Lamont had met up with Bob later that night in the *Golden Lion*. He shared the Sergeant's suspicions about Mrs. Coutts and had heard a few whispers himself. Putting Walter on the beat instead of Alec would lull Mrs. Coutts into a false sense of security. He was going to wait a while and then mount an undercover operation.

"What about Mullins?"

"I don't tell him about every CID job I'm doing. If he asks I'll let him in on it."

A couple of days later I was up at the Ingham Infirmary. The District Midwife had been down to Keppel Street the day before. A young woman had been admitted with serious stomach pains. It had not taken long for the Doctor to give a diagnosis: an abortion had been carried out and the woman was bleeding internally. She had been patched up but might not be able to have any more children; only time would tell. Abortions were of course illegal but human nature being what it is, people did have sex. Not that I was an expert on the subject – I was lucky if my Agnes let me hold her hand, let alone any more intimate part of her anatomy. Pregnancies occurred and if the woman was unmarried, or married with her husband away at sea, then it was a trip down the back-streets to find someone who would get rid of the baby. The District Midwives were always on our backs to put a stop to it but we rarely had any evidence – it was only in the odd case where something went wrong that we had any chance of finding the abortionist.

I went in to see the young woman – her name was Peggy

Morgan. She was deathly pale and had deep shadows under her eyes. I looked twice at her – I knew the face from somewhere. As soon as she saw the uniform she started to cry. I often had that effect on pretty girls.

"Don't worry, lass, I've just come to ask you a few questions." I took my helmet off and she looked again.

"Oh, I'm sorry, I thought you were someone else."

"A Constable?"

"It's just that I work in the *Wheatsheaf* and we see a few Bobbies."

I recognised her – I'd last seen her talking to Fraser Thompson.

"You'll know Fraser, then?" The tears started again. "Was he courting you?"

"Well, not really. He used to walk me home. We'd stop for a kiss in one of the back lanes."

It was often the only place in those days. I felt sorry for the young lass as she lay in her hospital bed.

> *"Then gently scan your brother Man,*
> *Still gentler sister Woman;*
> *Tho' they may gang a kenning wrang,*
> *To step aside is human."*

"Did you tell Fraser you were pregnant?" I asked.

"He said he couldn't marry me. He's got a wife in Scotland and he can't divorce her as he's a Catholic."

It was the first I'd heard of it.

"He said we'd have to get rid of the baby. He knew someone and it wouldn't cost me anything."

"Can you tell me who it was?"

"He said I mustn't say. Not to anyone."

I had a fair idea. A few weeks back we'd received an anonymous letter about Bella Riley. Fraser had made a few enquiries and was sure that she was the one who had been carrying out the abortions.

There was no real evidence but he'd gone to see her to give her a warning.

Peggy wasn't going to say anymore. Fraser was on the night shift so I held on a while to make sure I would see him. He was his usual self, telling one of the others about a girl he was seeing. "I was walking her home. I said I had to have a piss in one of the back lanes. She came with me and then I pinned her against the wall and started kissing her. I even got me hand in her knickers but that's as far as it went. She's a sure thing for tomorrow though."

"Don't they ever ask you to marry them before they let you have it?" I asked innocently.

"Och, aye. I tell them I've got a wife in Scotland. I say we're split up but that I'm a Catholic and can't get a divorce."

"You're not a Catholic, are you?" Alec asked.

"No, of course not," Fraser laughed.

He wasn't laughing five minutes later when I had him up against the wall of the Parade Room after the others had left. It took a while but a couple of punches in the kidneys loosened his tongue. After Peggy had told him she was pregnant he'd been to see Bella. She was more than happy to do Peggy for free. Fraser would make sure that any other investigations he was asked to do came to nowt.

"You'll not tell the Sergeant, Tom, I'd lose my job. I didn't mean any harm."

It was a hard choice but in those days you stood by your fellow officers. "I'll think about it. But on one condition."

"Aye, all reet!" He was in no position to bargain.

"You'll visit Peggy in hospital and take care of her until she's settled."

"Aye. I'll gan up the Ingham tomorrow afternoon."

"And you won't play around with any of your lady friends until Peggy's back on her feet."

That was a bit harder for Fraser but he agreed.

I was leaving the Station and nearly bumped into Teddy Denby. He looked as though he was in two minds about something. I could smell the beer on his breath but he didn't look the worse for it.

"Can I help you?" I tried to sound as helpful as I could.

"I thought I might see that other Scottish officer. The one that came round that day wor Alice fell doon the stairs."

"You're lucky, he'll be out in a minute." Fraser came down the steps just as I'd finished speaking.

"Here's Mr. Denby to see you, Constable Thompson." Fraser looked worried when he saw Teddy but the pitman was not aggressive.

"I'm sorry to trouble you, Constable, but I'm worried about wor Alice. Her sister doesn't kna' where she is and me mother says she can't look after little Teddy much longer. Well... I'm thinking of having her back but only if she mends her ways mind. I thought you might kna' where she is – me sister said ye'd been to see her."

Fraser looked at me. With a few drinks inside him it wouldn't take Teddy too long to lose his temper. We both had an idea of what was going on in Winchester Street.

"Och aye, she's started going to the Pastor Stevens' Mission and they've found her some lodgings in Winchester Street. I'm not sure of the number; I could find out and take you round."

Teddy Denby was happy with that. He was on an early shift the next day so he agreed to meet Fraser just after three outside the Town Hall and they would walk down. Fraser, who would be off duty, was more than happy to accompany Teddy.

It so happened that the next day Walter and I were both on at two so we'd agreed to have lunch together at the North of England Café. It was a higher class of eating house than I would normally frequent but Walter's girlfriend, Gertie Ruffle, worked there. He had tried eating there on his own but had had an unfortunate occurrence, and would only go in if he had a friend with him. We were enjoying our steak and kidney pie when Alec Dorothy came in. He was in uniform. He looked round the room, saw us, came over, pulled up a chair and sat down. "I had to come up from the Dock with some charge sheets. Bob Jamieson said I might find you here.

He wants me to ask you to do him a favour."

Gertie approached. "Is everything all right, Walter?"

Walter wasn't quite sure. "Ye'd better ask him, hinny."

Alec smiled at Gertie as he took his helmet off. "Wye aye, pet. It's just that we're having a bit of trouble with some French sailors. They've worked their way up through Holborn to the Market. There's already been two fights. Sergeant Jamieson was wondering if these two might come on early. They'll have time to finish their pie though."

He paused and looked thoughtfully at our plates. The pie had a thick suet crust and the rich savoury gravy seeped out over the succulent chunks of steak and slices of kidney.

"There's no chance of a piece of pie while I'm waiting, Gertie? Just on its own – I won't have time for anything else."

"I'll go and see."

There was no problem. In those days the Police were welcome and often had a free lunch. Gertie came back and put a plate of pie down saying it came with the compliments of the Manageress.

"I'm not one to hold grudges, Walter. I'm getting on canny down the Dock and I'm out of the way of Mullins," said Alec, his mouth full of pie. A driblet of gravy ran down his chin; he shovelled in another very large forkful and was just about to open his mouth to speak when Walter butted in.

"Can you not put so much into your gob at one time, Alec, particularly if you're gan' to speak as well. The last time I was in here a fellow at my table choked to death on a piece of turkey. I couldn't go through that again."

Alec laughed. He'd heard Walter's story but he was not to be diverted. "I won't forget auld Mother Coutts though. Have you seen any funny goings on down Winchester Street, Walter?" Walter said nowt. He was firmly on Mrs. Coutts' side. "Well I think you soon will."

He polished off the last chunk of pie and wiped his mouth clean with the back of his hand. Walter and I had already finished. We paid for ours while Alec chatted to Gertie.

We joined Alec in the Market Place about twenty minutes later. The foreign seamen usually kept to the pubs near the Riverside but today they'd come up to the Market Place. There was a French destroyer on a courtesy visit tied up at the Corporation Quay. I saw a group of the French sailors with red pompoms on their hats heading down Union Alley.

Walter and I were soon helping a couple of them who were the worse for wear out of the *Norfolk and Suffolk*. If they could walk steadily once out in the fresh air we'd point them back to their ship; if not it would be a trip down to Keppel Street. These two managed to move off.

"I wish you'd send them all back, the bloody French bastards. We'd hev' won the war a lot quicker if it hadn't been for them."

I recognised the voice. Hughie Ross was standing on the Market cobbles just across from us shaking his crutch in the direction of the departing French mariners.

"I don't know what they're all doing in the Market Place, Hughie."

"Daint ye?" He looked round. "Well I can tell ye. I've just come out of the *Tram*. Geordie Hepplewhite was in there. He can speak a bit of French. He was in the trenches. He got chatting to a couple of the sailors. They wanted to know where Winchester Street was, Number 44. There's supposed to be a knocking shop there. Well, ye kna' what the French are like, and they don't mind paying for it either. The funny thing is it was one of your lot that telt them. I expect they'll all be doon Winchester Street after the pubs shut."

Hughie put his hand in his pocket and rummaged about. "I don't think I've even got enough for a pint."

"Go on, Walter, let Mr. Ross have a few pence for a drink."

Walter did as he was told. He was preoccupied. "I bet it was that Alec, he's always causing trouble."

We walked over to Crofton's Corner – it was always a good lookout spot and Sam Beecroft was already standing there.

"Thanks for coming on early, lads. I dinna' why they all decided to come up to the Market. There's plenty of good pubs doon Holborn." He looked round. "It's getting a bit quieter now; they seem to be heading away to Fowler Street. Ye kna, I think I've got time for a quick one down the *Lifeboat*. Will ye watch out for five minutes?" He was just about to move off. "Yon Alec's a canny fellow. He's sending them doon Chapter Row." But Sam's thoughts were on the pint of foaming beer he would have. Walter and I looked across to where Alec was standing in front of St. Hilda's talking to a group of the Frenchmen and pointing down the Row.

"I think you're right about Alec, Walter. Let's have a word."

As we approached him Alec greeted us with a big smile. "Panic over. They're away down to Fowler Street."

"Have you been telling them to go to Winchester Street, Number 44?" I asked him straight.

"Well what of it?"

"Ye'd nae reet." Walter was annoyed and that was unusual. "Ye're just picking on poor Mrs. Coutts because she had you transferred – and her deein' the Lord's work."

"Calm down, man." Alec wasn't perturbed. "The Big Fella's had the house watched, and he's sure there's something going on. The trouble is all the girls have their own rooms. We'd have a job to pin anything on auld Couttsie unless we can prove she knows what's happening in her own property. He reckons she owns another house in the street and has girls living in number 44 and 38. Well, I put me thinking cap on this morning and came up with an idea. If all these Frenchmen arrive at once and auld Mrs. Coutts takes them in, then we'll have her."

"Well that's not very nice – isn't it entrapment?" Walter had been learning some big words at night classes.

"Wye no! If she's as innocent as you think she'll send them away and that'll be the end of that."

"Does Inspector Mullins kna?"

"I doubt it."

"Well I'm gan' to tell him."

"And what do you think he's going to do – stand in the road and tell the Frenchies they can't have it today? I'd leave things to the Sergeant; he'll make sure Mullins knows when it's time."

Walter wasn't very happy. I tried to reassure him.

"Look Walter, if Mrs. Coutts is making those poor women work as prostitutes then she's undermining the Pastor's good works and if she isn't then everybody'll be happy."

"Aye, I suppose so."

As soon as Sam came back from the *Lifeboat* we made our way to the Station. Sergeant Jamieson was already in the Parade Room. He'd asked a few fellows from the early shift, including Alec, to stay on for a bit of overtime – he needed about a dozen of us for the raid. The Detective Inspector was in the room; one of his men was already on lookout at Winchester Street. The only person who was missing was Inspector Mullins but someone must have tipped him off. He came storming in just as the Big Fella was about to start the briefing. Norman Lamont didn't give Mullins a chance to say much.

"Ah, Inspector, I'm glad you're here. We're going to need your help. We've had reports that there might be a disorderly house in Winchester Street, Number 44, and possibly number 38 as well. I've had a Detective keep the place under surveillance and he's fairly certain the reports were true. I was going to have a word with you and the Sergeant about it, but now we've just heard about the French seamen."

"What French seamen?" Mullins was trying to contain himself. If it had just been Bob Jamieson he would have had no compunction in dressing him down before the rest of us. Norman Lamont was a different matter and Mullins could not be certain of coming off best. The Big Fella explained the morning's events.

"Well I happen to know Mrs. Coutts and I can't believe she would have anything to do with prostitution. She's already made one complaint about being harassed." Mullins looked in Alec Dorothy's direction.

"You need not worry, Inspector. There'll be no heavy-handedness. We're going to keep a very low profile. If the sailors are refused admittance then we'll make sure they move on peaceably back to their ship. If they go in then we'll give them a few minutes to make themselves at home and then we'll have a look inside ourselves."

Mullins said nowt but his face said it all.

The plan was for us to wait in the Black Maria in one of the side streets off Fowler Street. As soon as a good few of the mariners were inside we'd be given the word – the Chief had signed the warrants. It was only when I was sitting in the back of the wagon at about a quarter past three that I thought about Fraser and Teddy Denby. They'd completely slipped my mind. If we didn't get the shout soon we might very well run into them.

"Walter, what number Winchester Street did you say Alice Denby was living?"

"38."

"Let's make sure we go in that one."

The penny dropped. "Isn't Fraser gannin' roond this after?"

"Aye, he is."

There was a knock on the van door. One of the plainclothesmen popped his head in.

"We're on. There must be about twenty. They came up Winchester Street in groups. One of them knocked on the door at 44 – a fellow came out. We've seen him before, he's Mrs. Coutts' lodger, but we don't think he pays any rent. He let about half in and sent some down to number 38 and the rest to a house in Winterbottom Street that we've had our eye on. It's all clear now so you can head on up. If some of you go up the back lane..."

"I'm more than capable of directing operations from now on, Constable." Mullins took control. Walter and I made sure that we were in the group calling on number 38. We waited until Mullins gave the signal and then knocked on the door. We could hear an awful racket coming from inside. The door flew open and a young woman in her underclothes came rushing out.

"Thank God you're here, there's bloody murder gan' on upstairs." I recognised her: it was Scotch Helen. She'd been taken down the Mission a few weeks earlier. We didn't hang about.

"Draw truncheons," I called out as I headed up the stairs with Walter just behind. We had to push past some girls and a couple of French lads with blood streaming down their faces.

As we reached the landing I saw the backs of half a dozen sailors. Teddy Denby was standing over Fraser, who was laid out on the floor, and was defending himself and the Scot. He was flailing away with his fists to good effect. I didn't wait. My truncheon flew through the air and cleared one of the attackers out of the way. Walter did likewise. I heard a shout from the stairs.

"Behind you, man, there's a knife."

I swivelled round and my truncheon hit the wrist of a vicious looking villain who was about to stab me, knocking his knife to the floor. Mullins came over and grabbed the culprit, bashing his head against the wall. "Well done, Duncan."

The other sailors did not put up any resistance and we carted those who'd attacked us off to the Black Maria which had pulled up outside. There'd been no trouble in the other houses where the sailors and the girls had been caught in all sorts of positions and states of undress.

We found out later that Teddy Denby and Fraser had turned up at number 38 not long after the Frenchmen had gone in. They'd arrived outside Alice's room just as two Frenchmen were starting to take her clothes off. As soon as Alice saw Teddy she screamed blue murder and started fighting them off. Teddy attacked the two French lads and was giving them the hiding of their lives. Their friends came out of the other rooms and then the fun really started. Fraser tried to calm things down but was knocked to the floor. He was getting a good kicking but Teddy Denby managed to push the attackers back. That was when we arrived.

After we'd loaded up the Black Maria I went back to have a

word with Alice and Teddy. Fraser had already been taken off to the Ingham for a check over. Teddy had his arm round Alice's shoulder.

"Thanks for your help, officer." Teddy held out his hand and we shook. "Those French lads were attacking my Alice. We arrived just in time and you saved my bacon. I don't think I could have held out for much longer. Wor Alice says that Mrs. Coutts was trying to get her on the game. She wouldn't have any of it though."

"Well, it was either that or being sent back to see Pastor Stevens. Some of the girls say he's worse than the ones that come here when he gets you in that little back room." Alice was beaming at Teddy. She was lucky. I didn't know how long it would last, but in those days it wasn't easy for a married couple to split up, particularly if there was a child. They set off back to Wilson Street holding hands.

I went and had a quiet word with Inspector Mullins. I thanked him for the warning. "It could have saved my life, Inspector." I didn't like saying it, but it had to be said.

Mullins looked at me. "No, I won't have that." He paused. "They say that if you save someone's life then you're responsible for them for ever after." He didn't need to say any more and I quickly changed the subject. I mentioned Alice Denby's comment about the Pastor. Mullins looked thoughtful.

"Aye. He has a very strict rule that when he's seeing someone – when he's saving someone, rather, he must not be disturbed for any reason."

"I was wondering if me and Constable Heron should call in at the Mission to tell him about the raid here and see what he has to say."

"Well somebody has to." I took it for a yes.

Walter came along but hardly said a word. The door of the Mission Hall was closed but not locked. We went in but there was no one there. Walter was about to say something but I put my finger to my lips. I thought I could hear a noise coming from the back of the Hall. I started tip-toeing across the wooden floor and motioned for Walter to follow me. We reached the far side where the noise was still muffled but a bit clearer. We went into the corridor. There was a door half way down with a large notice on it, 'PRIVATE'. I put my ear to the door and could hear a man breathing very heavily. I had no doubt about what was going on, nor had Walter from the look on his face. I tried the door knob very quietly; it turned but the door was bolted. I banged hard on the wood.

"Open up. Police."

There was a sudden silence.

"Open up. Police. At once."

The Pastor's voice boomed out. "You can't come in."

"If you don't open the door I'll kick it in." To reinforce my message I put my foot against the door and kicked.

The bolt slid back. The Pastor tried to block my entrance but I pushed past him. He was in his shirtsleeves and was buttoning up his flies. The young lass with him had a bit more to do. She was desperately trying to arrange her undergarments. It was Florrie, the girl we had seen the last time we were in the Mission.

"Was he forcing himself on you?"

"Say nothing," Stevens called out. "You have no business to come in here uninvited. I'm going to complain to Inspector Mullins."

"It won't dee ye any good." Walter's voice was as firm and determined as I had heard it. "He's just raided Mrs. Coutt's house in Winchester Street. She'd put all those girls you sent to her back on the game. Ye must have known, and you're taking advantage of them yourself. You're nowt but a hypocrite."

Florrie wouldn't say anything so there was not much else to do. As we left, Walter told Pastor Stevens that the whole Mission would know the truth about him.

When we arrived back at the Station the celebratory atmosphere of the early afternoon had quietened a little. The French Captain had arrived, and although he had been apologetic at first he was distinctly unhappy after he had seen his men. He spoke passable English and asked to see the Chief Constable. The Captain had been polite but was not pleased with the way his men had been treated. In addition to the three in custody he had two more out of action in the ship's hospital berths. He was due to sail the next day and needed all his crew. His men had said that it had been a Police Officer who had told them to go to Winchester Street. In France brothels were legal, so the sailors did not think they were doing anything wrong. The trouble had started because two of them had been viciously attacked without provocation as they were being entertained by a lady of the establishment. One of the attackers was apparently a Police Officer in plain clothes. The other French mariners were doing no more than coming to their crewmates' aid. The uniformed Police Officers who had entered the house had launched a cowardly assault from behind without any warning. The incident with the knife could not be excused, and the offender would be dealt with severely.

The Chief agreed to release the Frenchmen in custody on bail provided they returned to the ship. The Naval Captain was going to contact the French Consul in Newcastle to arrange for a lawyer to represent his crewmen.

The Chief had a long session with Mullins and the Detective Inspector but things got worse. The French Ambassador in London became involved and the next morning the Chief Constable received a call from the Permanent Secretary at the Home Office half an hour before he was due to be in Court. As a result the Chief did not oppose the application for a continuation of their bail. The French sailors left Shields later that day on the afternoon tide. No further action was taken.

When the case against Mrs. Coutts came to Court she was represented by King's Counsel from Newcastle and admitted one charge of keeping a disorderly house at number 44. The other charges were kept on the file. She was fined twenty pounds.

When he heard the outcome, Alec Dorothy was worried. He thought he'd be sacked. But that was not the way the Chief worked. When he asked for explanations from the Big Fella and from

Mullins, both defended the action taken. They did not condone what Constable Dorothy had done but they claimed that the opportunity for raiding the premises was too good to miss. Nobody could have foreseen that Teddy Denby would arrive when he did, let alone that he would be accompanied by Fraser Thompson. As it was, the link between the Mission and Mrs. Coutts' nefarious activities had been established. No more was said but Alec knew that his card had been marked; the next time he stepped over the line he would be out.

Fraser had only a couple of bruised ribs and Teddy Denby to thank for not faring much worse. He had a chance to visit Peggy Morgan when he was being checked over at the Ingham, and was true to his word. He went out with her for a good few months until she was back on her feet but he moved on. He had a roving eye.

Pastor Stevens left Shields soon afterwards. The Mission remained open but it was not the same without Stevens – he could pull them in. He was one of the best Preachers around. It was a shame; had he not had a weakness for the fair sex he could have done a lot of good.

Open Air Swimming Pool

A dish of panacklety

Walter and myself rarely had time off on the same occasion as
Agnes and Gertie but when it did happen, we would all try to go
out together. Agnes preferred this to being with me alone – she had
to spend less time avoiding my attempts to hold her hand. We had
decided to go to the new Open Air Swimming Pool. I was a keen
swimmer and had joined the Life Saving Swimming Association
as soon as I had come to Shields. I used the Derby Street Baths in
the winter, and as soon as the Open Air Pool was built I became a
regular. I had never been able to tempt Walter but Gertie was keen
to have a dip and so Walter agreed.

   We stood by the poolside in our swimming costumes. Although
it was a sunny June day there was a cool north wind coming off the
German Sea. The water was choppy and looked icy – there was only
one thing to do.

   "Come on, Walter." I grabbed his hand and ran towards the
edge. I sensed some resistance but he was soon running with me. I
dived in and Walter jumped. The cold hit me and I was breathless as
I reached the surface. It was exhilarating. The girls were laughing.
There was no sign of Walter, then he came to the surface only
to flap about and go under again. We were in the deep end and
it crossed my mind that I had never asked him if he could swim.
I dived down towards him and pushed him up to the surface. He
was struggling like a maniac and it was all I could do to keep his
head above the water. There was a splash and a young lad came
swimming up.

   "I'll help you, Mister," he shouted out. With four hands holding
him, Walter calmed down. We managed to reach the side and Gertie
helped us to get him out. He was coughing and spluttering and it
took him a while to come round.

   The young lad who had helped started to walk off. I went over
to him and shook his hand.

   "Thanks a lot, son."

"Aw, it's all reet. I could see he was giving you a bit of trouble."
He did a quick run and dived back in.

I went over to Walter who was looking sorry for himself, with
Gertie and Agnes fussing over him.

"Why didn't you tell me you couldn't swim?"

"Well, I've nivver been taught, and I didn't realise it was the deep
end."

I didn't push it; he was embarrassed but it didn't spoil our day.
Walter and Gertie stayed in the shallower part of the pool and me
and Agnes had a good swim. I complimented her on her fine crawl
stroke.

"It was Herbert who taught me how to swim. He could have
been a champion swimmer had he chosen." Herbert Jaggers had
been her fiancé – killed in the War and never forgotten.

As we were leaving I saw Jimmy Biddulph, the local leader of
the Miners' Union, and walking alongside him was the young lad
who had helped me to rescue Walter. I'd met Jimmy a couple of
times when we had policed meetings in the Market Place. We said
hello and started chatting. The young fellow walked on.

"The lad there helped me pull Walter out. I would have had a
job without him."

"Aye, I saw it. They should put up bigger signs for the Deep End.
He's a canny lad. You'll probably know his family – he's Johnny
Doyle, Bobby Doyle's youngest."

I knew the Doyles all right – a family of villains.

"Young John's the best of them. He was a friend of our Ernie."
Ernie Biddulph had died of pneumonia about a year before. "He
was always coming round, and he was always hungry. He still kept
coming after Ernie passed away and one night he just stayed. He
said he didn't want to go back home, his brother Bobby was always
clouting him, and with his father inside his mother had gone back
on the game and was bringing customers back. He used to be a
scrawny nowt but once he was living with us he started putting on
a bit of weight. I sent him down to the boxing club. Bob Jamieson

214

helps to run it. If it hadn't been for Bob I don't think they would have taken him. Stoker Armstrong said the boy was too weak – he didn't want a killing on his hands so Bob set him working on the barbells to strengthen him up. It was two months before they'd let him in the ring. He'll never make a champion but he's doing canny. He helps out in the yard at St. Hilda's Colliery and sometimes gans out with the wagons."

"He doesn't look like a Doyle." The other Doyles were all black haired and shifty looking. Johnny had an unruly mop of fair hair and clear blue eyes.

"Aye, well a good few Scandinavian ships come into the Tyne."

Jimmy didn't need to say anymore. He walked off to catch up with Johnny.

After that I took Walter in hand. We would go swimming together whenever we could, either to the Open Air Pool or to the Derby Street baths and I taught him how to swim. It took a while. Walter was never going to make a Channel swimmer but he mastered the basics.

My further acquaintance with Johnny Doyle was to come about in an unexpected fashion. It all started with Bill Spyles. I was in the Parade Room one night having a cup of tea. Bill for once was not playing 'fives and threes'. He must have arrived late – he might have been held up in a Public House. As well as the pots of whisky tied to the back gates of some pubs, it was not uncommon for an officer to be invited in if the Landlord was entertaining a few friends after hours. The Bobby would see the lights still on, usually through a chink in the curtains. He'd knock to see that everything was all right and the Landlord would ask him in for some refreshment. You could smell the alcohol on Bill's breath – together with the raw onion. The last Bobby away from the Market would fetch a sackful.

"Did you hear about the visitor to Shields?" Whether we had or not we were going to. "It was a lady. She told her friends how she had been surprised how religious the folks of Shields were. Her friend asked how was that. Well, she said, 'I was passing Trow Rocks and I saw a large crowd of men. They all raised their eyes to the heavens. They then lowered their heads and all cried out, 'The Lord be praised!'."

We had a good a laugh. Fraser Thompson who was sitting beside me couldn't see the joke. I explained it to him while the others listened in. Trow Rocks were just outside the Shields boundary and they came under the jurisdiction of the Durham Constabulary. They had one Police Constable in Whitburn who spent most of his time in the *Grey Horse*. Trow Rocks had become a gambling den – pitch-and-toss was the favoured game. What the lady had seen was the coins being thrown in the air – the men all looked skywards, they then looked down. It was two heads – 'The Lord be praised.' – they'd won. My little exposition brought a few more chuckles. Fraser looked at me.

"What's pitch-and-toss?"

Bill nearly choked on his onion. "You don't know what pitch-and-toss is?"

"I've never heard of it."

"Well," said Bill, a little glint in his piggy eyes, "would you like me to show you? I could give you a game." He took a few pence out of his pocket and looked round. "Anyone else want in?"

No one did. With dominoes you wouldn't lose much even if you lost all night. But with pitch-and-toss you could lose a lot of money very quickly. I tried to come to the young Scot's aid. "Why don't you just play for matches until Fraser picks it up?" Bill looked daggers at me but Fraser didn't seem bothered.

"No, I'll be all right. If Bill explains the rules I'll pick it up soon enough." He did. After about twenty minutes he was half a crown ahead and the game was over. Bill was furious.

"You've played this bloody game before!"

Fraser laughed. "And what if I have? You were all too happy to take advantage of me."

Bill said nowt and I tried to change the subject.

"Would anyone fancy a game of football next Sunday morning?"

There was no response. "Come on, fellas. The team's got its first fixture in a fortnight and we could do with a practice match beforehand. Bob Jamieson said he'd be willing to let anyone who wants to play swap shifts." There were still no takers.

"Och, they're afraid of being shown up." Fraser was one of our star players out on the wing. "It's all right – we'll go easy on you."

Some of us had got together to form a team. The problem was that the Chief would not let us have time off to play. Any practice sessions had to be in our own time and with people being on different shifts it was not easy. Bob Jamieson was as helpful as he could be and for once Mullins had not interfered. Our first fixture would be against the Gateshead Force and I was hoping that if we made a decent show the Chief might change his mind, but we needed practice and I was trying to encourage a few others to take part at next Sunday's session so we could have a proper game. It was looking like a non-starter. As I was leaving the room to go back on the beat Bill Spyles came out after me.

"Thompson plays for your team does he?"

"Aye."

"What position."

"Right wing. He's good and all."

"And you're trying to make up another team to play against you?"

I nodded. I was beginning to wonder what Bill was up to. It all became clear.

"Right. I'll play and I'll get a few others, so long as I can play left back – and not a word said to young Thompson; I don't want him catching cold."

"Well you might, Bill, when he runs rings round you."

Bill didn't laugh. But the look in his little piggy eyes gave him away. "I can look after myself."

Bill was as good as his word and by the next day we had the makings of a second team – it was mostly old timers, but at least we had a chance of having a game. We were only about three or four shy of a second eleven when I took the list to Bob Jamieson.

"Well, it's a start, Tom. I was thinking the other day, some of the lads at the boxing club were talking about starting a football team. Perhaps some of the older ones might be willing to turn out for our seconds."

Bob Jamieson helped to run a boxing club in Holborn. It seemed a good idea to me.

"We'll put the young lads up front – I can't see any of these doing much running about." He chuckled as he looked down the names. "John Burgess in goal and Sam Beecroft with Bill Spyles at the back. I'd tell your forwards to make sure they stuff plenty of cardboard down their socks." Shin pads were a luxury few of us could afford in those days.

The match was about two minutes old. Walter, who was playing centre forward, passed the ball back to me at right half. I'd shown off my dribbling skills by getting past one of the young lads from the club, and I sent the ball out wide to Fraser who took off at great speed, effortlessly going past two of the other side then cutting in to head straight towards Bill Spyles. Bill had a long sleeved jersey on with a white armband – the seconds didn't all have a strip – and his belly stuck out over his knee length khaki shorts. As Fraser got close he made to swerve past the full back, but Bill was too quick for him, made no attempt to play the ball but charged straight into Fraser and floored him. Bob Jamieson who was refereeing allowed play to go on. This set the pattern of the game. After three vicious shoulder charges Fraser at last managed to outsmart Bill. He'd got round him and was away for goal when Bill lunged with his right foot and scythed his legs from under him. This time the Ref gave a free kick. We had more success down the left wing where Alec Dorothy was giving Sam Beecroft a run for his money and by half time we were five one up. Fraser was limping heavily. Bob Jamieson called the two Captains over and suggested that we swapped a few players to even things up a little. He didn't want the lads from the club to become discouraged. Young Johnny Doyle had been up against Henry

Milburn at left back and having a hard time of it so he was swapped over to our team. Fraser moved to centre forward, Walter and Alec went to the other side.

I had been surprised to see the Chief Constable standing on the touchline with Henry Burnside. I hoped he had been impressed.

The second half got underway. As soon as I had the ball I passed it out to young Johnny. I wanted to see how he'd fare against Bill. Like most of the lads from the club, and some of our second team, Johnny was playing in an old pair of boots with extra segs hammered in but he was still quite nippy. As he came near to Bill he moved his body to the right, Bill anticipated his movement and went in hard. At the last minute Johnny swerved to the left, avoided Bill by a yard, and put over an inch-perfect cross which Fraser headed in. I had never seen the body swerve used before and neither had Bill. After a quarter of an hour of Johnny's tricks he realised he was being made to look foolish so announced he was out of puff and swapped places with John Burgess. Bill took John's cap and gloves and readied himself to keep goal. Johnny Doyle had even less difficulty against John Burgess. The cross came sailing over towards Fraser, but before the ball was anywhere near him the unfortunate Scot was on his back. Bill had come out quick and piled into him. This happened the next time Johnny sent over a cross so the young lad tried a new tactic. He ran in a lot closer to the goal before making as though to cross the ball. Bill went straight out towards Fraser. Johnny kept on coming and shot the ball into an empty net. Bill was stranded halfway out. Fraser went over to Johnny and slapped him on the back. "Well played, son."

The next time Johnny was on the ball it looked as though he was going to try the same tactic but Bill had learned his lesson. He came rushing out towards the young lad, Johnny quickly crossed the ball to Fraser who scored, but Johnny did not see the goal. Bill had decided he'd had enough of Johnny's tricks and had run straight into him sending him flying. Johnny was only a light weight; he hit the ground hard and didn't move for a good few moments. I was close to the lad and helped him to his feet. He was winded and shaken but otherwise able to continue. The Chief Constable had motioned to Bob Jamieson. They had a quick word. Bob came over, checked that Johnny was all right, walked over to Bill and sent him off the field. Bill went – in those days you didn't argue with the Ref.

He stood on the touchline for a while and then went over to the Chief Constable. He'd been one of the first recruits made by the newly appointed Chief Constable some twenty years before. He said a few words and then held out his hand in apology – accepted. When the match was over he went straight up to young Johnny, said sorry for his tackle and congratulated him on his game. Fraser was limping off. Bill held out his hand to him as well.

"We even now?"

Fraser thought twice but realised that it was not a good idea to have Bill as an enemy.

"Och aye." They shook.

Johnny Doyle's body swerve was the talk of the Shields nick. The Chief had also been impressed and later that week half a dozen brand new pig skin football boots and some tins of dubbin were handed over to the Boxing Club for use by the footballers. There had been some money spare in the Shoeless Children Fund.

The next time my path crossed with Johnny Doyle was in the line of duty. I was on the morning shift and I was patrolling down Long Row at about half past seven. I had my cape on as there was a persistent drizzle and a cold wind off the river. I was thinking that I might call in on one of the lodging houses. 'Everything all right?' 'Yes, Officer, would you like a cup of tea?' That was the usual drill, and if you were lucky and someone was having a cooked breakfast you might get a bacon sandwich as well, or a Shields kipper. I'd not seen Cuddie Cleghorn for quite a while and thought that I might look in at number 33. I was nearly there when a woman with a pinny on came running out the door. When she saw me she shouted out. "Thank heavens you're here. There's an awful barney gannin' on. A big fella's trying to murder Mr. Cleghorn."

Lodging housekeepers often had differences with their customers – you weren't talking about the best quality of people down the Long Row. They mostly took care of it themselves, but it looked as though I would have to earn my cuppa that morning. I ran in to the house. Cleghorn was on the floor holding on to the leg of a big, thickset, red headed man in his forties. The fellow was trying to get away but Cuddie was clinging on for grim death despite the thumps the other chap was giving him. I soon separated them. Cleghorn's customer calmed down as soon as he saw the uniform, but I still gave him a hefty clout in the shoulder to push him against the wall. Cleghorn had a nasty bruise to his left eye. He'd have a shiner and his glasses were broken. It was the old story: the lodger had tried to sneak out without paying.

"I thought you always took in advance."

"Aye I do. He weighed in two days ago and paid up for a night, but then came back yesterday and asked to stay for another. He seemed all right so I trusted him. He said he'd come to Shields to see an old friend who'd see him all right but was having a job finding him."

There was only one door in and out in most lodging houses so the landlord could make sure he was paid. If someone who was staying over didn't return then his belongings would be forfeit.

"What's your name?" I asked.

"'Arry Lacey."

"You got an address?" He shook his head again.

"I'm arresting you for assault."

"I was going to pay, but I 'ad one too many last night. I'm sorry, Mr. Cleghorn."

"I dain't want your apology I want me one and a tanner for the neet."

It didn't look like he was going to get it. I made 'Arry turn his pockets out – he only had a tanner left.

"You'll not leave me with nuffin'..." but Cleghorn was already pocketing the sixpenny bit.

I had to walk Lacey down to Keppel Street. He was a cockney. I didn't know what he was doing in these parts so I asked him who the friend was he was looking for. He didn't reply straight away; he was mulling over whether to tell me.

"Doyle. Bobby Doyle."

"Big Bobby or Little Bobby?" I asked. He didn't seem surprised that I knew the Doyles.

"The father."

"Is he out of Durham?" I asked.

"Oh, I didn't know he'd been inside."

"Well, if he's out, you won't find him round here. He lives down Holborn getting on towards Tyne Dock."

I explained how he could find the Doyles. It didn't do him much good. As I'd brought him in early we put him straight up to Court. He pleaded guilty and he was fined seven and six or six days for the assault. He had no money and no address so he would spend the next week in Shields nick. We could hold a prisoner for that long – it saved all the fuss of sending them to Durham.

It was well past eleven by the time I left Keppel Street. I crossed King Street and was walking up Salem Street when I saw Bill Spyles standing outside the Auction Rooms. He wasn't alone: Rosie Hindmarsh, the Auctioneer, was there. She was a big woman who always wore a tweed suit, a man's cloth cap and smoked cigars. You had to be very careful when selling anything to Rosie – she'd knock you down as low as she could. I went over. A horse and cart was standing outside and the carter was arguing with Rosie. A young lad was standing holding the horse's reins. As I came close I realised it was young Johnny Doyle.

"I thought you worked at the Yard."

"Aye I did. But it was only casual and me gaffer knows most of the carters. He got me fixed up with Mr. Simcox."

I knew Jack Simcox by sight; he did a lot of furniture shifting. If he didn't have a job on he would go round the houses asking if anyone had any old furniture they didn't want. He'd give a few pence and then take it round the Auction Rooms until he sold it.

I bid Bill a good morning. He didn't seem to be in a very good temper. "Rosie reckons she's had stock going missing over the past few weeks. I was down here yesterday and she made me search Bob Pratt's cart. There was nowt. Now she's accusing Jack Simcox."

"I'm doing no such thing." There was nothing wrong with Rosie's hearing. "All I'm saying is that things can't walk out of here on their own, and I've had no break-ins at night. If anything's leaving then the chances are it's going out on a cart."

I looked into the Rooms. Items were piled up all over the place. There were tables, desks, chairs, prams, sewing machines – anything you might want to buy or sell. I was thinking to myself that it would not be easy to see what was missing. Rosie read my thoughts.

"I know it looks a jumble but the things that have gone are quality – paintings, clocks, china, nothing too big but all good stuff – that's why I noticed."

"Rosie's well known for the quality of her stock, aren't you, dear?" Gilbert Hindmarsh's cultured tones interrupted his sister as he looked askance at an old mangle that was blocking the doorway. Rosie and her brother had inherited the family business but there had been a falling out. Gilbert was a well educated man but lacking in honesty. There'd been a scandal over some fake paintings and he'd narrowly escaped a spell in Durham. He no longer took an active part in the business but you'd often see him around.

Gilbert walked towards the cart. "I can't see what the fuss is all about. If Mr. Simcox took nothing then there will be nothing under his tarpaulin." He started to untie a rope. "Could you undo the other one, Officer?"

I looked at Bill, he nodded, the ropes came off and I rolled up the tarpaulin. There was a fair bit of junk.

"There I telt you. There's nowt of yours there." Jack Simcox was about to put the tarpaulin back when Rosie Hindmarsh pushed her left hand into a pile of rags.

"Wait a minute." She popped her cigar into her mouth and put both hands in. "Well, what have we here?" She pulled out a large porcelain jug.

"Yours, dear?" Gilbert enquired.

"You bloody well know it is, Gilbert. You were admiring it the other day. It's Staffordshire, eighteenth century and worth twenty quid of anyone's money. It's a quality piece, like the others that have gone."

Bill looked at Jack Simcox who didn't seem too bothered.

"Well, I've no idea how it got on the back of my cart. It's nowt to do with me. I unloaded a wardrobe and two chairs with young Johnny over there. He went out back to cover the cart up while I was in the office with Miss Hindmarsh. We had a bit of a natter and then I came outside. That's when Constable Spyles turned up."

"Well somebody must have put it there." Bill didn't have to say any more – all eyes looked at Johnny Doyle.

Gilbert Hindmarsh looked across at Simcox.

"How long's the lad been working for you, Mr. Simcox?"

"About six weeks."

"That's about the time I've noticed things going missing." Rosie Hindmarsh took the jug from Gilbert. "If you want to keep working for me, Jack, then the lad'll have to go."

"But I haven't done owt. Like Mr. Simcox said we unloaded, he went off with Miss Hindmarsh and I came oot here and covered up the cart. What would I want with an auld jug anyway?"

"Well, we'll have to take you and the jug down to the station, Johnny. We'll need to ask you some questions." Bill had no choice.

"You can do what you like to him, but this jug is going nowhere." Rosie could be an awkward customer and once she'd made her mind up it didn't change.

"We won't be able to bring charges without the jug, unless I arrest you as well for obstructing the Police." Bill was becoming a little tetchy. I thought it was time for me to step in.

"Are you saying you know nothing about the jug, Johnny? You

didn't take it?"

Johnny shook his head.

"I don't see how we could charge him anyway. Do you really think that a young cart lad could pick out a valuable jug from amongst all that?" I pointed into the shop.

"Well he's a Doyle. I had doubts about taking him on. He probably knows someone." Jack Simcox was starting to look worried; of course, if it wasn't Johnny then the finger pointed to him. Johnny said nowt; he knew that once his family was brought into it he wouldn't have much chance – everybody knew the Doyles.

"I'm sorry, Johnny, I should never have taken you on; you're sacked." Jack Simcox didn't mince his words. "And don't expect any pay for this week either."

It was Bill who jumped in this time. "I'm not having that. Tom's right: there's no evidence against the lad. You can sack him if you must, but you'll have to pay him what's due."

You didn't argue with Bill. Jack Simcox put his hand in his pocket and counted out a few shillings.

Young Johnny didn't know what to do with himself. He looked completely lost as he walked off. I caught up with him. "Do you want me to walk home with you and tell Mrs. Biddulph what happened?"

He shook his head. "She'll only worry the more if she sees me coming yem with a Bobby beside me." He looked down at his boots. "But could you have a word with me D... I mean Mr. Biddulph. You don't think I did it, do you?"

"No I don't."

I said I'd call round in a few days' time. I was taking Agnes to the Empire that night for the Music Hall and I had my weekly game of dominoes at the *Turk's* the night after.

Bill and I went our separate ways. I headed off back down to the Long Row – I still hadn't had my cup of tea. Cuddie Cleghorn was sat at the table going through the racing pages. I joined him without waiting for an invitation.

"Is there any chance of a cup of tea? I've been on the go since I left here." Cuddie shouted through to the kitchen and a few minutes later a middle aged woman brought two steaming cups of tea. I poured a couple of mouthfuls into the saucer, blew on it to cool, and gulped it down. I told Cleghorn about his cockney lodger who now had bed and board in Shields nick.

"It looks as though you won't get your money for last night."

Cleghorn looked at me and smiled. "Wo'nta?" He put his hand into the table drawer, pulled out a pocket watch and handed it to me.

"I'm always a bit suspicious of folk who want to pay later. He'd left his bag with me for safe keeping and I had a look through when he was oot. I found the watch; it's a good make. It doesn't work at the moment but it shouldn't cost much to put right. You'd better tell him I suppose. I'll keep it here for a fortnight and if he doesn't come back with what he owes me, I'll sell it."

"And you took a beating trying to stop him going out when you had that all the time."

"Aye. But it was on the spur of the moment and I didn't want the others getting any ideas." He took a sip of his tea. "You were a while getting back here."

I told him about the trouble at the Auction Rooms.

"That's funny, ye kna', I was looking round the Auction Rooms in King Street about a couple of months ago when the same thing happened. The Auctioneer, Mr. Sadler, was accusing some carter. I can't remember now who it was; it could have been Simcox. Anyway, something was found on the cart and it was the lad who took the blame. The carter said he'd only been working for him for a couple of weeks. He sacked him on the spot. Mr. Sadler said he wouldn't take it any further as the lad had lost his job."

I said nowt but I was thinking. It was quite common in shops for someone to pilfer a bit of money just after a new recruit had been taken on. The shopkeeper would almost certainly sack the new employee. Life could be hard. I decided to go back to Keppel

Street via the Market Place and I met up with Bill again. He was just coming out of the side room of the *Mariner's Arms*. I told him what Cleghorn had said to me. Bill may not have been the brightest spark but he had a lot of experience when it came to villainy.

"I never thought it was the lad. He's got an honest face and he didn't look worried in the slightest when you started rolling the tarpaulin back. How would he have known the value of that jug?"

"So you think it was Jack Simcox after all?"

"He's in on it but he needed someone this morning to put the jug on the cart when he and Johnny were unloading. That's the only time it could have happened."

"Gilbert Hindmarsh? You reckon he'd rob his own sister?"

"He'd sell his grandmother down the river for half a crown."

"Should we mention it to CID?"

"I want to find out a bit more first. You leave it to me, Tom."

I said no more. CID had their uses but most Bobbies preferred to do things the old fashioned way – leg work and talking to the right people. We all had our regulars who'd give us some information for the price of a pint.

It was a couple of days later that I thought to ask Bob Jamieson to tell Harry Lacey that he could recover his watch if he paid Mr. Cleghorn his dues.

"You're too late, Tom. He's out. Someone came in and paid his fine. You'll never guess who." My blank face must have given me away. "Bobby Doyle."

"Bobby Doyle? You mean he paid ten bob for Lacey's release?"

Bob Jamieson nodded. "I reckon they must have met inside. Lacey knew the drill in the cells. Bobby said he'd read about the fight at Cleghorn's in the Gazette. He's not been out of Durham long. I don't know where he got the money."

I was patrolling down the Long Row later that morning so I looked in on Cuddie Cleghorn. He was in a cheerful mood; Lacey had already been in. He'd worked out where his missing watch

227

might be.

"He had another fellow with him who paid the money."

"It was that bastard Bobby Doyle. Ye shouldn't let people like him in a respectable place like this." Hughie Ross came out of the kitchen, a drying up cloth in his hand. "It's bad enough the Polis callin' in every other bloody day after a cup of tea."

"That's a good idea. Why don't you bugger off and put the kettle on." Cleghorn and Hughie were as bad as one another.

"Well, if that was his name why did Lacey ask me if I knew where a Bobby Doyle lived?" Cleghorn asked.

"Did he tell you what the fellow he was after looked like?"

"Aye. He said he was a big lad, mind."

"Well, that'll Bobby Doyle's son, Little Bobby, but they usually live together – and thieve together."

A few minutes later Hughie Ross came in holding two mugs of tea by their handles in one hand and his crutch in the other. He put them down on the table. "I'm off oot noo." He stood waiting. Cleghorn put his hand in his pocket and gave him a tanner for the washing up. He picked up a slip of paper and handed it to Hughie.

"You'll put that on for me?"

"Aye, all reet, but if it wins you'd better give me a bloody tip."

I enjoyed my tea. I couldn't help thinking that Bobby Doyle must be up to something and I wanted to know where he had found his money, with him just out of Durham. Even if Lizzie was back on the game she was definitely past her best, and wouldn't be earning so much that Bobby could go splashing it about, particularly if Little Bobby had left home. I found out the answer to both these questions from an unexpected source.

That evening I called on Jimmy Biddulph. The Biddulphs lived in an upstairs flat on Green Street. Jimmy opened the door; he seemed surprised to see me.

"Did Johnny not tell you that I was calling round?"

"Aye, he did. It had gone clean out of my mind." He hesitated. "Tom, I've got a few comrades from the Union round tonight."

"Do you want me to come back later on?"

"Well, if you don't mind. We'll be finished in about an hour."

"I'll pop round to the *Queen's Head* then."

"Aye, all right then. I'll tell you what, Tom, these Union meetings make me thirsty. I'll see you in the *Queen's* in an hour. It might be better not talking in front of Johnny anyway. His father was round here yesterday, and Johnny's got a lot on his mind as it is."

An hour later Jimmy was sitting beside me in a quiet corner in the *Queen's Head*. The Landlord knew me so I had not had to pay for my whisky while I was waiting, and Jimmy bought me another when he arrived. I told him about the trouble at the Auction House and how I thought Johnny had been hard done by.

"Johnny told me about it. He said he didn't take owt, and I believe him, but it's good of you to back him up. I've managed to get him his job back at the Yard."

"Did you say that Bobby Doyle had been round?"

"Aye, we'd just finished tea when there was knock at the door. Wor hinny answered it – it was Bobby Doyle and she brought him up. Bobby said that he was just out of Durham. He'd returned to an empty house; Lizzie was out in the boozers, there was no sign of the bairns, no fire in the grate and only half a stale loaf in the larder. When Lizzie came back she'd told him that Johnny was living with us. Bobby and Ellen had left months ago, Lizzie didn't know where. He had come to ask Johnny if he knew where Little Bobby and Ellen were but Johnny didn't. Bobby asked if Johnny was working. When we told him that he had a job in the coal yard, Bobby said to get his things together, he was taking him back home. Johnny's face fell. He said he wasn't going. Bobby said that he was under twenty one and that he had no choice. The wife got up and went into our bedroom. I thought she was upset. I told Bobby Doyle that if Johnny didn't want to go then I wouldn't make him. He started shouting his mouth off. He said if he didn't come the neet, then he'd be straight down to Laygate nick to fetch a Polis. I was on the point of throwing

him down the stairs when wor Nell came back in. She had an old
baccy tin in her hand and she put it down on the table. 'I'm having
no barnies in this house. Not in front of wor Johnny. You look as
though you could do with something to eat, Mr. Doyle.' We'd had
panacklety for tea and there was still some left in the pan. It was
soon heating up on the coals. 'Now sit down at the table,' she said to
Bobby. I could tell by the look in his eyes that he was thinking about
the panacklety. She reached into the pantry and took out a jug.
'Johnny, you run down to the pub and fetch your Da' a pint of beer.'
Johnny took the jug and left. Nell spooned out a steaming dishful
for Bobby and cut him a couple of thick slices of bread. He didn't
wait for the butter and just sopped up the savoury broth. He must
have been famished. Nell sat opposite him. She opened the tin and
poured the contents on to the table, coins and notes. She counted it
all out as Bobby enjoyed his meal. 'Seven pounds five and tenpence.
When Johnny first came here he didn't work for six months he was
so thin, and we had to build him up. Now, we paid for all that. Since
he's been working he's given me his pay each week. He's never had
much more than ten or eleven shillings. I'd let him have a shilling for
himself and I kept the rest. I haven't told him but I put it to one side.
I thought he might need it later on – and feeding one mouth extra
doesn't cost much. I only took money out if he needed any clothes
or boots.' She looked Bobby Doyle straight in the eye. 'No Polis will
take Johnny out of here without a Court order and you'll see none
of this.' She was splitting the money into two piles as she spoke. 'I'm
going to keep the two pounds five and tenpence for what I've spent.
You can take the five pounds but you're never to set foot in here
again or come near Johnny, and you'll have to sign a paper saying
that you give up any claim on the lad and agree to us adopting him.'
Bobby Doyle said nowt but just pushed his plate forward. 'That's the
best panacklety I've had for years. Is there any more?' Nell gave him
another helping. 'I can see he's better off here, Mrs. Biddulph.' He
reached out for the five pounds. 'Just a minute.' Wor Nell opened
one of the table drawers and took out some paper and a pen and

ink. 'Here, Jimmy, you know how to write these things.' Well I just put down what she'd said and handed it to Bobby. 'Can you read it for me?' he asked me. I did and he then put a cross at the bottom. 'That's me mark.' He'd gone before Johnny got back. We shared the beer as a celebration."

"He sold his son for a fiver?"

"Aye, that's the Doyles for you. It was worth it to see the back of him."

That was the last I saw or heard of Bobby Doyle for some time. Henry Milburn who usually patrolled down the Long Row and Wapping Street told me that he'd come across the Doyles, father and son, fighting outside the *Burton House*. He'd broken the fight up and they'd each gone their separate ways. It must have been about the time that Bobby had been down Cleghorn's boarding house. After that he left Shields. Lizzie couldn't cope on her own and was taken to the Workhouse. Johnny didn't want to know, and Little Bobby and his sister had seemingly vanished.

About two weeks later Bill Spyles caught up with me in the Parade Room just before a shift.

"I'm going in to see the Big Fella, Tom. It's about that Auction House business with Jack Simcox. Will you come and back me up?"

"Aye, of course. Have you found something out?"

"Too bloody right. Jack Simcox and old Gilbert Hindmarsh have got a proper little racket going on."

Detective Inspector Norman Lamont was sitting at the big CID desk. The room was nearly full as there were two other plain clothes officers there, but we squeezed in. Bill described what had happened at Rosie Hindmarsh's Rooms and how his suspicions had been aroused by Cuddie Cleghorn's comments to me. He'd got the Bobbies with an Auction Room on their beat to call in, just as though it was routine, and to ask if there had been any thieving. There were about six big Auction Houses; four had had thefts over

the last year and in each case a new lad on Jack Simcox's cart had
been blamed. The lad had been sacked and so no report had been
made to the Police. Bill had got a couple of his informants to keep
an eye out on the two Houses that had not yet been targeted. Titch
Foster, a good for nothing who could blend into the background
anywhere, had kept an eye out at Bainbridges in Commercial Road.
He said that it had been done so slickly, that even he had nearly
missed it. Gilbert Hindmarsh had arrived at the Auction Rooms. He
had come to the front of the shop with a painting and had stepped
outside to look at it in daylight. Jack Simcox and his cart arrived.
Hindmarsh had placed the painting just inside the door while he
went off with the auctioneer to look at something else. Jack and his
lad unloaded a piece of furniture. When they came back to the front
door Jack gave the lad a piece of paper and sent him back into the
shop with it. He looked round, picked up the painting, put it on the
cart and covered it with some old rags.

"So old Gilbert Hindmarsh is up to his tricks again." The DI was
interested. "Do you know where they're taking the stuff?" he asked
Bill.

"Aye. Titch followed the lad after he'd left Simcox's yard one
evening and found out where he lived. I went round the next night
and had a word. He knew Mr. Hindmarsh. He said they'd made a
couple of deliveries for him to a shed down by the riverfront not far
from Kirton's Quay. He thought it was a funny sort of place to take
anything. He's a straightforward lad and he'll say nowt."

"Excellent work, Constable Spyles." The DI took things over
but kept me and Bill on the team. Jack Simcox was arrested two
days later at Bainbridges, stealing an antique silver plate and
Gilbert Hindmarsh who was on the premises was brought in for
questioning. Later that day Hindmarsh accompanied the DI down
to the riverside where the shed was searched. I was there. It was
quite a hoard but Hindmarsh did not seem too worried. He walked
over to a shelf at the back of the shed and picked up a thick sheaf of
papers which he handed to the Big Fella.

"There are my receipts, Mr. Lamont. I think you'll find them all in order."

There were receipts from all the Auction Houses in Shields. They were all similar – 'Item – Jug – oil painting or mirror, etc', with the price next to it; none were very expensive. The DI picked one at random. "Well which one does this apply to?"

Gilbert looked at the pieces which nearly filled the shed. "It would be hard to say, Inspector. Why don't you point to a piece that you think has been stolen and I will find the receipt."

All Bill's good work came to nowt. Rosie must have been round to her colleagues and when they were brought down to look at the collection, only one or two could identify something which they said might have been stolen. Gilbert picked out an invoice with a description resembling the piece and said he had paid for it. Jack Simcox was found guilty of stealing the one item from Bainbridges, given a ten pound fine and lost all his trade with the Auctioneers. Gilbert Hindmarsh was banned from all the Auction Houses. We heard on the grapevine that Rosie had given most of the stolen items back. She might have been sharp when it came to pricing but she was honest.

It was not a satisfactory result but at least we'd cleared Johnny Doyle's name, though little good that did for him as things were to turn out.

233

Long Bank

Toll for the brave

It was a time of unrest. Discontent was rife amongst the pitmen and
the colliery owners were refusing to make any concessions. Jimmy
Biddulph, the Miners' Leader, was often to be seen in the Market
Place where meetings were regularly held. They would mostly
pass off without incident, but occasionally you'd get a heckler and
there might be a bit of trouble. News of the agitation in Shields had
spread. Hedley Davies was becoming a popular figure in some parts
of the North. We had had dealings with him before. He had set up
a Party called Volunteers for Law and Order. His volunteers, thugs
by another name, had tried to break up one of the Miners' meetings
and they'd nearly succeeded.

Some of our old timers in the Force were not too keen on
the Union and would go in heavy handed. Jimmy Biddulph had
complained to the Chief Constable. He said that the Police were
siding with Hedley Davies' agitators. Inspector Mullins became
involved. He had been jostled by a couple of demonstrators after a
fight had broken out, and this had hardened his opposition to the
Miners' Union. He had asked the Chief to ban the next meeting.
The Chief was reluctant to do so but he had also been coming
under pressure from some of the Members of the Police Committee
to take a firm hand. He had decided to let the next meeting go
ahead but he warned Biddulph that if there was trouble future
meetings would be stopped. He then received a letter from Hedley
Davies who had heard of the Chief's decision and didn't like it. If
the Miners were going to be allowed to stir up social unrest then
the people of South Shields ought also to be allowed to hear from
those who stood up for law and order. He was proposing to hold a
meeting on the same day and at the same time as the Miners but on
the opposite side of the Market Place. The Chief felt that he had no
option but to ban both meetings. Jimmy Biddulph was furious. The
Miners' Union took legal advice and a Solicitor's letter landed on the
Chief's desk. It said that the Chief's decision was unlawful; he had

already given permission for the Miners' meeting, so he should only
have banned Hedley Davies's demonstration. The Miners would
go ahead with their plans and if any of their Union Stewards were
arrested they would sue the Chief Constable for false imprisonment.
Hedley Davies responded that if the Miners went ahead then he
would be there as well. The Chief had a top level meeting with
Henry Burnside, Mullins and Detective Inspector Norman Lamont.
He then spoke to the Chairman of the Police Committee. He told
the Miners and the Volunteers that he stood by his decision to ban
both meetings.

His plan for the day was that if the Miners and the Volunteers
turned up, plain clothes officers would mingle with the crowd and
take a note of the names of the ringleaders. If there was no trouble
then they could be dealt with later for breaching the banning order.
Mullins was to have a full complement of Constables on stand-by,
and if there was any breach of the peace then they would step in.
CID would be on hand to collar the ringleaders.

The Chief's strategy had caused a difficulty for the Big Fella. The
day of the Miners' meeting was a Friday, and every Friday morning
the money for the wages for Redheads at the West Docks was taken
by car from the National Bank in King Street to the riverside. An
armed detective accompanied the shipyard Wages Clerk and the
driver. In recent months there had been a spate of payroll robberies
in the North and the Detective Inspector had put on two of his
men as a precaution. It was agreed that on that particular Friday,
two Bobbies would be asked to go into plain clothes to cover. Bob
Jamieson asked for a couple of volunteers. It was no surprise to me
that Fraser Thompson was the first to step forward – he was always
keen to make a good impression. It was known that Bob Jamieson
would be retiring and it was an open secret that Fraser was after the
job – so was I, but for different reasons. The only chance I had of
going beyond the hand holding stage with our Agnes was to marry
her, and she had made it plain that she would never wed an ordinary
Constable. Bill Spyles was the only other one to come forward and

that was unexpected – Bill was one of the old school who never volunteered for anything.

I found out why a couple of days later. I was having a cup of tea in the Parade Room before going on the afternoon shift. Bill was there already with John Burgess.

"I hear you'll be looking after Fraser next Friday, Bill."

"Aye, but he'll have to look out for himself when the shooting starts. I only put my name forward on condition that I had the gun."

"You mean there's only one?"

Bill laughed. "You're not still in the Army now, Tom. There's one gun. The Big Fella keeps it locked up in his desk. He gives it to the Detective whose turn it is to act as guard and when he returns he gives it back. It's an old revolver from the Boer War. I've been itching to get me hands on it for years."

"Do you think the gang are going to have a go then?"

"It's very likely. They hit the payroll for Parsons at Sunderland a couple of weeks ago. They only managed to snatch one bag. I reckon Shields is a likely target."

"Were they armed?"

"Pick axe handles."

John Burgess chortled. "Pick axe handles or not, I wouldn't like to be in their shoes if Bill starts blasting off with his revolver."

"You mean you'd shoot them, Bill?"

Bill slurped a mouthful of tea from his saucer. "Of course I'll shoot the buggers."

I went on patrol. I was walking down King Street at about half past three and thought I would look in at the North of England Café. Gertie Ruffle, Walter's girlfriend, worked there. I popped my head round the door; it was quiet and Gertie waved me in. "Hello, Tom, I'm just going to have a cup of tea out the back. Would you like to join me?"

There was a room at the back of the Café where food brought out from the kitchen would be collected and where all the cutlery and table settings were kept. The waitresses would have their own meals there. Walter had started making a habit of popping in when it was quiet and the Manageress had suggested to Gertie that she should take him into the back room. I felt quite honoured. As I drank my tea Gertie said that she had wanted to have a word with me. I guessed what was coming; we shared a similar problem. I wanted to marry Agnes but she wouldn't have me until I became a Sergeant; Gertie wanted to marry Walter but he wouldn't pop the question. Walter couldn't understand why someone as pretty as Gertie could see anything in him, and he lacked the confidence to propose to her. I'd talked to him before but he just couldn't pluck up the courage. Gertie was not happy.

"Me Mam and Dad keep getting on at me. We've been going out together for four years and we're not even engaged. Do you think he wants to get married?"

"I know for a fact that you're the only girl for him. I think he's afraid that you'll say no."

"Could you say something to him?"

"I have before but he's done nowt about it."

"Well, I'm going to have to do something. I used to go out with Herbert Hodges. We've known each other since Sunday School. He's still keen on me. Me Mam keeps asking him round for tea on Sundays. She's never been over-fond of Walter."

The cook came in from the kitchen. He placed a large tray of treacle tarts on the table in the middle of the room. "I'm leaving them there to cool down. They're just out of the oven and I divvent want any gannin' missin'." He went back through the kitchen door. Gertie looked at me and we both got up and walked over to the table. The sweet smell of treacle was overpowering and the small golden brown tarts looked irresistible. She reached out and picked up two of them.

"Here. We'll have to be quick before he comes back in."

We started at the edges. The pastry was not too bad but the treacle filling was red hot. We'd nibbled our way through about half when we heard the heavy step of the cook. Gertie looked at me in panic. She put the whole tart into her mouth, I did the same. As the burning hot treacle touched the roof of my mouth I nearly leapt off the ground – Gertie grabbed my hand and pulled me into the linen cupboard. It was just big enough for two. We suffered in silence still holding hands as the cook's footsteps came into the room, stopped as he placed something else on the table, and then receded into the kitchen. The last of the tart had gone down what would be a blistered gullet. Gertie half opened the door and we looked at each other. She was trying her best not to laugh and cry at the same time. We were very close – I put my arm round her waist but she pushed me away still laughing. As we stepped out of the cupboard the cook came back through the door.

"Your helmet's on the table – it gave you away. These girls always fall for the hot treacle tarts but I'm surprised at ye." He laughed and went on through to the café.

I began to look at Gertie in a different light after that, but Walter was my friend. The next time we went swimming I told him that he had to put the question.

"I can't, man. I've tried to many a time, but at the last minute me legs gan to jelly."

"Well, if you don't someone else will."

"Who?"

"Herbert Hodges."

"Aw, him. I met him once. He's a Sunday School teacher. I've nowt to worry aboot there."

"I was having a cup of cha in the North of England the other day with Gertie who told me that her mother had started to lay down the law; she wants Gertie married and off her hands – if you don't ask her then she'll make sure that Herbert will."

Walter looked thoughtful for a couple of minutes until his normal blank look took over.

Nobody knew what was going to happen on the Friday of the Miners' meeting. They would normally advertise it with handbills but this time it was word of mouth. They didn't want us, or Hedley Davies' louts come to that, to know the start time. They would normally begin at about two and Mullins had asked the afternoon shift to report early for Parade. He'd doubled up the beats in and around the Market for the morning in case things kicked off early. It was just as well. Walter and I had decided to meet up on the Friday morning and have an early lunch at the North of England Café before heading into the nick. We were crossing the Market Place about half past eleven. Sam Beecroft and Alec Dorothy were standing on Crofton's Corner. Sam was starting to look worried.

"The pubs have been busy since opening time. It wouldn't surprise me if they were going to start early." There were a lot of people in the Market Place, most of them Miners. I thought that Sam could be right.

"Hey, look over there." Alec pointed to a cart that was approaching the old Town Hall in the middle of the Market Square. A couple of fellows started unloading planks and very soon a platform was being erected. Jimmy Biddulph came out of the *Tram* and waved at us as he headed out onto the Market Place.

"Tom, would you get down to the Station and tell Mullins. Walter, run down the Long Row and ask Henry Milburn and John Burgess to come up. They said they'd stay close so you shouldn't have any trouble finding them." Sam had had his orders from Mullins and he would wait for the others to arrive before doing anything.

As I reached Keppel Street I bumped into Bill Spyles and Fraser Thompson. They were waiting outside the Station for the Shipyard's car to pick them up and go on to the Bank. I was surprised to see them in uniform. The wages escort was usually in plain clothes. The gun was clearly visible in its holster around Bill's protruding belly.

"It's Mullins panicking as usual. He thinks that we may be needed to have a go at the miners on the way back from the docks. He didn't want us to waste any time coming back to Keppel Street to get changed."

"Well don't go shooting any miners, Bill!" was my retort. Bill just scowled and I went on in to the building.

Inspector Mullins was not too pleased at the news.

"That's all I need; CID are all right – they don't work shifts like us. I'm going to have to call out the Fire Brigade."

It wasn't to put any fires out. The men who went out with the tender were on standby. Once the Fire Bell was rung they'd come running; most of them lived in the houses in the Police building. Some would be on shift but Mullins would be able to raise a few others to help out in the Market Place until the two o'clock shift came on. Mullins left Bob Jamieson to do the necessary. He looked at me. "What are you waiting for, Duncan? Change into your uniform and then you can drive me up to the Market in the sidecar."

When we had arrived Mullins asked me to stay with him in case he needed to pass any urgent messages back to Keppel Street. I had a clear view of all that went on in the Market Place, but missed the attempt on the Dock's wages in King Street. I heard it at first hand when the dust had settled.

Henry Gill, the Wages Clerk, was matchstick thin and no more than five foot tall. He wore wire glasses and there was always a Senior Service cigarette between his lips. He had a rich bass voice which belied his small stature. The Dock car had picked up Bill and Fraser from Keppel Street and they accompanied Henry Gill into the Bank. The driver of the Rover – Jock Murdoch, a big surly looking fellow who didn't say much – remained outside. It didn't take Henry long to check that the money was all there; the notes went into a briefcase and the coin was in a canvas bag. Fraser offered to carry the bag but Henry declined.

"I'm responsible for the money once it leaves the Bank, Officer. Your job is to stop anyone from taking it from me."

The Bank Manager himself accompanied them to the door. Redheads was his biggest client. As they came out Big Jock slowly opened his door to come round to let Henry in the back. He was in no hurry. Suddenly four fellows with pick axe handles jumped out of a car parked across the road and came at them. Bill whipped the pistol from the holster and levelled it at the nearest attacker.

"Stop or I'll shoot."

The man kept coming. Bill pressed the trigger – nothing happened. The pick axe handle smashed into the side of his head and he went down. Henry had opened the car door himself and shouted to Jock to get in the car. Fraser pulled out his truncheon and got between the car and the attackers. He took a nasty blow on the arm but managed to knock one of them back. The man who'd felled Bill was about to finish Fraser off when little Henry jumped out of the car and shouted for help at the top of his voice. The assailant hesitated a second and Henry barged into him. He didn't have much effect and was knocked to the ground, but it gave Fraser a chance to steady himself against the car. Then Bill staggered to his knees spitting teeth and blood. He whipped out Gentleman Jim and it hammered into the legs of the man who'd put him down. There was a crack of breaking bone and a screech of agony as the man hit the pavement. Bill then went for the three men around Fraser. He was only just in time. The young Scot took another blow to his arm and had turned deathly pale but Bill meant business. A blow to the head felled one; Bill took a hit on the left forearm but got his own strike into the ribs of the third man who sank to his knees and who Bill finished off with a short arm knock to the head. The fourth man ran to the car but was too late. The driver had seen Bill at work and took off. Jock Murdoch slipped the Rover into gear, put his foot down and rammed the other car. He then got out and dragged the stunned driver from his seat and gave him a good punching. Unlike Henry Gill he preferred taking on the unarmed. The last of the gang stopped in his tracks, turned on his heels, and headed towards the Market Place. Henry Gill was on his feet – he shouted to the passers-by to stop the thief and a couple of men ran after him.

Those of us in the Market knew nothing of this at the time. We saw a man run up from King Street being chased by a couple of other fellows. As he pushed into the crowd one of the miners went to stop him. He blurted out that he was a pitman himself from Harton Colliery and that he was being chased by the Volunteers. Then the fun started. The miners let him through and stopped the pursuers. Mullins saw the disturbance and shouted out to draw truncheons and move in. Norman Lamont, who was in the crowd with three of his detectives, went to arrest Jimmy Biddulph and one or two of his Committee men. Things looked as though they could turn nasty. I could just about see the raised platform from where I stood. Norman Lamont was talking to Jimmy. Jimmy then stood up and raised his loud hailer to his mouth. He asked all the miners to remain calm. They were not to resist the Police. There was a lot of muttering but slowly things quietened. He then thanked the crowd for their support but told them that the Police insisted that the meeting could not go ahead. He was going to accompany the Inspector to the Police Station of his own free will. The Union would challenge the Chief Constable's decision in the Courts. He was formally arrested as he stepped down from the Platform but the Big Fella only lightly touched his shoulder and they walked together through the crowd.

Whilst this was going on the Bank Manager had come running up from King Street. He had first spoken to Walter who was standing on the edge of the crowd. Walter had waved me over and ran to get Mullins. When we got to the Bank, Fraser and Henry Gill were sitting on the running board of the Rover. They didn't look good. Bill was a real sight, with the right side of his face all smashed in and blood running down his cheek, but he was on his feet and in charge, standing over the robbers with Gentleman Jim ready to lash out. The Bank Manager had rung the Station and it was not long before Henry Burnside came striding up. He'd brought with him the two old timers who manned the Chief's Office, the only two Constables who were not out on duty. He was out of breath when he arrived – Henry was not used to physical exercise.

"The Black Maria's on its way." He paused and looked around. "A bloody ambulance is what we need. Well done, lads. I'm glad you didn't need to use the gun."

Bill just stood there saying nowt, then he picked the gun up, pointed it at Henry, raised the barrel to the sky and pulled the trigger. Nothing happened. Bill could hardly speak but he managed to get in a few words I'd prefer not to repeat in a book that might be read by women and children. We later found out that the gun had not worked for years but no one had thought to tell Bill.

Henry Burnside was a big man who had got where he was as much for his brawn as his brain. He put his hand round Bill's shoulder.

"I'm sorry, Bill. You did bloody well. Now we'll have to get the payroll down to Redheads. Inspector Mullins, can you organise two replacement guards?"

Before Mullins could say anything Bill spoke, quietly but firmly, blood still trickling down his chin.

"There's no need. I'll finish the job and so will Fraser."

Fraser didn't look quite so sure about it as Bill did, but said nowt. He was deathly pale, and barely made it to his feet, his left arm hanging useless by his side. Henry Gill had a nasty gash on his forehead but he said that he too must go.

Henry Burnside was visibly moved.

"Aye. But you go strite to the Ingham afterwards. All three of you. You'll drive them, Jock?" Jock nodded.

"Just had on a minute first." He then strode across the road and went in to the *Golden Lion* – he was a regular. He came straight out again holding a bottle of whisky in one hand and five glasses in the other. He poured out a stiff measure and gave a glass to each of the wounded, then one to Jock and he downed one himself. Bill had a job drinking but he managed and returned the glass to Henry with a grateful look of thanks. Suitably fortified the four men in the car made ready to move off. The Superintendent looked at me. "What are you waiting for, Duncan? You gan ahead and give them an escort."

By the time we'd reached the dockyard word had already

reached them of the attempt on the wages. We were greeted like heroes. There was a big crowd outside the offices. If the wages had been snatched then they might not have received any money until Monday and that would have meant no beer at the weekend for the men and in some cases no food for the family. Henry Gill went in with the money and we stayed outside. The effects of the Super's whisky had worn off and Fraser in particular was looking distinctly fragile. I had a quiet word in the Manager's ear and in a couple of minutes his Secretary came out with a tray carrying a bottle of Malt and some glasses. I had my share this time. By the time we left the Yard the wounded heroes were in better shape but we wasted no time in going to the Ingham Infirmary. The doctors had been forewarned of our impending arrival and Henry Gill, Bill and Fraser were taken straight into the accident ward. The three robbers had been given some preliminary care but they were moved to one side so that our men could be tended first. Sam Beecroft and Alec Dorothy were on guard. I went over to join them and cast an eye over the three villains.

"I know him," I said. "It's Harry Lacey. He's a friend of Bobby Doyle. I bet he was the one who got away."

"Aye, they already know, Tom," Sam responded. "Jimmy Biddulph recognised Doyle in the Market Place. He's told the Big Fella. They're on the lookout for him now."

As soon as I returned to Keppel Street I went along to the CID Office to see the Detective Inspector. I told him that I had heard that Bobby Doyle's son Little Bobby was living down the Wapping Street area, and that I suspected that Big Bobby would try to contact him.

"Thanks Tom, I'll tell Mullins but I don't want us going in mob-handed this time." We all remembered the troubles that had been caused by the raids led by Mullins looking for Mickey Jobling.

"We'll ask the beat Bobbies to keep their eyes peeled and I'll send a couple of plain clothes men down there as well."

Most of the shift was in the Parade Room having a cup of tea. I sat down beside Walter who looked thoughtful for once. "I've made up my mind. The next time I see Gertie I'm definitely gan' to ask her."

"Well make sure you take her somewhere romantic before you pop the question."

"Aye, I was gan' to take her for a walk roond the South Park this Sunda'." I said nowt.

The next day I was on the lookout for Hughie Ross. If you stood in the Market Place long enough you'd see him. At about half past three he came out of the *Mariner's Arms*.

"What d'ye want?" was his greeting as I walked over to him.

"You know Bobby Doyle, don't you?"

"Aye and before ye ask I've not seen him, and even if I had, I wouldn't tell ye."

"Do you know his son Little Bobby?"

"No. That bastard Bobby Doyle tricked me oot of some money before the War and I've had nowt to do with him since. Besides they live doon Holborn and I divvent get roond there much."

"Little Bobby's left home. He's been seen down by the *Burton House*. There might be some money in it for you if you could find him."

"What's he look like?"

"He's a big fella with black hair and a shifty look, just like his old man. He might have his sister living with him."

"Well, I'll need a few pence for a pint if I'm gannin' into the *Burton Hoose*."

I gave him a tanner. "And that's all until you find him."

"Reet, well bugger off noo. I'll get a reputation talkin' to ye all the time."

A couple of days later Cuddie Cleghorn was waiting in the corridor outside the Charge Office at about ten o'clock at night as I came in at the end of my shift.

"I'm glad to see you. Auld Hughie's taken a beating. They brought him up from outside the *Burton Hoose*. He's got a black eye, a cut lip and a couple of sore ribs, the poor bugger. I've patched him up as best I can. He's no money for a doctor. He said I had to tell you."

It was the end of a long day but I had an idea what had happened to Hughie so I went back down the Long Row with the boarding house keeper. Hughie was in a room with three others who were trying to get off to sleep so we couldn't say a lot. Even by the light of the flickering candle I could see that Hughie had been given a right going over.

"It was that bastard Little Bobby all reet." Hughie's whisper reverberated round the room. "I clocked him in the *Burton Hoose* the other neet. He's gannin' by the name of Anderson. He works at Coulson's Tallow factory. I went roond there the next day and followed him yem. He lives in Wapping Street just past Shotton Bank. Him and his wife have the top room. I hung around a bit and saw Tommy Surtees – I've known him for years – he says they keep themselves to themselves. It was a shame aboot the bairn. It died a couple of days after the birth. I saw Little Bobby in the *Burton* last neet. I asked him if he was any relation to Bobby Doyle from doon Holborn way. He said nowt but when I left he came after me and gave me this to keep me mouth shut."

"Aye and if you divvent keep it shut ye'll get another bloody beltin'. I've got to get up at six."

I put my hand on Hughie's shoulder, slipped a florin into his hand and left him to his sleep.

The DI was interested.

"There was one thing that worried me, Sir. I don't believe for a minute that Bobby's married, and why would he change his name? Do you remember when we nicked him down Holborn he was very protective of his sister? I can't see him going anywhere without her."

He looked at me. There were certain things you didn't like to mention and incest was one, but it did happen.

"Talk to the District Midwife and if you're still suspicious we'll go round. You can identify her?"

I nodded. I had been very close to Ellen in a yard up from the *Queen's* in Holborn. The District Midwife remembered the Andersons as a slovenly couple. The baby had been born with a crooked backbone and was covered with black hair. It had been a blessing that it had died. She suspected that they'd smothered it – that wasn't too uncommon but you could never prove anything. Babies like that were often the results of incestuous relationships, but she'd had no reason to believe that Mr. and Mrs. Anderson were other than a normal couple. She gave me a description of Ellen Anderson – it fitted.

The next evening at half past six I accompanied the Big Fella and the District Midwife. Henry Milburn was with us and we had Walter and John Burgess not far behind in case of trouble. As soon as Little Bobby answered the door the Big Fella pushed past him into the room and we followed. Ellen was standing by the table.

Norman Lamont looked at the Midwife. "Is that the woman you know as Ellen Anderson, living with this man as his wife?"

"Aye, and they had a bairn together."

Lamont looked at me. "Do you know this woman, Constable Duncan?"

"She's Ellen Doyle and that's her brother Bobby."

The Detective Inspector's face was grave and his voice deadly serious. "Ellen and Bobby Doyle, I'm arresting you for incest."

I had noticed that there were two empty plates on the table and a pudding basin tied in a cloth. I went over and placed my hand on it. It was hot. I untied the cloth, the savoury smell told me what it was.

"I know someone who's very partial to a dish of panacklety. It's for your father, isn't it?" Bobby said nowt. Ellen was crying and wasn't in any state to talk. Henry Milburn and the Midwife led them outside. The Big Fella motioned for me to stay.

"We'll never find him in this warren at night. He's probably in one of the old sheds down by the River. We'll get a search organised for tomorrow."

"It's a cold night out, Sir. If no one turns up with his grub I'd put money on Bobby coming knocking on this door."

Norman Lamont paced the wooden boards. "You could be right. I'll get Heron to keep you company and you can wait here. I'll tell Inspector Mullins. If Doyle doesn't turn up by ten o'clock he'll have to relieve you or call it off."

It was better than walking the beat. There was a cold nor'easter blowing with showers of icy rain.

Walter and I settled in for a night by the fire. There was only an oil lamp for light but there were plenty of coals. The bowl of panacklety was still on the table. Walter kept looking at it. "D'ye think that panacklety'd gan to waste?"

I was feeling a little peckish myself. We found some bread in the pantry cupboard but no butter. It didn't matter. We shared the dish and then Walter put the kettle on for a brew. There was no milk so we were having it black. Then we heard footsteps coming up the stairs. We put our cups down and went over to the door. Walter drew his truncheon. There was a quiet tap on the door. I pulled it open and grabbed the caller by the lapels.

"Hey what y'er deein'?" It wasn't Bobby Doyle's voice. I pulled him inside – it was young Johnny – he seemed relieved to see us. "I thowt it was wor Bobby gannin' to give us a hidin'. He doesn't like me coming roond. I just wanted to check that wor Ellen was all reet." He looked down at his boots. "I was gannin' to tell them to turn the auld fella' in. Mr. Biddulph had told me that you were after him and that you thought he might be with wor Bobby."

"I'm sorry, Johnny. We've just arrested Bobby and Ellen."

"For hiding the auld fella'?"

There was no way round it. "No, Johnny, for incest."

Walter chipped in. "Did ye kna' what they were up to?"

Johnny didn't answer straight away. "It wasn't Ellen's fault. You can't say no to Bobby when he wants something. That's why I left home. Me Fatha' was inside, me Mutha' was always drunk and didn't care. But after I left the neighbours started talkin'. That's why

251

Bobby moved doon here."

"Come and sit down, Johnny; Walter's just made a pot of tea."

"Na, I'd better gan yem."

I explained to Johnny why we were here. "It would be awkward for us if you met your old man coming up the stairs."

He didn't say much. He sat in the chair I'd vacated and sipped his tea. He wasn't in the mood for conversation. Walter made up for it. He'd finally put the question to Gertie and she'd accepted. They were going to keep the engagement quiet until Walter had bought a ring. Her parents wouldn't be able to object then.

It was about nine o'clock when we heard a noise on the landing. There was a very gentle knocking on the door panel. "Are ye there, Bobby?"

It was Doyle all right. I went to the door and was just about to open it when Walter stood up and stamped his boots on the wooden floor. Bobby Doyle didn't wait. He knew the sound of a copper's boot and was off down the stairs like a flash with me after him. When I got outside the cold rain hit me. I cursed the Doyles but it was too late to go back inside for my greatcoat and cape. Bobby was racing along a deserted Wapping Street – there was no one else about. I put my whistle to my lips and blew it hard. Henry Milburn and John Burgess wouldn't be far away. I could hear Walter's boots clattering over the cobbles behind me. Water was streaming down my face. My helmet was back in the room. I was not made for sprinting and Walter soon overtook me. He'd brought his lantern with him.

"Keep blowing your whistle, Walter," I shouted. Johnny Doyle had followed Walter out and he flew by me over the cobbles. We'd reached the foot of Long Bank then I just caught sight of Johnny turning down an alley off Shadwell Street. When I reached the corner I couldn't see much. I stayed put. Every time I heard Walter's whistle I gave a blast on my own. I saw a headlight coming towards me. It was the motorbike. I could see two Bobbies running behind – John Burgess and Henry Milburn, no doubt. Mullins stepped out of the side car.

"They're down there," was all I said and off we went. Mullins shouted to the motorbike driver to head back to the nick and send out the Black Maria.

When we reached the end of the alley there was an old warehouse. I blew my whistle and Walter responded from up river. We went round the old building and found ourselves on a derelict quay. At the far side a lamp was swinging backwards and forwards to attract our attention. Johnny Doyle was holding Walter's lantern.

"They're up there," he shouted pointing to a dilapidated old shed – a beam led up to the ramshackle hut. Walter had reached the top; he was clinging on to the door and we could hear Bobby Doyle shouting – he wasn't going to give himself up. Then Walter managed to push in the door. A moment later there was a crash of splintered wood and two entwined bodies fell into the Tyne.

We shone our lanterns over the water. The tide was on the turn and the river was full. The water was inky black. I was a qualified lifeguard but I did not fancy going in. The decision was made by someone else. I heard a helmet and cape hit the ground and the next thing I saw was Mullins diving into the murky waters. I didn't wait. Walter was my friend and I was not going to let Mullins take the glory. I undid my tunic and kicked my boots off – you needed as little as possible to pull you down. As I hit the water the cold sliced into me like a blade. My breath was nearly sucked right out of my body. I surfaced and tried to stay calm but could see very little. Then a light from a lantern found me. I caught sight of a head just downstream. The current had me and I was travelling fast. I kicked with my feet and swam on. The head had become a hand waving out of the water as the river pulled downwards. I dived as hard as I could. I could see nothing but my hand touched something. I grabbed a body and pushed hard towards the surface. It was Mullins. As we both gasped for air he started struggling. I gave him a slap and shouted to him to hold on. It was pitch black and I could barely make out the shore. I then heard a whistle and kicked in that direction. A lantern appeared and I saw the quayside. I was starting to feel the cold now and Mullins was a dead weight. I managed to grab hold of a wooden pillar that supported the quay. There were no ladders. A lantern shone down. I then heard John Burgess's voice.

"Had on, Tom. We've got a rope."

A rope came over the edge. I tried to get it round Mullins but my fingers were frozen and my strength had gone. "I can't do it."

"Had on." I heard voices. If I let go of Mullins I would be saved. Otherwise we'd both go under. The next minute Johnny Doyle was dangling on a rope next to me. He said nowt, just tied the rope under Mullins' arms. Even with the two of us it was a job. He then held on to me while they tried to pull Mullins up. He was too heavy. I heard John Burgess say, "You'll have to come up, Johnny, to give us a hand; had on, Tom." I put my arms round the wooden post and held on for grim death. Johnny went up quickly and then all three pulled up Mullins. Even so it seemed to take an awful long time. Then Johnny was back down with the rope. I was not in good shape and was of little help. Johnny went up again and then I was being pulled upwards. I felt a strong hand on my shirt collar and I was on the quayside. Henry Milburn and John Burgess took off their capes and greatcoats and wrapped them round me and Mullins. He was lying on the quay beside me. "Thanks, Henry. Thanks, John," was all I could mumble.

"We couldn't have done it without the lad. He was the only one light enough to gan' doon. But he's strong for his age; we couldn't have hoiked you out without him." Johnny was hugging himself with his arms and I could hear his teeth chattering. We then saw lanterns coming towards us.

We went back to Keppel Street in the Black Maria and were soon huddled round the stove in the Charge Office. We'd taken off our wet clothes and were wrapped in blankets from the cells. The Police Surgeon was on his way to check us over. Henry Burnside was there; he had been in his office upstairs. He often called in of an evening as it gave him a chance to get away from the wife, and he'd have a drink on the way home. He looked us over, then went up to his office and came back with a bottle of whisky. He laced the hot tea we were drinking.

"Is there any news of Walter?"

Sergeant Jamieson shook his head. "I've got half a dozen officers down there combing the river bank but it's as black as pitch. The River Police have put a launch out."

We were all quiet. The whisky was poured out again. Henry and Bob had one as well. Jimmy Biddulph and his wife turned up with dry clothes for young Johnny. The Sergeant had sent a man round to their house. I shook young Johnny's hand. He was a bit unsteady on his feet; he wasn't used to strong drink and his exposure to the cold was taking its toll.

The Chief came in just as Johnny was leaving. He had a few words with the Biddulphs and patted Johnny on the back. His first words to Bob Jamieson were the same as the Superintendent's. "Any word on Constable Heron?"

He came over to me and Mullins. He put his hands on our shoulders and said, 'Well done'. It was all that was needed. He left with Henry Burnside. He was going to see Alderman Heron, Walter's uncle, to break the news. He would then head down to the riverside to show support to the officers. When he arrived there and saw the conditions he called the men back to Keppel Street until dawn.

The Police Surgeon checked us over. Mullins was to have bed rest for a couple of days, but I was told to keep warm and have a good night's sleep. Bob Jamieson had found some spare uniforms and a couple of old overcoats. He said he'd get his wife to wash our old ones. Mullins had not said much. He was still shivering. As he was about to leave he held his hand out to me, "Thank you, Tom, you saved my life."

I shook my head. "No, you can't say that."

He looked at me but before he could say any more I just said, "They say that if you save someone's life you're responsible for them for ever after."

Bob Jamieson chuckled. Mullins merely nodded his head. He'd told me the same after he'd stopped a Frenchman from knifing me in the back. He patted me on the shoulder and went out.

Bob Jamieson came over to me. "When McIver's dropped the Inspector off he'll take you home, Tom." McIver was not on duty but he'd heard what had happened and had offered to help. He was driving the motorbike and sidecar.

"Thanks. I'm going to have to tell Gertie Ruffle. I'll ask McIver to take me there first if it's all right, Sarge."

"Aye, of course it is."

McIver did not mind. When we reached the Ruffles' house it was nearly midnight and there were no lights on. I gave the heavy cast iron knocker a good belt. It took a while before I saw a light through the transom. The door opened a few inches and I saw Mr. Ruffle's head looking out. He saw the uniform and called out into the room where his wife would have been standing. "It's the Polis."

"Can I come in, Mr. Ruffle. I've got some bad news for your Gertie."

"Wor Gertie? Aye, well you better come in." McIver had pulled the canvas cover over the bike and he came in as well. It was still pouring down.

There were only a few dying embers on the fire and it was cold. Gertie guessed as soon as she saw me that something had happened to Walter. She listened to what I had to say.

"But you haven't found a body?"

McIver answered. I was starting to feel my own grief.

"There's nae hope, pet, I'm sorry. Not in this weather. Tom here and the Inspector were only in the watter themselves for five minutes and they wouldn't have lasted much longer."

Gertie started crying. She looked at her mother.

"We were going to get engaged."

Her mother put her arms round her. There was not much left to say.

The search started again at dawn but no bodies were ever found. The Doyle name was condemned throughout Shields, and news of the charge of incest against Bobby and Ellen only deepened the sense of outrage. Jimmy Biddulph later told me that Johnny didn't go out for a fortnight.

They had a memorial service for Walter. It was a moving occasion. All the Force was there along with the Aldermen, Councillors and Magistrates. The Chief had wanted to put Mullins and me forward for a medal but we'd declined. Walter had been the hero and it had cost him dear. He was awarded the King's Police Medal for gallantry – posthumously.

I carried on the beat as usual but my heart didn't seem to be in it. Agnes and I would take Gertie out with us whenever we went to the pictures or just for a walk. I would often pop in to the North of England Café for a cup of tea.

Bob Jamieson announced his retirement. Walter's sudden death had made me realise that you had to take your chances while you could. I told Agnes that I was going to apply for the job and that afterwards I'd be popping the question whether I was successful or not. She gave me a strange sort of smile. Fraser Thompson was also in the running. He was a strong candidate, had been part of the team that had stopped the payroll robbery, and he had not put anyone's back up. Whilst he had been recovering from the injuries he had sustained outside the National Bank he was seconded to work in the Chief's Office. Fraser had gone out of his way to make himself helpful, and had even asked to borrow the Chief's copy of the Justices' Manual to study at home in the evenings.

I was at home myself one night warming my feet by the fire and reading some Burns. I had a glass of whisky on the grate. There was a knock at the door; I went down; it was McIver. I asked him in.

"Can you come round to our house, Tom? Gertie Ruffle came calling about an hour ago. She's in an awfu' state."

"I'll just put my coat on." I could see McIver looking at my glass of whisky. "I'd offer you a drink but don't you think we'd better go straight away?"

"Well, it's bitter cold out there and a wee drop would no doubt quicken my step." I poured him a glass.

When we arrived at the McIvers' Agnes took me straight into the scullery. She wanted to have a word with me.

"Gertie's pregnant." Agnes never minced her words. "She gave in to Walter when he asked her to marry him. She told her parents tonight and they threw her out."

"They what?"

"Showed her the door – they're strict Methodists and Mr. Ruffle wasn't having disgrace brought on the family."

"I suspect it was more Mrs. Ruffle. She never liked Walter."

"Well, there's only one thing to do."

I looked at her. I had a feeling that I wasn't going to like what was coming.

"You're going to have to marry her."

"What?" My Agnes had had some strange ideas but this took the biscuit.

"You were Walter's best friend."

"Aye."

"You'd bring his child up as your own."

"Aye."

"If you don't Gertie will be on the street and the baby will no doubt be born in the workhouse."

"But Agnes, it's you I want to marry."

She looked me straight in the eyes. "Tom Duncan, you're a good man, you're steady and honest, but I'll always compare you to Herbert and you'll always come out second best. If you become a Sergeant I'll have to marry you and I think I'll regret it. If I do take a man it'll have to be someone completely different from my Herbert."

I didn't know what to say so I said nowt.

"You'll have to persuade Gertie. Once she's agreed the Ruffles'll have no choice but to accept her back."

I was sent into the front room and as I sat down the McIvers left. It took me an hour to talk Gertie round and she insisted on speaking to Agnes before making her decision. That clinched it.

I went with Gertie to her parents' house the next evening. Gertie had gone to see her brother Billy's wife during the day and Mr. and Mrs. Ruffle knew what to expect. They took us into the front room. There was no fire on and the room was as cold as the welcome. I explained that I'd asked Gertie to marry me and that she had accepted. I hoped that they would take her back until the wedding. We were going round to see the Minister that evening. Mr. Ruffle was about to speak when his wife started.

"I always said that Walter was a bad influence on wor Gertie."

I wasn't going to let anyone criticise Walter.

"Mrs. Ruffle, I'll not have you say a bad word about Walter. He loved Gertie and she loved him. Walter's dead and gone now and he can't marry Gertie so I will, and I'll bring up his child as my own. I think it's disgraceful the way you've treated Gertie. I only came here to ask you to take Gertie back until the wedding. If you're not prepared to do so then we'll leave now." I made as though to stand up.

Mr. Ruffle gestured to me to stay put.

"Me wife didn't mean anything by it, Mr. Duncan. She only wanted the best for our Gertie. Gertie, you can come home now you're getting married."

We were married in four weeks. McIver stood as best man and Agnes was the bridesmaid. Word soon got round the Station and there were some raised eyebrows, but McIver made it known that I was doing the right thing by Walter. If there was any talk, it was behind my back.

Fraser Thompson was appointed Sergeant. In a way I was glad; I preferred being on the beat. I applied for a married officer's house and agreed to join the Fire Brigade. We were well settled in one of the Police Station houses by the time the baby was born. It was a boy, Walter. We lived a few doors down from the McIvers. Agnes had left a few days after our wedding. She'd ran off to Scotland with Dapper Digby, the bookies' runner.

Johnny Doyle left Shields not long after his brother and sister were sent down for seven and five years respectively. I was coming out of the nick one afternoon at about half past two after my shift. Johnny was waiting for me just across the street. He was holding an old cardboard suitcase under his arm. He wanted a word so we went in to the *Havelock*. He couldn't have been much more than seventeen, but he was with me and was served without question. He was going to join the Foreign Legion. It was one way of cutting himself off from his past completely. He had not told the Biddulphs. He wanted me to go round and tell them how grateful he was to them for looking after him, but he had to get away from Shields and from the name Doyle. He didn't have a trade, and if he joined up in the British Army the chances were that he'd meet up with someone who knew him. I didn't try to dissuade him; he'd made up his mind. I walked him up to the station and saw him on the train.

I went round to the Biddulphs' at tea time. They were starting to worry. Mrs. Biddulph had to go into her bedroom for five minutes after I'd told them. Jimmy went to the pantry cupboard and brought out a bottle of whisky. Mrs. Biddulph came back in. Johnny had taken the money from the old baccy tin that she'd been putting aside for him. I stayed for tea – it was panacklety. I understood why Bobby Doyle had wolfed his down – Mrs. Biddulph was a dab hand as a cook. "He'll miss your cooking," I said as I savoured the dish.

"I only hope he'll be all right." Mrs. Biddulph looked as though she was going to break down again so I said no more about Johnny.

Jimmy Biddulph became a good friend of mine and we stayed in touch. He would occasionally receive a postcard from Johnny, usually about Christmas time. There was never a return address – the cards had come from Africa or the Far East. They stopped altogether during the War. Jimmy came to see me one evening in 1946. He had a letter. It was from France and was written in French. Jimmy asked me if I could make sense of it. He knew that I'd picked up a bit of the lingo during the last War. I couldn't help but I knew someone who might be able to. I took Jimmy round to Beaky Thomas's house. He was in his eighties now but was still mentally alert. There was no reply so we went down to the *Wheatsheaf.* Old habits die hard. Beaky was there sitting in a corner nursing a pint. He was glad to see me, drained his glass and handed it to me for a refill. He used to teach French and was more than happy to translate Jimmy's letter. He read through it first.

"It's bad news I'm afraid, Mr. Biddulph." Beaky looked quite emotional.

"I'd better get us something stronger then," said Jimmy and went to the bar for three whiskies.

"I'll just read it out then," said Beaky after Jimmy had returned with the three glasses. He spoke slowly as he translated the letter.

"It has taken me a long time to decide to write to you. When one joins the Legion it is often with the intention of never returning nor ever sending any message. I was a friend of your Johnny. I am a Norwegian and Johnny and I joined at about the same time. In the Legion you have to speak French. Neither of us knew the language so we had to learn. I didn't speak English either but many of the words Johnny spoke were similar to Norwegian words. We became good friends. He had given his name as Smith. No one ever enlists under their real name. I saw him writing a card to you one day and he told me that his name was Biddulph and that you had brought him up as your own child. By then we would have trusted each other with our lives. When War broke out we were in Indochina and we stayed there. The French had a pact with the Japanese."

Beaky paused and took a sip of his whisky.

"There was not much to do and Johnny and I planned our future. We had both already served our twenty years and we decided that as soon as the War ended we would leave the Legion and with the money we had saved we would open a bar in France.

"In 1945 the Japanese attacked us without warning. It was a massacre. Somehow Johnny and me got out and joined the remnants of the French Forces heading south for safety. The Japs harried us every step of the way. The Lieutenant who was leading our Unit was killed. Johnny had been made up to Acting Sergeant two days before and he took charge. He led us for more than a hundred miles through jungles and swamps. The Japanese Forces launched a last attack. Johnny was wounded badly. We retreated as far as a narrow defile. Johnny gave orders that we were to carry on to the South. He would stay behind with two other wounded men who could not walk so well but could still shoot. They had machine guns and would delay the enemy as long as possible. I wanted to stay with him but he put me in charge of the others – they needed me more. He gave me his passbook and said that I should still open the bar in France with our money. He said he would be back after the War. That was the last I saw of him. We heard his gun blazing away for a long time. We made it."

Beaky paused again to take another sip of his whisky.

"He was awarded the Croix de Guerre posthumously. The citation said that by his actions he had saved many lives and had upheld the highest traditions of the French Foreign Legion. The medal is in the Legion's Museum as there was no record of any next of kin. It is in the name of John Smith.

"I was wounded myself and it took me a long time to recover. I now own a little bistro in Marseilles. I have a lot of ex legionnaires as customers. There's a picture of Johnny with me in uniform at the back of the bar and I've a copy of his citation next to it.

"I know nothing of Johnny's early life but I thought you should know that he was one of the bravest and best of the men I have known

and a credit to you."

Beaky took another stiff drink. "It's signed *Jan Andersson*."

We drank our whiskies. Jimmy went up to the bar and brought back three more large ones. He put them down on the table. "Thank you, Mr. Thomas." He raised his glass.

"To Johnny."

"To Johnny," we replied.

Extracts of Poems by Burns

from: *ADRESS TO THE UCO' GUID, OR THE RIGIDLY RIGHTEOUS*

p2

"Oh ye wha are sae guid yoursel,
Sae pious and sae holy,
Ye've nowt to do but mark and tell
Your Neebour's fauts and folly."

p197

"Then gently scan your brother Man,
Still gentler sister Woman;
Tho' they may gang a kenning wrang,
To step aside is human

from: *EPISTLE TO A YOUNG FRIEND*

p60

'I'll no say men are villains a';
The real, harden'd wicked,
Wha ha nae check but human law,
Are to a few restricted.'

from: *TAM O' SHANTER*

p188

"Auld Ayr, wham ne'er a town surpasses
For honest men and bonnie lasses."